Archibald Zwick
and the Eight Towers

Robert Leslie Palmer

CROSSBOOKS
PUBLISHING

CrossBooks™
A Division of LifeWay
1663 Liberty Drive
Bloomington, IN 47403
www.crossbooks.com
Phone: 1-866-879-0502

Scriptures taken from the Holy Bible, New International Version®, NIV®.
Copyright © 1973, 1978, 1984 by Biblica, Inc.™ Used by permission of Zondervan.
All rights reserved worldwide.

First published by CrossBooks 11/23/2010

ISBN: 978-1-6150-7649-9 (sc)
ISBN: 978-1-6150-7650-5 (hc)

Library of Congress Control Number: 2010940876

Printed in the United States of America

This book is printed on acid-free paper.

Dedication

This book is dedicated to my parents, **Harrison Rowe Palmer** and **Margaret Elizabeth Palmer**, whose love and encouragement shaped my life.

Contents

Acknowledgments

This book would not be possible had it not been for the loving support of my wife, **Huisuk Kim Palmer**, and son, **Aaron Rowe Palmer**, who not only encouraged me to write this book but supported my decision to take a sabbatical from the practice of law in order to do so. In addition, they both offered invaluable advice about the manuscript.

I am also indebted to several other people, mostly friends and family, who agreed to read my manuscript and make comments. They include my sisters, **Coralie Maples**, **Claire Ferguson**, and **Charlotte Podsednik**, my brother, **Bill Palmer**, my sister-in-law, **Rennie Palmer**, and my niece, **Jasmine Lee**. My friends who reviewed the manuscript include **Carri Bass**, **David Bass, Anthony Cooper, Amelia deBuys, Ben Hogan, Bill Lewis, Susan McPherson, Clint Neumann, Erica Neumann, Ken Riddle, Siham Shunnarah, Barry Stalnaker,** and **Randy Tribble**. Although I could not incorporate all of the comments they made, I used the best suggestions to improve the book.

I would also like to thank **Steve Drake** of **LifeWay** and **Phill Burgess** of **CrossBooks**, both of whom graciously reviewed my manuscript and assisted me in many other ways. There are many others at **CrossBooks** who offered invaluable assistance, many whose names I do not know. I want to thank the very talented artist, **Mark Anthony Pino**, for his excellent work in capturing scenes in the novel as well as for his patience in making the numerous changes I requested. I also thank **Kelly Barrow** and **Sam Fitzgerald** for their invaluable assistance in the production of the art. I appreciate the hard work that **Joel Pierson** and his team put in to edit the novel. Finally, I would also like to thank **Beth Ludema, Courtney Packard, Rebecca Roberts, Matt Campbell, Brian Martindale,** and **Stefanie Holzbacher** for their assistance.

Chapter One
A Terrifying Night at Sea

Archie was cold, wet, hungry, and exhausted. But he was alive, and that was reason for hope, especially now that the storm had passed.

He did not know how long he had been clinging to his overturned kayak, or where the storm had taken him. It was now pitch-black, and Archie guessed that it had been hours since sunset, though the sudden darkness brought by the storm made it difficult to know just when the sun had gone down. As the waves gently rocked him, Archie's thoughts drifted to his parents, who were no doubt very worried by now.

The Zwick family was vacationing on a small island in the Bermuda archipelago, and Archie had been so eager to use his new kayak that immediately on arrival he had run directly to the water after they arrived, pausing just long enough to shed a few articles of clothing. Because it was already late in the afternoon, his mother had called after him, using his full name "Archibald," as she always did when she wanted him to know that she really meant what she was saying. She had instructed him to come in out of the water in half an hour. Archie's parents had then gone inside the house, and Archie, determined to enjoy the precious moments in the water, had paddled out farther than he should have. Before he realized the danger, a strong current had pulled him out to sea and then the sudden storm had erupted.

Hours of sheer terror followed, for his kayak soon capsized. It was all Archie could do to hold on to it during the terrible storm. He was a very good swimmer for a boy of sixteen, and he was now thankful that his

1

parents had insisted that he complete every swimming course available at the local YMCA. But this gave him very little comfort as he struggled in the rough waves. With each swell, Archie had been certain that he would lose his grip and be swept away from the kayak. And with each terrible gust of wind, his face and body had been sprayed with a salty ocean mist that had found its way into his eyes and mouth and nostrils, despite his best efforts to protect his face.

Now, hours later, Archie did not even know which way he should paddle, even if he had not lost the paddle. And although he had been trained in righting a capsized kayak, he now lacked the energy to try such an ambitious project. Instead, he scanned the horizon, hoping to catch a glimpse of lights indicating a shoreline. He wanted desperately to be out of the water, filled with a hot meal, dry and warm, and resting in a cozy bed. There was still just enough of an ocean spray to sting his eyes with saltwater, and so, after a while, Archie grew weary of looking for the shore. He held on to the kayak, struggling to stay awake, for he was afraid that if he fell asleep, he might release his grip, drift away from the kayak, and drown.

Afraid of what might happen if he continued in his current predicament, Archie decided that if he drowned, it would not happen because he failed to act. He began to drain the seawater from the kayak by lifting first the bow and then the stern, holding each end up for as long as he could in his weakened condition. He then stared for some time at the overturned kayak, mentally preparing himself for the daunting task before him. Suddenly, with one mighty shove, Archie managed to right the kayak on his first attempt. Mustering the little remaining strength in his weary body, he began pulling himself up onto the kayak, which rocked with each movement he made. Because he feared that he would not have the strength to right the kayak if it capsized again, Archie took his time, inching gradually up and over the cockpit. Once his body was centered over the kayak, Archie slowly began turning until he lay lengthwise, face down. He raised his torso and allowed his feet to dip into the water. Then he began maneuvering his legs into the cockpit.

When at last he was sitting in the kayak, Archie took a deep breath, sighed, and began sobbing uncontrollably. The flood of tears sprang from a multitude of emotions—from joy, despair, terror, anger, and longing. Joy, because he had righted the kayak and crawled into it. Despair, because he was uncertain whether he would ever find his way back. Terror, because he feared the unknown: the storms, the sharks, and other ocean perils. Anger, because he felt his parents had failed to protect him. And longing, because he missed those same parents, his home, and school, and every part of the life he now felt was being snatched from him.

The crying released all of the emotions Archie had pent up during the storm, but it also sapped his remaining strength. When he no longer had the energy even to cry, Archie began to think of what might happen even if he could find his way back. He assumed, at a minimum, his parents would ground him for the whole summer vacation. He knew that his father would be especially angry, for he had sternly warned Archie to stay close to the shore. In his mind's ear, he could hear his father say, "The boy thinks he invented the wheel," his father's way of saying that Archie did not know as much as he thought he did.

Archie was now as tired as he had ever been, and he wanted more than anything to sleep. He struggled to remain awake, because he was afraid if he fell asleep, the kayak would capsize again and he would drown. But the physical need was too great, so Archie leaned forward and allowed his heavy eyelids to close. Although he quickly drifted into sleep, fear and discomfort precluded a deep sleep. Caught between the world of dreams and the nightmare of terrifying reality, Archie simply floated in his kayak. After a while, he opened his eyes and sat up, not really refreshed, but unable to continue in this awkward half-sleep. He sat quietly and once again, began searching for lights. For quite some time, success evaded him.

The monotony was finally broken when Archie caught a glimpse of a greenish, glowing light in the distance. His heart racing, he was suddenly energized to begin paddling, but because he had lost his paddle in the storm, Archie was forced to use his hands. He had floated silently for so long that the sound he now made as he splashed his way through the water seemed odd to him—odd and very loud.

So happy was he to see the light that he never took his eyes off of it as he paddled. After studying it for some time, Archie decided it must be a small island, perhaps even the island on which his family was vacationing. Lights from a larger island would surely be spread out. At last, Archie would be out of the ocean and safely on shore. He would be able to make a telephone call to his parents, who would certainly come to get him. It would be very pleasant, indeed, to get out of his wet clothes, eat a meal, and lie down to sleep in a warm, *dry* bed.

As Archie relished these thoughts, he continued to study the glowing green light, which gradually took shape before him. Although Archie expected the single light eventually to divide into a multitude of distinct lights emanating from various buildings along the shore of the island, it remained curiously united, yet continued to grow in size and actually began to take shape. Archie soon realized that the light he had observed consisted of a structure that was *glowing* in the dark! There were no lamps, floodlights, beacons, traffic lights, neon signs, or other lights—just a glowing edifice! While his brain was still trying to process this strange fact, it received another shock. There was no island at all. Instead, a glowing, green castle seemingly arose directly out of the sea!

Archie rubbed his eyes in disbelief, expecting the glowing, green castle would simply be transformed into more familiar forms as he drew nearer. Instead, vivid details of the medieval castle came sharply into focus the closer he got to it. A wall at least one hundred feet high surrounded the entire fortress, parts of which were visible beyond the towers that punctuated the wall. Everything seemed to be constructed of the mysterious, glowing, green substance, which appeared to be the only source of light. And Archie's first impression had been right: the walls of the castle rose directly out of the ocean itself. It was not sitting on land at all!

Archie's focus on the strange sight was broken by the sound of rowing, and he soon spotted a small boat approaching him. At first he thought the splashing oars and lapping waves were muffling the voices of the men aboard the small craft, for Archie could not understand what they were saying. Soon, however, he realized that they were speaking a strange language. Their appearance frightened him, for as the boat neared, the men stood up in the boat, and Archie could see that they were wearing strange clothing—loosely fitting, knee-length tunics over pantaloons. As he strained to make out more detail, Archie's focus shifted from the clothing to the men's eyes, in which he saw a kindness that quickly eased his fears. He was glad when they lifted him out of the kayak and took him into their craft. He was soon wrapped in a blanket and lying in the boat as the men rowed it toward the floating castle. Archie closed his tired eyes and quickly fell asleep.

Chapter Two
A Strange Awakening

Archie awoke in the quiet darkness of night and found himself in a small room lit only by a single lamp. He was warm and dry, and the terrifying night he had spent alone in the sea now seemed like a strange dream to him. He rubbed his puffy eyes in the vain hope that he would soon recognize his surroundings, but when he was fully awake, his heart quickly filled with panic.

Archie did not know exactly how long he had been asleep, but he knew it had been a very long time. He also knew his absence had ripped apart his parents' world, for he was their only child, born long after they had abandoned any hope of having children.

This single fact—that he was an only child born to parents almost old enough to be his grandparents—had molded Archie's personality more than any other, for he found himself able to relate more easily to adults than to children his own age. But even that was hard, so Archie spent most of his time alone. When he was inside, it was not unusual for him to be found using his computer or reading a book. And when he was outside, although he was quite athletic, Archie avoided team sports. Instead, he invariably chose athletic activities that required no team and no opponent—swimming, kayaking, and mountain biking.

But Archie spent most of his free time tinkering. He loved to take things apart and put them back together, just to see how they worked. Whenever anyone discarded an old machine or electronic device, Archie would always be there to retrieve it from the trash. He would then fix the device or cannibalize it for parts. He even tinkered with creating his own

5

gadgets from some of those discarded parts, and he fancied himself an inventor. Even his selection of books reflected this love of tinkering, for he would read anything that described how things work.

Archie knew that his parents loved him, and this made him feel guilty that he so strongly disliked their old-fashioned ways. His father, especially, was too regimented and disciplined for Archie's taste. Yet, now that he had been torn away from them, their idiosyncrasies no longer seemed to matter. Archie's longing for his parents was greater than he had ever expected it could be. He sat up, determined to contact them as soon as possible.

As he eyed his surroundings, Archie began to notice just how unusual they were. What he had taken for a lamp looked nothing like any lamp he had ever seen. Instead, it consisted of a glass bowl filled with water in which a ball-shaped object glowed, not unlike the glow sticks that kids buy at carnivals. This suddenly reminded Archie that the last thing he had seen before falling asleep was a greenish, glowing, castle wall rising directly out of the water. Archie jumped out of the bed and hit his head on the low ceiling. A searing pain shot from his head down his spine, and Archie's heart began to race, though he did not know whether it did so because of the pain or his increasing fear.

Still in pain, Archie noticed that he was no longer wearing his own clothing. Instead, he wore some unusual silken garments that did not fit him very well. Though loose-fitting, the garments had sleeves and legs that were too short, and the torso was longer than any shirt he had ever worn, for it ran well below his waist. Archie suddenly remembered that the men who had rescued him had worn the very same type of garment, but with one very important difference. On the front of Archie's tunic was a sophisticated embroidery of what appeared to be a coat of arms. Yellow gold cord was in abundance, forming the embroidered field of this work of art. At the top was a thick black bar with six white towers. Beneath that, the yellow gold field included a smaller, internal black shield with a single white tower, over which there was a gold crown. The entire shield had a simple black border. Archie did not know what any of it meant.

Then looking around the room, Archie saw that it was smaller than he had realized, possibly about six feet by six feet, and not quite five feet high. Not only was the ceiling too low, but now he realized that even the bed in which he had slept was shorter than his bed at home. Although quite comfortable, the bed was somewhat firmer than he was used to. The sheets and blankets, on the other hand, were woven of a much finer and softer material than he had ever seen. What he had used as a pillow just moments before was actually tubular and, like the bed, very firm. Archie recalled that the "pillow" fit perfectly in the small of his neck, and he now wondered why all pillows weren't shaped like it. He picked it up and noticed that there were elaborate symbols embroidered on the silky material covering it.

Archie grabbed the lamp and began to examine it closely. Removing the ball-shaped object, he immediately noticed that its feel just did not match its appearance. It was neither warm nor did it emit any fumes, and it felt very smooth and yet very firm. What was it? Squeezing the glowing ball, Archie observed that it was as hard as concrete or steel, but unlike concrete, it was very smooth, and unlike steel, it was very light. Despite his initial impression, the ball was also unlike any of the glow sticks that he had ever bought at a carnival, for they were never very firm and had to be broken to start the glowing. This lamp was unlike any he had ever seen. Archie dropped the glowing ball back into the bowl, and to his surprise, the ball began to glow brighter. He hadn't noticed that while he was examining the ball, it had gradually dimmed.

Holding this strange lamp in his hand, Archie began to inch around the room, still hoping to make sense of his surroundings. Touching the wall, he realized that it felt just like the glowing ball, for it was as smooth as steel and unlike the walls in Archie's home or school. The only obvious difference was that the ball was glowing, but the wall was not. But then, the wall was not wet. Archie immediately splashed some water from the bowl onto the wall, but to his disappointment, nothing happened.

After getting down on his hands and knees, Archie slowly made his way around the rest of the very small room, noting that the only furnishings were the small bed in which he had slept and the small night table on which he found the lamp. The floor and the ceiling appeared to be made of the same substance as the walls and the glowing ball. There were no windows or doors, and Archie wondered just how he had gotten into the room. It also occurred to him that unlike the bedrooms in his own home, this room really was a bedroom, with only one purpose—sleeping. But then it occurred to Archie that with no windows or doors, this "bedroom" could actually be a tomb. He shuddered at the thought.

With his heart pounding for the third time since he had awakened, Archie frantically renewed his search for an exit, but to no avail. Feeling his way first along one wall and then the next, until every wall had been thoroughly examined, Archie next turned his attention to the floor. Feeling and looking for a trapdoor or a knob or something—anything—different, his search soon led him back to the bed. Crawling under the bed was difficult, for Archie was tall and muscular for his age, and the space between the floor and the bed was scarcely more than one foot. But that effort, too, was fruitless, for there was nothing under the bed.

Crawling out from under the bed, Archie sat down and sobbed. Having failed to find an exit, and unable to think of any way out of the tiny room, he was soon overwhelmed with terror. Could this actually be a tomb? Could it be that his hosts thought he was dead? Archie began yelling at the top of his lungs. He pounded on the walls, the floor, and the ceiling. After some time, he slumped down, resigned to his fate, for he did not believe anyone could hear him. Emotionally unable to cope with terrifying reality, Archie allowed his thoughts to carry him away to more pleasant times and places.

He thought about the blond-haired, blue-eyed beauty of his dreams, Lauren McManus, a cheerleader at William McKinley High School. Her charms had captivated Archie the very first time he had seen her, but he knew that she would never fill any major role in his life. She was popular and he was not. She was beautiful and graceful and always knew just what to say and when to say it. Archie, on the other hand, though quite muscular and not at all ugly, was awkward and shy and sometimes very clumsy. And he was bright enough to realize—or so he thought—that the social order in his age group had already been cast in stone, before he and his classmates had even darkened the doors of college. Lauren was but a pleasant diversion for Archie's daydreams, and he knew that it was best that way. Somehow, he knew deep down that if he ever really got to know her, her charm would soon evaporate. He would rather keep the daydream.

Archie's thoughts next drifted to his best friend, Ted Dugan, who sometimes served as Archie's liaison to the rest of the world. Ted straddled the divide between geek and jock, never really fitting into either world but easily navigating between them. Archie had known Ted since they were both scarcely out of diapers, for they lived next door to each other, and they were like brothers. Ted was more disciplined than Archie, but less creative, more athletic, but less adventurous, more obedient, but less empathetic. Had they met later in life, they never would have been friends, but now they were practically joined at the hip. Somehow, each boy used his character traits to positive effect on the other.

On one occasion a few years earlier, the boys had been playing in the woods behind their homes when Archie had been struck by one of his all-too-frequent inspirations. They simply had to build a tree fortress

(Archie had convinced Ted that although other boys build tree *houses,* nothing short of a tree *fortress* would do for them). And so, the two boys had gathered the raw materials—and in a few cases, persuaded their fathers to buy some of the indispensable things they would need—and began to build the tree fortress. When they had almost finished, Archie had been struck by another inspiration and forced poor Ted to tear down a substantial portion of the fortress to begin anew. The new design would conceal the way in and out of the—

Archie jumped out of the bed and once again hit his head. Ignoring the pain, he wheeled around and began pulling on the bed. Nothing moved. He then shoved the bed, which suddenly receded into the wall. At the same time, a concealed door opened in the ceiling and a ladder thrust forward from the opposite wall. He was not trapped after all!

Pausing just a moment to take in the result of his efforts, Archie looked at the wall from which the ladder had come and saw that there was now a depression in the wall in its exact shape. He knew that he had carefully examined the wall earlier and that there had been no cracks or other hints of the ladder, and this he knew was remarkable. Positioning himself at the bottom of the ladder, Archie looked up and was amazed to see a sky full of stars—more than he had ever seen at any time in his life. He then climbed the ladder quickly, at least until his head rose through the ceiling and into the night air.

Archie froze at the sight that lay before him.

Chapter Three
A Beautiful Girl

tanding in a rooftop park, Archie looked down at a beautiful, green, glowing city below him. Although every building glowed with the same intensity, Archie once again noted that there were no lights of any kind. Yet, despite the fact that it was night, he could clearly see an enormous city that appeared to extend to the horizon in every direction. Indeed, he could no longer see the ocean. He stepped up and off the ladder.

Suddenly, the stillness of the night was broken by a single, melodic voice.

"K'truum-Shra d'jeo jönpelæo?"

Archie wheeled around and stood staring at the most beautiful—and strange—girl he had ever seen. She was short and very slight in figure, had very thin facial features, long dark hair, and an olive-green complexion. Her eyes were the most unusual and brilliant shade of green, and in the darkness, even they appeared to glow. He sensed in her a gentleness of spirit, and he felt oddly drawn to her, though he was unable to speak. A puzzled expression soon came over her sweet face.

Bowing her head, the girl slowly approached Archie and gently placed a sort of necklace made of what appeared to be seashells over his neck and then spoke again.

"K'truum-Shra you like?"

"I don't know," Archie replied, "What is K'truum-Shra?"

The girl giggled. "K'truum-Shra our city-home is, and you our most venerated guest be. Mókea my name."

"And I am Archie. Where am I?"

Mókea giggled again. "K'truum-Shra."

"I have never heard of K'truum-Shra. Where is it? Is this an island? Are we close to Bermuda?"

Mókea smiled and explained, "K'truum-Shra our ancient city is. Bermuda I not know."

Stunned by this response, Archie realized that finding his way back to his parents might be more difficult than he had expected. It was obvious that the girl had no answers for him. He changed the subject. "I did not understand you at first. How is it that I can understand you now?"

"You most sacred neck-ornament for K'truum-Shra wear. It you understand make. We you many generations await."

"But your speech is still very different," Archie observed, "and why have you expected me?"

Mókea took Archie's hand and said, "You many questions have. I answers not have. You come."

Mókea led Archie to a broad sidewalk, where he saw that the park was well above the streets. As far as Archie could tell, the only parts of the city that were not glowing were the park on top of the city and the streets below. Archie counted the flights as Mókea led him down some stairs. After four flights, they emerged at street level, where they stepped onto a sidewalk that appeared to front the street. Archie noticed a shimmering in the street itself and then he heard the sound of gently lapping waves. He instantly realized that the streets were not really streets, but canals!

Mókea and Archie briefly walked along the sidewalk, which was several feet above the canal. The structure along which the sidewalk ran was occasionally punctuated by massive columns that were somewhat thicker in the center, but the structure was otherwise open. Mókea stopped, wheeled around, and spoke.

"Here you wait."

Before Archie could respond, Mókea disappeared, and he stood alone on the sidewalk. In less than a minute, she returned, carrying some clothing, and the couple returned to the stairs and ascended the four flights back to the park at the top. As they walked, Archie spoke.

"Where are you taking me?"

Without turning her head, Mókea replied, "To Palace of Elders." She then added, "I answers not have. You come. You find out."

Archie realized that he would still get no answers from this strange girl, so he gave up trying. At the top of the stairs, they emerged onto the broad sidewalk at the park level, which they followed for what seemed to Archie to be about forty-five minutes. From time to time, they would come to a cross-street—or cross-canal. The sidewalk on which they walked bridged each canal. In fact, at every intersection of canals, there were four broad sidewalks, each of which bridged the intersection, so that the bridges formed a square over the intersecting canals. At each corner, there was also a set of stairs descending to canal level. As he observed all of this, it occurred to Archie that there were no individual buildings, houses, shops, or other structures. Instead, each structure was connected to others, and it appeared that the entire city was one single, very large building.

Archie concluded that although it was nighttime, it was not too late, for the couple would occasionally pass other people with the same general features as Mókea. Had it been much later, he surmised that they would pass fewer people. Had it been earlier, they would likely have passed more. Most of the people they encountered said nothing but simply smiled. A few gawked at Archie's sandy blond hair and fair complexion, and one or two said to Mókea something along the lines of, "Take care of the venerated one," but did so in the same broken language Mókea used.

Although all of the people they passed wore the kind of silken clothing that Archie now wore, they were not all as elaborately embroidered. Only infrequently did he see tunics with embroidered shields, and all of those tunics were white. In contrast, the tunics that bore no coat of arms were of many colors, primarily pastels, but none was white. And those tunics also appeared to be made of a coarser material, though they were still beautiful and light. The way the gentle breeze made the loose, "bell-bottom" sleeves flow was somehow soothing. But Archie's most important observation: of the few who spoke, only men did so, and only if they were wearing a coat of arms.

Eventually, they approached a dark spot with a large, glowing building in its center, with glowing walkways leading to it. But at least four or five blocks away, the elevated walkway ended, and the couple descended to canal level. The canal-level sidewalk also had bridges that spanned the last few blocks before the large building, but these bridges were narrow and were obviously drawbridges. Archie also noticed that within these last few blocks, the buildings were distinct, not joined as the other structures had been, and the density of their construction diminished as they approached the large building in what he now realized must be the center of the city, for it was encircled by a grand canal from which eight intersecting canals emanated.

On crossing the last drawbridge, Archie noticed that what he had perceived as a dark spot was, in fact, a large and very neatly trimmed garden. The glowing building in the center was imposing in nature, and Archie assumed that it was the seat of government. This was where Mókea was taking him. Despite her apparently gentle nature, Archie immediately began to feel uneasy. Nevertheless, because he had no alternative, he continued walking with her.

Palace of Elders

They crossed the threshold of the enormous doors that led into the building and entered a fabulously ornate room, with dozens of the glowing lamps similar to the one Archie had seen in the bedroom in which he had awakened. But Archie did not have any chance to examine this first room in the government building, because Mókea quickly ushered him into another room, even larger and more ornate. This room, which appeared to be in the center of the building, was the largest one Archie had ever seen. And unlike other large rooms, this one had no columns supporting what must have been the largest dome in the world. Archie estimated that the top of the dome was at least three hundred yards high.

Archie remembered watching a program on the Discovery Channel or the History Channel about the architectural strength of domes and arches, and he wondered about the absence of any columns in a structure of this size. But then he remembered how light the ball in the lamp was, and it occurred to him that a substance that light and yet so hard would be very useful in constructing enormous buildings. Then something else occurred to Archie: he remembered that when he had first seen the castle-like walls of the city, he had noticed that it arose directly out of the sea. Suppose the city was one enormous, *floating* construction. That would require some really light material.

The enormous room was very well lit, with thousands, or maybe even millions, of the glowing ball lamps. They lined the walls at regular intervals, and hundreds of chandeliers, each the size of a small house, hung from the domed ceiling. Unlike the glowing ball lamp in his bedroom, these ball lamps did not glow with a greenish tint, or even a yellowish tint, but with a pure white light.

The walls were covered with ornate tapestries and embroideries of many vibrant colors. Together, they formed a pleasing atmosphere, not at all the jarring, discordant feeling Archie would have expected from so many different works of art. As he looked more closely at the artwork, he could see tapestries and embroideries of several coats of arms. At the top, was the largest embroidery: the coat of arms that was on Archie's tunic. This stopped him momentarily. There, right before him, was the same yellow gold shield, bordered in black, topped by a thick black bar in which six evenly spaced white towers stood, and including a smaller, internal black shield with a larger, white tower topped by a gold crown. Mókea gently nudged Archie, who began walking again, but not without noticing that her tunic bore the same coat of arms.

As they approached the center of the room, Archie saw that it had seating resembling a theater, yet was circular and surrounded a central floor on which sat a large, circular table. Surrounding the central floor was stadium seating, with each row significantly higher than the one directly in front. As a result, the round table was much lower than the rest of the room. Mókea led Archie down an aisle of steps to the table, where several distinguished-looking men were seated. The men shared the same general characteristics as Mókea, and though clearly adults, not one of them was larger than a typical American twelve-year-old. As Archie and Mókea approached the men, all but one arose, almost in unison. When everyone else was standing, the remaining man, the tallest in the group, arose. To Archie's surprise, his attire matched Archie's, down to the coat of arms. Then he spoke.

"I am Mókato, the Eldest of the Elders of K'truum-Shra. Welcome to our city. You have already met my granddaughter, Mókea, and these are the Elders of our city."

"Thank you," said Archie, "but where exactly am I? And can you call my parents and tell them I am okay and ask them to come get me?"

"We do not know your parents," Mókato said, "for they have never come to us, and we do not know how to reach them. But we are certain that you will soon discover for yourself how to find them."

"But I don't understand anything here," Archie protested. "I don't even understand where I am, who you are, or how I got here. I don't even know how it is that I can understand you perfectly but could not understand your granddaughter."

"That is easy. You have now been wearing the sacred necklace long enough to hear us plainly and for us to hear you plainly. But do not take it off, for it will not work again."

"Can you at least tell me where this city is located? How far is Bermuda?"

"We do not know Bermuda," Mókato replied. "And K'truum-Shra is right here. All that you see is K'truum-Shra."

Archie looked into Mókato's eyes. He could see only gentleness there, but that did not assuage the anger he now felt. "If you aren't going to help me, then why did Mókea bring me all the way over here to you?" A sad expression came over Mókea's face, and Archie felt ashamed. He knew that embarrassing his hosts would not help him find his way home. And when he looked at Mókea now, he could not tear his eyes away from hers. Here, in the light of this enormous room, he could truly see how beautiful she was. Her eyes were even brighter than he had realized, and even her complexion and hair clearly had a green tint.

In the white light of this room, Archie now realized that Mókea and her people were *green*! Not pure green, but green in the way Europeans are "white," Africans are "black," Native Americans are "red," and Asians are "yellow." Mókea's skin was really an olive-green color, and her hair was dark brown, but in the light displayed just the slightest hint of green. And all of this was put together in the most amazing way so that Archie marveled at Mókea's beauty. Archie's attention snapped back into place as Mókato spoke.

"We have brought you here to the Palace of Elders, because you are the one whose coming was foretold so many generations ago. We have brought you here so that you can begin preparing for the mighty quest that awaits you."

Chapter Four
The Fortress City

efore Archie could ask any questions, Mókea gently thrust the clothing she had been carrying into Archie's hands.

"You will find that these fit you better, for they have been tailor-made for you."

At that, she directed him to a small door that led into a room beneath the lowest rows of stadium seating. As Archie changed his clothing, he looked around the small room and decided that it must be a toilet, though he was not certain. Water flowed into a small bowl somewhat lower than a typical American sink, but it also flowed into a bowl built into the floor. Archie assumed that the bowl in the floor was the toilet.

The new clothing fit Archie better but was identical in design to what he had been wearing. The pantaloon legs and the tunic sleeves were now the appropriate length, but the pantaloons were still baggy, and the tunic now extended all the way to his knees. When he stepped out of the toilet, Mókea took the old tunic and pantaloons and handed them to a servant.

Archie's hosts then led him to an ornately decorated banquet hall in the same building, where he was to be the guest of honor at a feast. Though enormous by any reasonable standards, the hall in which the feast took place was nevertheless dwarfed by the central, domed room in which Archie had met Mókea's grandfather, whom he now knew to address as "Lord Mókato." Once the food was placed before him, Archie's stomach suddenly came to life, and he realized just how hungry he was. He ate everything placed before him. Much of it was made from the ordinary foodstuffs he was accustomed to eating at home—mostly vegetables and fruit—though it was sometimes prepared in ways that were quite unusual. But there were also many foods that Archie did not recognize at all, and he immediately noticed that the seemingly wide variety of meats consisted entirely of fish.

Archie did not sleep again that night but remained with his hosts in the ornate palace. First, the feast itself took several hours, during which his hosts evaded answering Archie's many questions. Instead, their conversation focused on the politics of the city, all of which was very foreign and very boring to Archie. Though they confessed that they knew nothing of Bermuda, America, or the outside world, they did not seem curious at all. After the feast, they returned to the central hall of the palace, in which they listened to a unique orchestra that played very odd instruments. After what seemed an eternity, and to Archie's relief, his hosts announced that he would now be given a tour of the city.

Mókato and Mókea led him out of the central hall, through a narrow corridor, down some stairs, and into a somewhat darker room apparently beneath the courtyard surrounding the palace. Though large, the room smelled like the sea, and except for a walkway around the perimeter of the room, was full of water. Piers extending from the walkway were punctuated with stalls. Mókato and Mókea led Archie down one pier to a carriage floating in the water.

"Watch your step," Mókato said as he stepped off the pier and into the carriage.

Archie followed and was, in turn, followed by Mókea. Mókato and Mókea insisted that he take the seat between them, and as soon as he had, the carriage began moving. To his amazement, Archie realized that two dolphins were pulling the carriage! They departed the livery stable and passed through an ornate gate into the daylight and a broad and beautiful canal.

Archie immediately saw that the broad canal, which encircled the island on which the Palace of Elders was situated, was full of traffic—vessels of many types drawn by teams of two, four, and six dolphins. Some of the vessels were completely enclosed and resembled stagecoaches; others had fabric tops, some of which were down, and still others had no tops at all. There were vessels that vaguely resembled just about every kind of horse-drawn carriage or wagon. And the larger the vessel, the greater the number of dolphins that pulled it. There were even a number of dolphins bearing riders sitting on finely decorated saddles. It was quite obvious that the canals in K'truum-Shra served as the principal means of transport.

Archie's Dolphaeton Tour

Although the city did not glow during the day, it was, nevertheless, breathtaking in its beauty and size. Every structure was brilliant white and appeared to be made of stone, at least from a distance. However, having inspected the Palace of Elders closely, Archie knew that it was definitely not stone. The surfaces were smooth and highly polished, more like steel, and the palace was clearly monolithic in construction. Indeed, despite decorative touches that made them look like they were made of individual stones or bricks, it was clear that even the sidewalks surrounding the palace were monolithic. Perhaps the entire city was one single, gigantic structure.

Turning to his hosts, Archie asked, "Everything glowed green last night, yet now is white. What kind of building material does that?"

"Everything is made of k'truum," Mókato explained. Then, clearly puzzled, he asked, "Have you never seen k'truum before?"

"No, I haven't," Archie replied. "Why does it glow at night?"

"During daylight hours, it soaks up sunlight. If exposed to daylight long enough, it can be regulated with water, so that it glows brighter or dimmer, as desired. Of course, if never sufficiently exposed to sunlight, no amount of water will make it glow."

Archie immediately thought about the little experiment he had conducted in his cramped bedroom, casting water from the lamp onto the wall.

"What do your people use for building?" Mókato asked.

"Many things," Archie replied. "But mostly concrete, steel, and wood."

"What are concrete and steel?" Mókea asked, "And do you actually cut down trees for wood?"

Realizing that concrete and steel were made from substances found in the earth and obviously not available to these people, and not knowing what to make of Mókea's question about cutting down trees, Archie decided that it would be better to learn more about this strange city before revealing too much about his own world. So, he evaded the question by asking another question.

"Where do you get k'truum?"

Mókato pointed to a sort of scum that appeared here and there on the surface of the water and to men who were scooping it out of the water with a fine mesh net on a long pole.

"The k'truum rises from the ocean floor and washes into our city. Harvesting the k'truum from the surface and then drying, treating, and shaping it is a lucrative vocation for many of our people. These men are called k'truum-smiths."

Mókea joined in, saying, "The name of our city—'K'truum-Shra'—means 'the city made of k'truum.'"

Barely acknowledging this additional information, Archie changed the subject, asking another question that had been on his mind. "What is beneath the grass around the Palace of Elders?"

Mókato looked puzzled, but Mókea laughed and replied, "The grass grows on soil, silly, and the soil rests on a bed of k'truum. You didn't think that the grass grew directly out of the sea, did you?"

As they made their way through the canals, Archie could see that every part of the city was connected to every other part by the numerous sky bridges he had seen the previous evening. Lord Mókato explained that these bridges served in a double capacity, as bridges and as a sort of superstructure. Near the center, where the drawbridges spanned the canals, the city blocks were connected by an underwater superstructure composed of k'truum, but beyond the first few blocks, the only apparent connection between city blocks was the series of bridges.

The entire city was octagon shaped, with a grand canal surrounding the Palace of Elders in the center. From there, eight canals emanated from the center. These were called "tower canals" and led directly to the towers at the eight corners. There were also sixty octagonal canals crossing these tower canals, called "ring canals," with the distance between them increasing toward the outskirts of the city. Within a district formed by the five ring canals closest to the government building were the major institutions, the universities, banks, libraries, and other public institutions. Beyond that were distinct districts, defined by ring canals, for workshops, markets, dining and entertainment facilities, and finally, farms and orchards.

The buildings located in three districts—the workshop district, the market district, and the dining and entertainment district—were very similar. Each block in these districts was a single four-story structure that occupied the entire block. Viewed from the canals, these structures were open and consisted of stacked pavilions. The lowest floor was at the same level as the sidewalk abutting the canal. Large pillars stood at that level and supported the third floor, on which similar large pillars supported the park level. Additional floors—the second and fourth—were inside the structure and supported by smaller pillars.

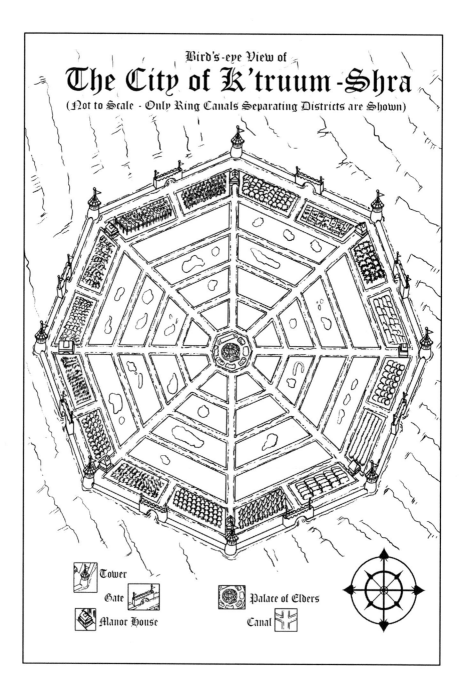

Bird's-eye View of
The City of K'truum-Shra
(Not to Scale - Only Ring Canals Separating Districts are Shown)

Tower

Gate

Manor House

Palace of Elders

Canal

As they made their way down one of the tower canals, Archie saw that the city was vibrant with life. T'lantim—Mókea explained that her people were called by that name—were busy in their workshops, on their sidewalks, at their markets, and in their homes. Archie also noticed that the stacked pavilion structures that comprised the bulk of the city were completely open to the outside, separated only by occasional sheer drapes that were almost transparent. He wondered whether the room in which he had slept was the only enclosed room in the entire city, and then it occurred to him that perhaps T'lantim desired privacy only when they slept. Mókea must have known what he was thinking. She explained that the reason the bedrooms, most of which were located at park level, were enclosed is so that they would be dark. If exposed to the sunlight very long, the K'truum walls inside the bedrooms would soon glow. But when they were not asleep, the T'lantim preferred open, airy spaces and seldom divided their living and working spaces into separate rooms.

Walking on the skybridges on the previous evening, Archie had not seen the artistic detail adorning the bridges. From the canal, he could now see that each skybridge was arched and that on either side of the arch was a decorative relief that reminded him of seashells.

Before long, they entered the workshop district, with entire blocks devoted to a single craft. Archie observed one block filled only with craftsmen making what appeared to be saddles, and Mókato explained that the saddles were made from k'truum, over which the skins of sharks were stretched.

Approaching some pavilions that appeared to be dining facilities, Archie asked if they were restaurants. Mókea smiled and explained that the T'lantim did not typically prepare meals or eat in their homes, for a strong sense of community precluded the segregation of families, one from another, when it came to the celebration that was every meal. Large communities of families ate together and shared in communal chores associated with those meals, including preparation, setting tables, and cleaning up.

At the outer edges of the city, there were no buildings, but only farms and orchards, each sitting on top of a bed of k'truum. Just past the farms and orchards stood the one hundred-foot high wall that surrounded the city. At each of the eight corners that formed the octagon-shaped wall, there was a single tower. At the center of each of the eight sides was an enormous gate, through which traffic could enter the city.

Skybridge Intersection

Although the vessel in which they were traveling, a "dolphaeton," as Mókato and Mókea called it, moved rapidly, the trip from the Palace of Elders to the outer wall of the city took a full hour. At the wall, the dolphaeton turned right and began to make its way through the broad canal that bordered the enormous wall encircling the city. During the trip from the central city, Archie had counted the ring canals and made a mental note of the number of canals comprising the various districts: the institution district, five; the workshop district, twenty; the market district, fifteen; the dining and entertainment district, fifteen; and the farm and orchard district, four, with the sixtieth and final ring canal being the one that bordered the great wall.

Now in the ring canal adjacent to the great wall, Archie noticed elaborately uniformed soldiers marching in the fields to the right of the dolphaeton and other soldiers standing guard on the wall on the left. Archie was struck by the fact that the soldiers' uniforms resembled those of medieval knights, except that their armor was obviously made of k'truum and their capes were black, with just a hint of green. In addition, their helmets had an unusual shape, for they each resembled a shark, with an obvious fin where Western helmets had in ancient times borne a plume. A few of the men wore capes with one or more green stripes along the borders, and Archie guessed they were indications of rank. Mókato explained that the soldiers' barracks were located inside the enormous wall, which housed one hundred thousand men. Every male citizen of K'truum-Shra was required to serve a minimum of two years in the military, though some volunteered to serve longer. But only thirty-six hundred were actual knights. Instead of the black capes, the knights wore only white tunics over their armor. Each knight's coat of arms was emblazoned on his tunic.

The dolphaeton did not make a complete transit around the ring canal adjacent to the great wall, but only went halfway, and yet it took two hours. At long last, they turned right, into one of the tower canals leading back into the city. As they returned to the dining and entertainment district, Archie realized that the rooftop parks extended throughout every district of the city, other than the farm and orchard district close to the great wall and the institutional district close to the Palace of Elders. Because the crossover bridges were also located at park level, residents could literally walk or run for miles.

Canal Level View

As Archie had seen on the previous evening, broad sidewalks also surrounded each city block, several feet above the water level. An occasional staircase permitted access between the walkway and the canal, for the boarding of vessels navigating the canal, and just beneath the walkway, gates received dolphins and the vessels they pulled into livery stables. As they passed some of these stables, Mókato explained that beneath the surface of the water, each city block was supported by columns mounted on a "floor" about two stories below the entire city. The underwater floor, however, was punctuated by giant chain screens that permitted fish and other seafood the people enjoyed to come and go freely, while keeping sharks and other predators out of the city.

As they approached the Palace of Elders from the side opposite from which they had departed, Archie saw a long, rectangular pond on this side of the palace. Around the pond were flags of many colors, and as they got closer, he could see crowds of people watching some kind of spectacle. He strained his eyes to see what they were watching and saw several men wearing armor, though their appearance was very different from the soldiers he had seen earlier. These men wore white tunics over their armor, tunics on which their coats of arms were embroidered in bright colors. Just then, men at each end of the long, rectangular pond walked down some steps into the water and mounted dolphins. Archie realized that these men were knights about to engage in a jousting tournament. At the sound of a herald's trumpet, the two dolphins sped toward each other, and each knight tried to unseat the other. Neither was successful, but the crowd cheered anyway.

The sun was bright, the day beautiful, and Archie had long forgotten his worries. As his eyes eagerly swallowed the colorful jousting match, he felt Mókea take his hand and gently squeeze it. He looked into her eyes, and she smiled, but Archie saw something else in her eyes. Just as he realized that what he saw was fear, a tear rolled down her cheek, and Archie wondered what it was that he was expected to do.

Chapter Five
The Eight Towers

rchie remembered that on the prior evening, Lord Mókato had avoided answering his many questions after telling him he was, "the one whose coming was foretold," and that he must begin preparing for a "quest." But he had endured all the polite waiting that he could, so Archie made up his mind that he would demand an explanation from Mókato.

No sooner had he steeled himself for confrontation than Mókato spoke, almost as though he could read Archie's mind.

"Patience, my son. After the jousting tournament, much will be made very clear to you."

The dolphaeton had just arrived at the island on which the Palace of Elders stood, near the jousting pond. A group of T'lantim Elders greeted Mókato, Mókea, and Archie, while the driver of the dolphaeton drove his team into the livery stable beneath the Palace of Elders. During the largely ceremonial meeting, several men helped Mókato put on a very large robe, in the center of which was the large shield that Archie had come to associate with Mókato. Surrounding that shield were those of many other important men. Mókea explained to Archie that the shields of Mókato's allies were given places of greater honor, deemed to be near the top half of Mókato's own shield. She also pointed out that the families whose knights had dishonored K'truum-Shra, the T'lantim, or themselves still bore arms, but their shields were depicted at the bottom edge of the robe, near the ground. If three generations of sons could not redeem the family name, the shield was retired, and the family lost its social station as part of the nobility.

Once Mókato had donned the enormous robe, his entourage made its way to a colorfully decorated and ornamented grandstand overlooking the jousting pond. The tournament, already in progress, came to a standstill. The heralds sounded their trumpets to announce Mókato's arrival, and the small group took their seats—the best in the grandstand. Mókato sat on a sort of throne above everyone else. Mókea and Archie each sat beside him, but at a lower level.

Mókea began pointing out knights and describing to Archie their relative strengths and weaknesses. The armor and shields borne by these knights were very much like those borne by knights in medieval Europe, except they were so light they floated on water. In addition, the animals and other things emblazoned on the shields often had a marine motif. One knight's shield bore the image of three green sharks on a field of black. Archie recalled seeing this shield in the Palace of Elders, very close to Mókato's own shield. Another had a large red octopus on a white field, and three others had variations on the same theme: the distinctive towers of the City of K'truum-Shra. Although Archie could not see any color that was not represented, it was clear to him that various shades of green, blue, black, and white predominated. As far as Archie could tell, gold appeared only in the shield of Mókato. Mókea explained that gold symbolizes the golden sun from which all abundance comes to the sea and that only the heads of the "Eight Families" could achieve the position of Elder of Elders or incorporate gold into their shields.

Mókea became more excited as she pointed out the knight whose shield bore the three green sharks on the field of black, telling Archie that his name was Thlū'taku. She seemed to favor this knight, and even though he had known Mókea for less than a full day, this made Archie jealous.

"Thlū'taku is the best dolphin rider in K'truum-Shra. This is only his second year in the tournaments, but he has never lost a match."

"You like him, don't you?" Archie asked.

"I like everyone," Mókea protested, "because of my grandfather's position."

"You like him, and it is definitely *not* because of your grandfather."

A blush swept over Mókea's delicate face, and she turned to look Archie directly in the eye. "For a little more than fourteen years now, since the first anniversary of my birth, I have been betrothed to Thlū'taku. His is an old and powerful family, and I am fortunate that my parents chose well."

The heralds sounded their trumpets, and Mókea turned her attention to the jousting pond, where several attendants were preparing Thlū'taku for the next match. For a moment, Archie continued looking at Mókea, who pretended not to notice. He grappled with what she had told him, for Thlū'taku, who appeared to be in his mid-twenties, was much too old for Mókea. When the shock had worn off, Archie also turned to watch the match.

Thlū'taku's opponent—Pwrádisa—carried a shield very similar to Mókato's: a gold field with a black border, a black bar on top, and a smaller, internal black shield in the center. The difference, however, was that the white tower in the center of Pwrádisa's shield had no crown over it, and the black bar had three white objects rather than six white towers. Those objects appeared to be some kind of fruit, a fish, and a stalk of corn.

Mókea explained that Pwrádisa was also a talented knight starting his third season, though he had lost two matches. Archie could see that Pwrádisa, like Thlū'taku, was in his twenties. While Mókea was adding that it had been generations since Pwrádisa's family had wielded much power, Archie realized that with the gold field, Pwrádisa was eligible to be the Elder of Elders, and perhaps one or more of his ancestors had been. Mókato sat quietly elevated above the couple, with his ceremonial robe located at their eye level. Archie's gaze was suddenly caught by something on that ceremonial robe, and as he turned his head, he found what he thought he had seen: Pwrádisa's shield at the bottom of the robe, near the hem.

On their first pass, Pwrádisa's lance made contact with Thlū'taku, catching him off guard and almost unseating him. Without thinking, Archie cheered, an action that was immediately met with the silent but disapproving eyes of Mókato and Mókea. Archie struggled to find any clue to Thlū'taku's feelings right then, but this was difficult to read at a distance. Nevertheless, it appeared to Archie that Thlū'taku was embarrassed by the blunder. But if he was, he got over it quickly, for he showed a gritty determination as the dolphin riders sped toward each other on the second pass. This time, it was Thlū'taku's lance that made contact, and Pwrádisa reeled in his saddle but did not fall off. By now, Archie was caught up in the excitement of the sport and let everything else slip to the back of his mind.

Jousting Tournament

On the third pass, Thlū'taku unseated Pwrådisa, not only knocking him off his dolphin steed, but knocking him completely unconscious. Pwrådisa lay floating in the water, face-down, for what seemed to Archie to be a painfully long time. Then, all at once, everyone seemed to realize that the poor knight was helpless, and men began running everywhere. Thlū'taku jumped back on his dolphin steed, raced to Pwrådisa, and pulled him to the edge of the jousting pond. There, several men extracted Pwrådisa from the water but left him lying on the grass.

When it was clear to Archie that no one knew what to do, he jumped out of his seat and ran down the stairs and over to Pwrådisa. He removed the knight's helmet and checked his breathing. All the while, Archie struggled to remember what he had learned in his CPR and first-aid classes and wondered whether what he had learned would be appropriate for the T'lantim, a people who were smaller and slighter in build than most American twelve-year-olds. Still, he went to work and cleared Pwrådisa's airway and began to administer CPR. After a short while, Pwrådisa began to breathe, and all around him, T'lantim began to weep for joy.

"The outsider has breathed life into one of our own."

"The hand of God is truly on him, for he has been given the power to bestow life."

"He will truly bless our people."

Mókato gracefully descended the steps of the grandstand and walked right toward Archie. Though his eyes still had a gentle appearance, they also hid something else. Was it disappointment? Anger? Sadness? Archie could not tell. All he knew for sure was that Mókato was not completely happy with the events that had just transpired, and so he just listened.

"On your knees," Mókato demanded. Archie complied immediately.

Drawing a long, slender, slightly curved sword out of his garments, Mókato raised it high over Archie's head. Then, while Archie's heart pounded, Mókato gently lowered the sword, touching each of Archie's shoulders and proclaiming him to be the newest knight.

"By the power vested in me, the 613th T'lantim to wear the crown and title Elder of Elders, I dub you knight of the realm, and hereby command your fealty, not to me or to any individual, but to the City of K'truum-Shra and the T'lantim people."

But before Archie could say anything, Mókato moved to the now-recovering Pwrådisa, who lifted himself up and knelt before Mókato. Mókato, a tear in one eye, then spoke. "You know that our law forbids more than thirty-six hundred knights. You also know that you are the third son in your family to struggle to regain your family's honor. But because you were unable to do so before another became entitled to join the ranks of the peerage, you must now forfeit your shield, title, family, and honor." While uttering these words, Mókato used the sharp edge of his sword to gently snap the threads holding the crest on Pwrádisa's tunic. Then, shifting his piercing gaze from Pwrádisa to Archie, Mókato added, "It is indeed ironic that the one who today earned the right to become a knight did so by saving the life of his adversary."

Archie protested. "But this man is not my enemy, and I did not save him to take from him what is dear to him. Anyway, I did not even ask to become a knight! Are your laws so cruel that no one can celebrate victory unless another celebrates defeat?"

"Can joy exist without sadness," Mókato asked, "or life be full without impending death?"

After a brief moment of contemplation, Archie retorted, "Then I reject your shallow joy, your empty glories, and your compassionless life. I do not want to be a knight if it means inflicting pain on those who have not hurt me, those whom I would be sworn to protect."

The words Archie uttered did not seem to be his own, and they were greeted by silence. As he looked up into the eyes of Mókato, Mókea, the other Elders, Pwrádisa, and Thlū́taku, he realized they were also surprised. Everyone appeared to be pondering the words he had spoken as though they had heard them before and knew them well. Archie could not bear the silent inspection any longer, and spoke again.

"What I *will* accept as a reward, if it is offered, is to serve Pwrádisa as his squire—that is, if he will take me. I don't really know what a squire does, especially in this mixed-up place. In any event, isn't it only natural that I learn to be a squire before becoming a knight?"

After another agonizing moment, Mókato smiled, not in an artificial or even condescending way, but rather in the way a good and wise man smiles when he realizes that someone else—particularly a child—has taught him wisdom.

"Archie, stranger whose foretelling has been known by many generations of T'lantim, by your actions today, you have already demonstrated that not even our fathers and grandfathers knew of the wisdom you would bring to us. Honoring your humble request, I hereby award to you the station of squire, to serve at the pleasure of Lord Pwrádisa, if he will have you. And finally, although not yet a knight, I nevertheless dub you Archie the Bold, for that is what your actions demonstrate and that is what your name means."

Then Mókato turned again to Pwrådisa. "Lord Pwrådisa, saved twice today by the same man, I shall remove your shield from the hem of this cloak and place it in an honored position not because of anything you did. So shall your family once again rise in honor, but not for great deeds. A wise stranger has taught us that our character and our worth are not always measured by what we have achieved but sometimes—and perhaps more important—in the love and respect of others around us."

Mókato turned again to Archie and placed both his hands on Archie's two shoulders. "Son, I am proud of you, as a father for his own son. But now I must ask you to remove the tunic bearing my shield, for you were a guest in my royal house but have, by your brave actions, chosen more humble accommodations." Archie complied, and as he did so, Mókato continued. "There is no dishonor in this, only honor. I did not compel you to leave for some offense, and you did not choose to leave because of some fault of mine. Rather, it was your wisdom and humility that dictated your choice, and that has honored not only you but my own family, for you did this while wearing my coat of arms."

Archie had not forgotten Mókato's promise that Archie's quest would become clear after the tournament, so he decided now was the opportune time to raise the subject again. "Last night, you told me that a mighty quest awaits me and that my coming was foretold many generations ago. What is my quest?" Archie insisted.

Mókato paused briefly, looked Archie in the eye, and said, "You have waited long enough. There have been 613 who have held the position of Elder of Elders, and these out of only eight noble houses. Each of the eight noble houses is symbolized by one of the corner towers on the city wall, and the shields of the male heirs of these eight families all had a gold field with an internal black shield on which was depicted a white tower. Only these eight great houses were permitted to depict either the gold field or a tower. Unfortunately, over the generations, and possibly because of our very strict laws, four of those houses ceased to exist when no male heir was born, for names and houses and honors in our society follow the male line. Then, two other houses disappeared, when the heirs were unable to uphold the honor of their families. Over time, other nobles began adding towers to their shields to signify that one or more daughters of the families of The Eight had married into their own, lesser families, and so now it is not so uncommon to see towers on shields.

"Of the two remaining houses, that of Lord Pwrådisa, which is associated with the Tower of Humility, almost died out today, for had you not first breathed life back into his lifeless form, there would have been no male heir, and had you not made your noble sacrifice, Lord Pwrådisa and his heirs would have forever lost any chance of ruling again. This brings us to my own house, which is associated with the Tower of Purity. Sadly, my own two sons have not survived me, and I have only one grandchild, Mókea. But because Mókea is a female, it appears that my line, too, will vanish."

"But what does this have to do with my quest?" Archie insisted.

"Do you see this crown of leadership I wear? Of the 613 Elders who have worn it, more than two-thirds of them have done so since it was first foretold that during a crisis, an outsider would come and restore our society. Over the generations, this was progressively revealed through several more prophets. We have the accumulated writings of 'The Twelve,' as we call them, in our *Sacred Book of The Twelve*. But the writings are not clear, and our priests struggle over what they mean and have even divided into factions. In this way, endlessly bickering about the true meaning of the prophecies, the priests have made themselves useless to those who need them.

"Because my two sons were killed in the same storm that brought you to us, we were assuming that you would bring some miracle that would restore my house. Instead, you have already demonstrated that you are, indeed, The One, by breathing life into the sole survivor of a dying ruling house and then elevating that same house to its former glory. By your actions this afternoon, you have proven that you are The One."

"But what of my quest?' Archie implored.

With a smile overflowing with not only kindness but also true joy and peace—and not a little bit of pride—Mókato replied, "I have given you enough to digest tonight, and you have much to learn and do on the morrow."

Chapter Six
The First Tower

As Archie stood silently for a moment, his attention was abruptly diverted to a group of young boys bringing him a new tunic. As he examined it, he noticed that it bore the shield that Pwrǎdisa had carried into the jousting match. Like the coat of arms borne by Mókato, this shield was also gold with a black border, a black bar, and a smaller internal black shield. Unlike Mókato's shield, the white tower inside the smaller black shield had no crown over it, and the black bar at the top had a white fruit, a white fish, and a white cornstalk instead of six white towers. This, Archie now knew, was the coat of arms of the only other house whose sons were still entitled to seek the office held by Mókato, the Elder of Elders.

The new tunic bore the gold that signified a family of power, but Archie knew that the shield and its owner had just been rescued from destruction. With the help of the servants, Archie slipped the new tunic over his chest and was surprised that it fit him as well as the tailored tunic, as though it had been prepared for him in advance. He still wore the pantaloons he had received from Lord Mókato's house, and the difference in the fabric was astounding. From a distance, perhaps, no one would notice. But because he was now wearing the two garments together, he could see that the pantaloons were of a much finer weave and had a much silkier touch. The new vestment from Pwrǎdisa's house was nice but did not match what Archie had worn in its place just moments before.

After he was fully dressed, the servants guided Archie to the livery stables beneath the Palace of Elders. He could hear the Elders speaking above him and occasionally heard the voice of Mókato. Somehow, Archie surmised, if he had not intervened, he would have been upstairs in the glorious chamber housing the Elders rather than in this dark, damp barn, smelling of fish and who knows what. He had always been impetuous, but that impetuosity had been correct, more often than not (or so Archie comforted himself).

The servants led Archie to take a seat in an older vessel, a completely enclosed coach, but with windows and curtains. The coach itself was bright red, and on its two doors, one on each side, it bore the shield of Pwrådisa's house, the Tower of Humility. Inside, the coach was smaller than the stagecoaches Archie remembered from westerns. This coach was a two-door coach and had just one seat inside, a leather-upholstered bench, facing forward. The coachman called the carriage a neroh-brougham. Outside, almost at water level, there was another seat for the coachman, lower than the internal seat and closer to the water. At the rear were two seats of sorts, where two footmen stood guard.

Just as he sat down within the coach, Archie saw that the servants were all sitting in a pile of grassy hay inside an open vessel that was to be pulled by the coach. As daylight gave way to twilight, the evening air was still warm. Archie envied the servants their open-air ride, for it looked like it was more comfortable and more fun.

Although Archie was alone in the coach, he welcomed it. He had not been alone since he met Mókea upon awakening from his long sleep. As the small coach, pulled by a team of four dolphins, left the livery stable in the Palace of Elders and began navigating the ring canal surrounding the palace, Archie thought about Mókea, whose beauty maintained a firm grasp on his attention. It did not seem fair that she had been betrothed to Thlū'taku, a man much too old for her, since infancy. As the sun receded from the sky, the buildings gradually transformed from brilliant white, stonelike edifices to their nocturnal greenish, glowing, other-worldly appearance. There was plenty of activity, for the T'lantim filled the streets above and the sidewalks beside the canals, and their vessels, of every shape and size, transited the canals. As the neroh-brougham approached the dining and entertainment district, music filled the air, and Archie saw that the crowds were very large.

Soon, they had passed the bright and active dining and entertainment district and were now making their way through the farm and orchard district. Gazing out the window became dull after a while, and Archie, who had been awake many hours, curled up on the seat and fell asleep.

It seemed like he had hardly fallen asleep when there arose a commotion that awakened him. As he lifted his weary head, he realized that they had arrived at their destination. Archie sat up and examined his surroundings. Nighttime had now fully descended, and they were far enough from the center of the city that the greenish glow that had become so common to him came from just two places: the one hundred-foot-high city wall just a short distance away and a large manor house that straddled the tower canal in which they had been traveling. Steps going up both sides of the canal made their way to sidewalks on each side, which in turn led to an arched bridge on which the manor house sat. A deck surrounding the manor house provided an ideal place to observe canal traffic.

Before he could ponder more, Archie was ushered out of the neroh-brougham by servants apparently awaiting his arrival. While the coach and team were driven into a livery stable behind the canal wall, the servants led Archie through one of four doors in the arched bridge, which, he later learned, were the only way into or out of the manor house. After climbing several flights of stairs, they entered the main level of the house.

While the home was as stately as any he had ever seen, the one factor that Archie could not miss was that there was a large opening in the roof for the collection of rainwater. From the pool beneath that opening, water flowed into a waterfall on the side of the home facing the Palace of Elders. Unlike the pavilions he had seen earlier, the manor house had exterior walls, all of which were elaborately decorated. There were no doors to the deck on which the manor house sat, but only large openings that were covered by very large sheer drapes. If the drapes were intended to maintain privacy, they could not do a very good job, for the ocean breezes would catch them and keep them indefinitely suspended in the air. The rooms were large and had a very comfortable appeal to them, but they were not as well lit as the Palace of Elders. Most of the light came from the glowing walls and fire pits that were built right into the floors. When they had finally reached one large room, Archie saw Pwrâdisa, who politely gestured for him to take a seat.

Manor House

"Welcome to the house of my ancestors," Pwrådisa offered. "I am grateful that your actions have saved both my life and my family's house."

"It really wasn't anything," Archie said sheepishly. "Anyone could have done it—just took a CPR class before summer break."

Like all the T'lantim, Pwrådisa was short and of very slender build, and his complexion had a definite green hue, but he was somewhat darker than either Mókea or Mókato. Though slender, he was also very muscular, and his face bore a few mild scars. Archie could see a mixture of peace, confidence, deep sadness, and an even deeper anger in his eyes. But there was also gentleness. Not the kind of open and free gentleness of Mókea but rather the protective gentleness of a seasoned warrior who, though a survivor, had not forgotten the delicate and good things that make life worth living.

"You know so little of the struggle ahead, or even of the rivalries that mar our city. And yet you have a wholesomeness that defies your birth as a barbarian."

Archie suddenly realized that while he was "reading" Pwrådisa, he, too, was being read.

Walking around Archie in the manner that a rancher might examine his cattle or a king his subjects, Pwrådisa continued. "Though taller than most of our men, and certainly fleshier, I surmise that you are yet but a child. There is much that you know that we do not, and yet much of what is common among us perplexes you. That you can help us is doubtful at best, but I will not deny you your chance."

Archie then repeated the question he felt would never be answered: "Lord Mókato spoke of a quest that I must make, but he did not explain to me what is meant by 'quest,' what I must do, why I must do it, or how. To tell you the truth, I have just about had it. All I really want is to go home!"

"Perhaps his answers were not clear because you do not yet understand that it is you who have the answers. If we could tell you what to do, there would be nothing for you to do, for we could do it ourselves. At best, we can show you our society, and when you have learned enough, you will realize what must be done. It may be simple, or it may be dangerous and difficult. It may bring great joy, or it may bring terrible despair. This, only the future knows."

"Then start teaching me now!" Archie begged, "so that I can start as soon as possible."

"First, you should know that you have chosen well, to begin as the squire to a knight, so that you can learn from the bottom up. This shows humility and eagerness to learn. Second, your choice is also wise, because you have sought to learn from one whose family, name, and title mean almost nothing. By so doing, you will be an impartial observer, so that truth cannot evade you.

"Tonight, we begin with the basics about the eight towers. As you have seen, the city is surrounded by an octagon-shaped wall, and at each corner, there is a turret, or tower. The towers are identical in form and function, but not in history. First, the towers were each given names; they are the Towers of Humility, Mourning, Surrender, Morality, Compassion, Purity, Peace, and Sacrifice. Each tower was assigned to a single family to assist in guarding the city. These families became known as 'The Eight,' and the head of each family became one of the 'Eight Lords,' who formed a council, the Council of Elders. Originally, the eight lords each spoke with equal authority. Each assumed certain responsibilities, including the cultivation and harvesting of fruit, fish, and grain so that all of the people of the city would have a balanced and nutritious diet. Each lord undertook to harvest a different fruit, a different grain, and a different fish. My own house is associated with the Tower of Humility and raises and harvests pomegranate, tuna, and corn. Tomorrow, you will see my pomegranate orchards and cornfields."

"Over our long history, we have seldom seen battle. But each of the eight lords was responsible for commanding a division in our citizen-army should war erupt. Each division consists of twelve thousand men, including its staff, so that the strength of our army is about ninety-six thousand. Our soldiers are commoners, and the thirty-six hundred knights make up our officer corps. All males must serve two years in the military, and longer if war ever erupts. But we have not been at war in more than two thousand years."

Archie marveled at this fact, for he could not remember a time when his own country was not involved in some conflict around the world.

Pwrãdisa continued. "Although each lord's civil offices are located in the Palace of Elders, his military offices are located within the tower associated with his house. For this reason, each lord's manor faces both that tower and the Palace of Elders, while straddling the canal dividing the fields in which his fruit orchards and grain fields are planted.

"The shields borne by the eight lords were originally very similar. Each was on a field of gold bordered with black. At the top of the shield was a bar, called a 'chief,' on which there were representations of the fruit, fish, and grain for which the lord was responsible, all in white. At the center of the gold shield was a smaller black shield, called an 'inescutcheon,' on which there was a single white tower.

"In time, the eight lords realized that there was a need for someone to preside over their meetings. They created the office of the Elder of Elders and began electing him from among their ranks, to serve for life. Lords from each of the Eight Houses have served in that office, and while any of the Eight Houses filled that role, its patriarch was entitled to have a gold crown on his shield over the white tower.

"But as the lords disappeared, one by one, Lord Mókato's house began altering its shield. As you have seen, it no longer depicts the fruit, fish, and grain for which his house is responsible, but instead depicts six smaller white towers in the chief. Those towers represent the lines lost either through failure of the male line or failure to uphold honor. Each of those families is now under the complete control and patronage of Lord Mókato, and a steward runs their state affairs. But enough for tonight. You must be very tired."

Pwrådisa led Archie to his bedroom, which was located in a section of the home just above the arched bridge but beneath the deck. As Archie expected, access to this bedroom was gained through a trapdoor. As he entered the room and pondered Pwrådisa's words, Archie felt a sinking sensation in his stomach. For the first time, he began to see his new paradise in a more sinister light. Up to now, he had enjoyed truly noble impressions of both Lord Mókato and his granddaughter, Mókea, completely undisturbed by anything dark. But if what Pwrådisa had told him was true, Lord Mókato and his family were trying to seize complete control of K'truum-Shra. Who could he trust? They were certainly all strangers to him. Archie once again realized how much he missed home, and he wondered how he would ever find his way back.

Chapter Seven
A Squire's Training

Archie awoke early the next morning, and having previously learned how to navigate his way out of a T'lantim bedroom, he climbed out of the small room and made his way to the deck surrounding the manor house. He felt very refreshed and thankful for the sleep, because he had been awake for a full twenty-four hours before going to sleep in Pwrădisa's manor. This sleep had been more restful, for not only was it not preceded by a terrifying storm, but he was already beginning to know his hosts.

Archie stood at the center of the large upper deck of the manor facing the heart of the city, which now seemed so far away. He watched as traffic began to build in the canal. A variety of vessels moved up and down the canal, and laden with pomegranates from Lord Pwrādisa's orchards and corn from his fields, they made their way toward the city. Similar vessels, hungry for their loads, awaited workers to bring the produce to them. The pomegranate orchards extended as far as Archie could see to the left, and the cornfields extended as far as he could see to the right. For the first time, Archie realized that he had not seen a single wheeled vehicle, or any animals to pull them, during his entire stay in K'truum-Shra.

In some ways, T'lantim technology appeared to be more sophisticated than even American know-how, but in this one area, it definitely lagged: Workers in the fields and orchards were actually carrying their burdens in large baskets on their heads.

Just then, Pwrădisa called to him from across the veranda. "Good morning, Bold One. Did you sleep well?"

"Very well, thank you," Archie replied.

"Are you ready to become a squire?"

"As ready as I will ever be," said Archie, neatly tucking away in his brain the following note: invent wheel, impress Mókea, become hero. Only faintly aware that Pwrådisa was still talking, Archie's attention was quickly jerked away from his pleasant daydream when Pwrådisa snapped at him.

"If you are going to be my squire, you must pay attention! I have given you some latitude because you saved my life and my house, and because you are a stranger to our ways. But now that you have taken this responsibility, remember this: it is no light duty!"

Pwrådisa turned and walked down some stairs. Archie followed. The pair climbed down the stairs all the way to the canal level and then up the stairs from the canal to the pomegranate orchard. Several hundred yards into the orchard they came to a group of four boys, all about Archie's age, circled around one old knight, sporting a long white beard, fully armored, and wearing a white tunic with the embroidered image of a blue shield on which there was a single white flame. His tunic had no sleeves, and Archie remembered from the jousting tournament that the tunics worn by knights in armor had no sleeves. The boys, like Archie, wore tunics bearing the embroidered image of Pwrådisa's shield. As Pwrådisa approached, the boys all stood, some trembling, some happily, but all with tremendous respect.

"This is our newest page, 'The Bold One,' the stranger whose coming has long been foretold. He is to be trained as a squire, and when he is ready, he will be my personal squire."

At this, Pwrådisa turned and left, without as much as a farewell. Archie could not tell whether Pwrådisa was angry with him, or he was making some kind of point, or if this was normal under the circumstances. In any event, he decided that he had chosen to become Pwrådisa's squire, so he would do whatever was required of him.

"Young man, are you accustomed to sleeping in so late?" asked the old bearded knight. After a painfully long pause, accompanied by the worst stuttering that had ever issued from Archie's mouth, the old man laughed heartily. "We will not hold it against you, but you must learn discipline. My name is T'lôt'aris. And we shall call you 'Sleeper,' for you slept for two full days after we found you, and yet, on the very next morning, you slept in again."

Gesturing to four of the most uncomely boys Archie had ever seen, T'lôt'aris said, "These are W'mat'thop, K'ram'vl, K'lud'pe, and N'joph'n.

But don't bother learning their names. In this class, they will be 'Whiner,' 'Sloth,' 'Glutton,' and 'Liar.' Now, back to the lesson.

"You have each been chosen to become squires. This is an honor, for if you learn well and discharge your duties faithfully, and you demonstrate the high character required, in time, you will become eligible to be dubbed knights. As squires, some of your duties will be exciting, for you will accompany the knight to whom you are pledged to tournaments and to battlefields."

At this, the boys smiled and laughed, and some even elbowed others. But Archie recalled that K'truum-Shra had been in no war for more than two thousand years.

"Nevertheless, you will find that most of your duties are not so exciting but rather dull and tedious. You will take care of your knight's steed, feeding and caring for the dolphin so that you learn to think like a dolphin. You will even smell like one."

The boys laughed, and Sloth even offered that Glutton already did.

"You will also serve in the kitchen, wait on your master's table, care for your master's clothing, maintain his arms and armor, run errands, carry messages, and guard your master while he sleeps, even if you yourself are in need of sleep. And in your spare time, you will prepare yourself to become a knight by learning the Code of Chivalry, the rules of heraldry, the art of riding dolphins as though you were part dolphin, the art of arms—including both swordsmanship and marksmanship—individual tactics, leadership skills, strategy, and survival skills. In all of this, you will develop the qualities of character that mark a knight: *physical* strength, *mental* acuity, and *moral* might. These virtues cannot be taught, but you will develop them through rigorous discipline and testing. If, and only if, you develop these strengths, will you become knights.

"Now, for the first phase of your training, you will eat, sleep, and live outside, and you will be tested to the limits of your physical endurance. Look at what you are wearing. These are your clothes, your shelters, and a good many other things. Look at those around you. They are your society, your best friends, your worst enemies, and even more. Look at the dirt on which you sit. It is your mother, your kitchen, and your bed.

"Let us now run!"

Without another word, the old bearded knight suddenly began running and was soon moving faster than Archie could have imagined was possible for someone so old, but after the shock wore off, the boys followed. They began by running the distance of the pomegranate orchard and back, over the bridge on which the manor house straddled the canal, through the cornfield and back, and then into one of the doors in the arched bridge supporting the manor house and down a long underwater tunnel. They emerged inside the Tower of Humility and began climbing a spiral stairway until every one of them—except the old bearded knight—was huffing and puffing and panting as hard as he could. When they arrived at the top, they did not stop to admire the view but pushed on, running along the wall itself. Before they even made it up the stairs, Sloth and Glutton had both fallen out, and so it was just the old bearded knight, Whiner, Liar, and Archie. The small group ran for hours, and Archie felt that he was ready to quit this nonsense and find his way home. Worst of all, Whiner remained true to his nickname and complained about every uneven spot, every obstacle in the way, and anything else his mind could seize. Archie secretly wished that Whiner had dropped out of the run rather than Sloth or Glutton, but after a while, he simply mused about home, computers, Mókea (who had now usurped Lauren McManus in his daydreams), and anything pleasant. So Archie simply looked out at the sea on his left or off to the city on his right.

But this was not always possible, for every time they approached another tower, the old bearded knight led them down the spiral stairway and then back up, sometimes doubling or tripling the agonizing experience. This, Archie found, was most likely to happen when Whiner was loudest, so Archie began singing pleasant songs to amuse the small group. As they learned the lyrics, the others, even Whiner, joined in. The towers were not all bad, for there, the boys could grab a quick drink of much-needed water. At first, they were very clumsy, but after observing the old bearded knight, they soon learned how to handle the ladle in one sweeping motion: scoop—drink—pass.

After they had emerged for the second time from the Eighth Tower, Archie knew that the next tower would be the one from which they first emerged, the Tower of Humility. Archie assumed that this signified the end of the run, but when they arrived at that tower, they descended its stairs and ascended again. When they reached the top of the wall, the old bearded knight began running in the opposite direction, the direction from which they had come, thereby sending the obvious message that the run was not nearly over yet.

When the small entourage finally made its way back to the Tower of Humility, through the underwater tunnel, and back into the pomegranate orchard, the old bearded knight finally stopped, and the boys collapsed on the ground. It was almost dusk, and the boys had not eaten all day, so they were excited when the old knight told them that they would now gather their meal. He warned them that they could not collect any of the pomegranates or corn, because those belonged to Lord Pwrådisa, and they needed to learn to survive on their own. The old knight took the boys out through the field and pointed out various edible plants that had not been cultivated, as well as some edible—or so he said—worms. When they had each collected what seemed a fair meal, the famished boys returned to their base, where they found Sloth and Glutton. They did not return the happy and excited greetings of the young runners but explained that by failing to complete the arduous run themselves, they had been dismissed as potential squires. Now they would fulfill their commitments as mere servants in Pwrådisa's household. As if this were not enough to discourage the boys, T'lôt'aris, the old bearded knight, spoke again.

"It is not healthy to eat just before going to sleep. You will sleep more restfully when your stomachs are not digesting, so we will prepare this food tonight and eat it two hours before daybreak."

The old knight showed them how to prepare their feast and to preserve it until the morning. As he lay on the ground, Archie reviewed the day in his mind, wondering whether he could ever become a squire, much less a knight. He shifted his weight on the hard soil, hoping at least to make his sleep a little more comfortable. But just as he settled down, it began to rain, and Archie knew that his night would be no better than his day had been. But the cold wet drops did not prevent Archie's weary body from demanding its due, and Archie soon fell asleep.

Chapter Eight
The Art of Arms

It seemed to Archie that he had hardly dozed off before he was being awakened by the old bearded knight. It was still dark, and a heavy mist—the kind that follows heavy rainfalls—was hanging in the pomegranate orchard. Although it was no longer raining, the ground was saturated, as were Archie's clothes, and everywhere there was the musky odor of damp clay and mildewed vegetation, mixed with a sickly sweet scent that Archie assumed came from the pomegranate blossoms. Although his sleep had been heavy, his drowsiness was gradually replaced by awareness of the cold chill that had penetrated his body during the night. As the boys arose, the old bearded knight built a fire.

"We will dry your clothes," he said, "and if we have time, I will teach you how to avoid being soaked while sleeping in the rain." Staring at the shivering boys, he added, "Are you so dull? Strip off those wet clothes now!"

Though naked, it did not take long for Archie to warm up as he stood close to the fire. This made him appreciate the old bearded knight, for Archie now realized that it was the wet clothing that was making him cold and that the misty morning was not nearly as chilly as it had seemed just moments before. Archie looked at the old bearded knight, whose bone-dry clothing made him stand out even more than his aged appearance.

"When you feel warm enough, go ahead and eat your meal. We have a long day."

More welcomed words were never spoken, and the boys immediately ran to gather their food, which they had buried just a few hours before, protected only by a leafy wrapping that the old bearded knight had instructed them to use. As they sat around the fire, devouring their meals, wearing not a stitch of clothing, Archie felt that he had been transported back in time to some primitive culture. It dawned on him just how easy it was to shed the largely useless ornamentation of "civilized" life.

As he ate his meal, he marveled at the fact that it was quite warm and tasty. The leafy wrapper had somehow "cooked" his meager food, and he was reminded of watching his mother prepare fish without cooking it. He had seen her make a dish she called ceviche, putting raw fish into a pan with a lemon juice and vinegar solution. When she removed the dish from the refrigerator just a short time later, the fish looked and tasted like it had been cooked over a fire. Something in the large, broad leaves the old bearded knight had pointed out not only preserved the boys' meals from pests and decay, but chemically cooked the raw vegetables and worms.

As the boys ate, the old bearded knight constructed a rack out of branches and placed their clothing over the fire. This created considerable smoke, and soon, the boys saw steam rising from their clothes. Before long, the clothes were dry, though they remained covered with stains from the muddy clay in which the boys had slept, and they smelled of smoke. In contrast, the old bearded knight's tunic appeared as clean as it did the day before, and Archie wondered whether he had disappeared into the manor house while the boys slept in the rain.

As soon as they had eaten and dressed, the old bearded knight told Sloth and Glutton to put out the fire and clean up the campsite, leaving no trace that it had ever been there. He then turned his attention to Archie, Whiner, and Liar and uttered the words that had been at the back of each boy's mind, but that all of them had been afraid to even contemplate.

"Let us run."

Whiner let out an extraordinarily loud groan, even for him, but Archie and Liar quietly shared his sentiment. As they began to run, the soreness he had been feeling all morning suddenly assumed the center of his attention, for the prior day's run had been longer than his young body was used to, and his muscles now made it known that this run would be much more painful. The meal he had just consumed began to cause its own troubles, as an aching sensation began to grow in Archie's abdomen. He looked at Whiner and Liar to determine whether they were suffering as he was, but he could not tell.

They ran through the pomegranate orchard, across the bridge supporting the manor house, into the cornfield, and then to an uncultivated portion of that cornfield near the canal that bordered the great wall of the city. In that field, there was a large, octagonal arena surrounded by a fence. Next to the arena, there was a one-story building that resembled either a small barn or a large shed. To their surprise and satisfaction, their run—very brief by the prior day's standard—ended at the little structure. The old bearded knight opened the door and they entered.

Dozens of suits of armor, shields, swords, other weapons, and similar equipment filled the building, clearly an armory. Without any instructions, the old bearded knight began grabbing various equipment and shoving it into the hands of Archie, Whiner, and Liar. He then turned around and exited, and the boys followed.

When they were in the middle of the arena, the old bearded knight finally spoke. "Today you will have your first lesson in swordsmanship. The swords you will use have no edges and are designed for instruction and practice, but they can still hurt you. If you do not listen to every word of instruction, you will likely hurt the boy against whom you are matched. And I can guarantee you that your punishment will be at least as severe as the injury you inflict through your negligence."

Sloth and Glutton appeared out of nowhere and began helping Archie, Whiner, and Liar dress in suits of armor. They had been made servants in Pwrâdisa's House, and it was now clear that they had been assigned to serve their former comrades. This made Archie uncomfortable, for he felt their shame and humiliation. But these sympathetic thoughts quickly fled his mind as he realized that the suit of armor selected for him was far too small.

The old bearded knight looked both amused and perplexed, and led Archie back into the armory. Rummaging through the equipment, he finally pulled out a musky smelling older suit of armor and thrust it into Archie's arms.

"This is the largest suit of armor we have. Let's see whether it will fit."

Archie carried the armor back to the arena, and, with the help of Sloth, he put it on. It was old, smelled bad, and looked uglier than any armor he had ever seen or even imagined, but Archie was thankful that it at least fit him reasonably well.

For the rest of the morning, the boys sat around the old bearded knight as he demonstrated techniques with a sword, thrusting, parrying, defending, and guarding. This took several hours, during which Archie worried that he could not recall everything that the old master was teaching them. During the same time, Whiner shifted around, obviously uncomfortable, and complained without any apparent need to rest his vocal cords. Although Liar paid attention to the instruction, he periodically let it be known that he was a "natural" and that he could undoubtedly best any other squire without the necessity of further instruction. Sloth and Glutton spent the time cleaning the armory—or at least pretending to do so.

About midday, the boys were instructed to find and prepare their own meals, this time without help. After collecting their food, they returned to the arena, where all of the boys other than Archie quickly consumed their meals. Having carefully observed the old bearded knight, Archie found one of the broad, protective leaves they had used on the previous evening and then collected his food, wrapped it up, and buried it. After Whiner, Liar, Sloth, and Glutton had finished eating, the instruction continued, but now with some actual practice.

Standing well apart from each other, the boys thrust, parried, defended, and guarded as instructed by the old bearded knight. They learned and practiced dozens of techniques. Soon, the excitement of "air swordsmanship" wore off, and the repetition became tiresome and downright boring. In addition, the swords became heavier as the afternoon wore on, and all of the other boys, even Sloth and Glutton, began to sweat and breathe heavily. When at last they ceased their practice, all four of the other boys walked a short distance away and began to vomit. Archie did not feel ill at all, just tired, and he followed the old bearded knight a short distance, where both of them dug up their meals and ate them. Archie was not certain, but he believed that the old master smiled and winked at him.

When they returned to the arena, Archie was ready for more practice, but he could see that Whiner and Liar were still ill and that Sloth and Glutton had disappeared. For the rest of the afternoon, the air swordsmanship continued, but only Archie tried in earnest to maintain the proper form and timing. Whiner and Liar just mimicked the techniques, trying to expend as little energy as possible.

As dusk approached, they ran back to the pomegranate orchard and prepared for bed. Once again, there was no evening meal, but everyone prepared breakfast before going to bed. As promised, the old bearded knight showed the boys how to make a shelter with their garments, covering them with a kind of straw that was abundant in the pomegranate orchard. He also showed them how to make a bed of that same straw and to cover themselves in it to keep warm at night. It did not take long for the boys to fall asleep.

During the days that followed, their lives developed routine. In the mornings, they would arise, dress, and eat the breakfasts they had prepared the night before. They would then break camp, and Sloth and Glutton would remain behind to eliminate all trace that they had been there, even though they all knew they would return that night. The boys were never told why this was necessary, and only Archie was curious enough to ask the old bearded knight to explain.

"If we are coming back this afternoon, why not just keep the same campsite?"

The old bearded knight's response was mysterious. "Do the birds of the air make for themselves permanent homes?"

"But we are not birds," Archie protested.

The old knight smiled and then asked, "Do you know the future, Sleeper? Are you certain when you leave in the morning that you will return in the afternoon?"

Archie had no response and did not press the issue.

The mornings were filled with exercise, mostly running around the city wall, but also lifting and carrying heavy objects, while the afternoons were filled with training at the arena. At midday, when they typically arrived at the arena, the first order of business was to prepare their lunches, but no one ever made the mistake again of eating his meal before it was ready.

For several days, they continued with the air swordsmanship, but after about a week, they graduated to practice against scarecrow-like dummies. After another week, the boys were finally ready to fight one another, but this was preceded by another lecture about the dangerous nature of the practice swords and the consequences of injuring one another.

The first match was fought between Whiner and Liar, neither of whom was able to best the other. Then Archie was matched against Liar and quickly defeated him, which prompted Liar to insist that Archie had cheated and that he had actually won. This earned him a single cold stare from the old bearded knight. Archie was then matched against Whiner, who objected that he wasn't ready and that he had been tired out by his match against Liar. But when the old bearded knight matched Archie against each of these boys again, without any rest for Archie, the result was the same, because Archie had been listening and learning. He had really made the old master's techniques his own.

Soon, Whiner and Liar were routinely matched only against each other, while Archie found himself matched against the old bearded knight. For the first time in these matches, Archie had to struggle, and he was soundly defeated time after time. But he never quit trying, and the old bearded knight never tired of fighting Archie. Gradually—and imperceptibly—these matches against the old master honed Archie's skill so that the techniques became natural. And then, without really even thinking about it, Archie began devising his own moves, and the matches increased in ease for Archie while increasing in difficulty for the old bearded knight. One day, to everyone's surprise, Archie defeated the old master in just a few minutes. Liar gasped, but it was Archie who truly felt the emotion expressed by the air and noise that issued from Liar's mouth.

On the very next day, the boys began a new type of training: archery. That training progressed in much the same manner as the training in swordsmanship. When Archie bested the old bearded knight in archery, the training again changed, to dolphin riding and the use of the lance. During this phase of training, the boys did not run but instead swam every morning in the canal that bordered the wall surrounding the city.

Although Archie was accustomed to horseback riding, his experience offered no help in riding a dolphin. First, horses are much larger animals, and they are not at all slippery. In addition, a saddle fits neatly on a horse's back, because the horse has no dorsal fin. On a dolphin, the saddle sits in front of the dorsal fin and just behind the flippers, making the rider sit farther forward than he would on a horse. This creates the need for an acutely developed sense of balance. Also, horses don't suddenly get the urge to submerge, and a dolphin rider must learn to restrain his steed from doing this. But most daunting of all, Archie felt that he was too large to ride a dolphin comfortably, and he knew that he would eventually have to compensate for this. Nevertheless, he carefully absorbed all that the old bearded knight had to offer and learned to ride quite satisfactorily.

And when the art of riding dolphins had been mastered, the boys were trained in the use of a lance. The boys had learned to ride dolphins in the canal that bordered the city wall, but they would learn to use the lance in a jousting pond. Archie soon learned that there was a jousting pond associated with every one of the eight towers, although none of them was as nice as the one located next to the Palace of Elders. These other ponds were used for training and for practice matches between the riders representing different towers, while the larger jousting pond he had first seen was used only for championship tournaments.

Archie found jousting to be difficult, and it seemed to him that using a lance while riding a dolphin required a whole new set of skills. Even holding a lance made him feel that he had never really learned to ride at all. But Archie applied himself as he had in all his prior training, and he was soon able to use a lance nearly as well as the old bearded knight.

In the evenings, when the boys had all been released for the day, Archie would remain with the old bearded knight and ask him questions about the day's training. Sometimes—because Archie's questions would lead them there—they would discuss tactics and strategy. Archie gradually began to understand not only the weapons themselves but how they were best deployed.

One night, just as they were all returning to their camp, the old bearded knight turned to Archie. "Lord Pwrådisa has summoned you to the manor house. Go immediately."

It had been weeks since Archie had spent any significant time indoors. He welcomed the change and was thankful that he was ready. During all of his training, Archie had kept his eye on the old bearded knight, studying everything he did. By doing so, he learned things the other boys did not, things that made life easier. While the other boys had grown accustomed to wearing their filthy clothing and not bathing, Archie had observed how the old bearded knight cleaned his clothing, his armor, and his body, and did the same. Living outdoors did not mean living like an animal, and now he could return to the manor house without offending Lord Pwrådisa.

When he arrived, the lord of the manor greeted him warmly.

"I have heard good things about you, and I am happy that you are part of my household. Because you have learned so well, as of today you are no longer a page, but my personal squire. But before you perform any other services for me, I have a special project for you. I have decided to enter you in a tournament matching squires rather than knights."

Archie was both stunned and excited but stood mute before Pwrådisa.

With an expression that Archie could not quite read, the lord of the manor added, "Oh, Mókea will be there, and I understand that she is eager to see you again."

Chapter Nine
Everything New

Early the next morning, Archie arose before the old bearded knight. For the first time in quite a while, he felt refreshed, and it seemed that all of nature was rejoicing with him. Though still dark, the early morning sky was very clear, a fact betrayed by the multitude of brilliant stars. Despite the early hour, it was warmer than it had been for many nights, and the warmth was carried throughout the campsite by a gentle breeze. Even the fragrance of pomegranates penetrated Archie's consciousness for the first time in weeks. This caused him to pause, breathe deeply, and wonder why it had taken him so long to appreciate this gift of nature, just as he was arising from his last slumber in the camp.

He had much to do, for the tournament was scheduled for the following week. Although Lord Pwrádisa had already commissioned brand new armor and weaponry for Archie, he had instructed Archie to select a dolphin from his own stable, a steed that Archie would keep as his own. This was serious business and would require considerable time and effort. It is not enough that the dolphin and rider both have good lineage and training; to really work well together, they must know and trust each other. That would be difficult to accomplish in so short a time.

Archie left the camp before anyone else had awakened and made his way to Lord Pwrádisa's stables, which were located behind the walls of the canal straddled by his manor house. Once there, Archie had to awaken the stable master, who made no effort to hide his contempt for the youthful intruder. He muttered, just loud enough for Archie to hear, "Just made a squire and thinks he owns the place. Hmphh!"

Lord Pwrádisa's stables had a large variety of dolphins, including white-sided dolphins, white-beaked dolphins, striped dolphins, spinner dolphins, and many other breeds. But Archie knew exactly what he wanted and quickly found the stalls in which the bottle-nosed dolphins were housed and waded in. For at least two hours—and much to the stable master's annoyance—Archie painstakingly examined each dolphin from fin to flipper to teeth, for on the previous evening, he had discussed with the old bearded knight how to select a dolphin. During all this time, the stable master continued to mutter, more than once suggesting that the "child" now considered himself an expert in dolphin flesh. Finally, Archie's attention fixed on one of the largest bottle-nosed dolphins in the stable, a steed at least fourteen feet long and weighing no less than six hundred pounds.

Turning to the stable master, Archie asked, "What's his name?"

The stable master was stunned but finally spoke, "Name? What do you mean, name? Who gives names to dolphins?"

Ignoring the stable master's disrespect, Archie simply replied, "Well then, I'll call him 'Splasher.' Get your largest saddle and a bridle so I can ride Splasher and get a feel for him." Finally worn down by the young squire and resigned to his duty, the poor stable master simply obeyed—and without further muttering.

Soon, Archie had the saddle on his new steed and rode out into the broad canal. Splasher's size and muscle tone had been a good indication of his quality, for he was strong and fast and full of spirit, and the early morning light showed that he was also a handsome dolphin. Archie was not disappointed. For most of the morning, he rode Splasher through the various canals, testing the dolphin's reflexes and endurance. The pair quickly bonded, as though God had created rider and dolphin alike just for the moment.

Though Splasher showed no sign of tiring, Archie realized that he had much else to do, so he returned to Lord Pwrádisa's manor house, tied Splasher's reins to a hitching post, and was soon on his way to inquire about the new armor and weaponry. As he ascended the steps leading from the canal level to the manor house above, he was met by Glutton, who handed him a scroll. Archie knocked crumbs from Glutton's last meal off the crumpled scroll and gave him a stern look of disapproval. But the scroll quickly regained Archie's attention, because it bore the seal of Pwrádisa. Upon breaking the seal and removing the ribbon, Archie read his master's directive to proceed immediately to the workshop of Kótan, the premier armorer of K'truum-Shra, where his new armor would be properly fitted. Archie had not been aware that the armor had to be fitted and wondered whether he had missed something in his conversation with Pwrádisa on the previous evening. But Pwrádisa must have understood that, for the scroll gave precise directions to Kótan's workshop.

Without speaking a single word to Glutton, Archie wheeled around, hurried down the steps, and ran out to the canal-level sidewalk. He jumped into the water and mounted Splasher, and in an instant, he was riding Splasher toward the center of the city. In less than twenty minutes, he was within the workshop district, which was located inside the space of twenty ring canals situated closer to the center of the city than to its great wall. Turning left into the third ring canal in the workshop district, Archie began looking for a suit of armor suspended over the canal and marked with three yellow stars, the emblem of Kótan's workshop. It did not take long to find the workshop.

Archie tied Splasher to a hitching post, climbed the steps to sidewalk level, and looked for Kótan's workshop. He soon discovered that the workshop occupied the entire block, so he simply entered and began walking around. There were dozens of men employed in the workshop, doing everything that turned raw k'truum into arms and armor. Many were common laborers, carrying buckets of the scum Lord Mókato had pointed out on the surface of the canal waters. Others were treating the k'truum in various ways, and still others were shaping it into suits of armor, swords, lances, arrows, and other weaponry. Those who were treating the k'truum were the most fascinating to Archie, but they eyed him with suspicion. It was obvious that they intended to guard the master craftsman's ancient secrets. Still, Archie could see that the treatment of the k'truum involved the liberal use of fresh water, fire, and some other substances that Archie did not recognize.

Before he could get a better idea of how the whole process worked, Archie stumbled into Lord Pwrádisa, who was accompanied by a very muscular T'lantim man. Lord Pwrádisa introduced Archie to Kótan, who looked Archie over, chuckled at his sandy blond hair and fair complexion, and then instructed him to remove his tunic and pantaloons. Walking around Archie for just a moment, he then summoned four apprentices, who brought large buckets of the fresh k'truum over to the group. Just as Archie was noticing that the k'truum in each of the four buckets had a different consistency, one of the men began slapping the slimy contents of his bucket onto Archie's chest and back. Archie jumped, but Lord Pwrádisa put his hand on Archie's shoulder and gave him a reassuring glance. Kótan directed the laborer, instructing the removal of excess k'truum here and the addition of extra k'truum there. When at last Archie was covered with the slimy substance, the next apprentice began applying the contents of his bucket, and Archie realized that they were building layers over his body.

"I guess that this is the armor?" Archie weakly asked.

"Yes and no," Kótan replied. "This is the suit upon which the armor coating will be applied."

"How do I take it off?"

"Although as hard as any other armor, this armor will also be *flexible,* which will serve you well in combat, whether ritual or real. It will stretch enough to pull over your body. Once it has dried, we will cut the armor into six pieces: a hauberk for your torso, armored trousers for your lower body, a pair of gauntlets for your arms and hands, and a pair of sabaton for your feet. I will then harden these individual pieces and at Lord Pwrådisa's direction, add decorative touches."

Pwrådisa then added, "And you will have some of the finest and most beautiful armor in all of K'truum-Shra, for Kótan is the finest armorer in the entire city. Indeed, no other armorer has yet developed a technique for making armor flexible."

After about an hour, Kótan's apprentices carefully cut and removed the dried k'truum suit from Archie's body, and carried the six pieces into one of the few enclosed rooms Archie had seen in K'truum-Shra. They soon exited the room, and Kótan closed and locked the door behind them.

"Although he shares many of his secrets with his most trusted apprentices, this secret process is far too valuable to share even with them," Pwrådisa explained. "We will come back in three days. The armor will be ready then."

By the time Archie and Lord Pwrådisa left Kótan's workshop, it was getting dark, and Archie knew that there would be no jousting practice that day, so he resolved that he would arise all the earlier on the following morning. That evening, on his master's orders, Archie returned to the bedroom in which he had slept on the first night he arrived at Lord Pwrådisa's manor house. This bedroom was to serve as his quarters while he was squire to Pwrådisa.

On the following morning, Archie arose early and went straight to the jousting pond on Lord Pwrådisa's estate, because he intended to spend as much time as he could in practice before the tournament. Sloth met him at the pond, for Archie had instructed him to bring Splasher from the stable and have him ready. After Sloth helped Archie into the old armor suit that he had used in his training, Archie jumped into the water, quickly checked the saddle and bridle, and mounted Splasher. For most of the morning, Archie and Splasher made passes at a "quintain," a wooden target that was mounted on a horizontal pole. Whenever Archie's lance struck the quintain accurately, it would swing harmlessly aside. But on the few occasions that his lance was just a little bit off-center, Archie would be unseated, for the weighted arm would swing around with considerable force and strike him from behind. This made Splasher nervous, and Archie found that Splasher would increase his speed during the next pass.

That afternoon, the old bearded knight arrived, together with Whiner, Liar, and Glutton. For the rest of the day, Archie and the old bearded knight jousted as the other boys watched. Toward the end of the day, Lord Pwrådisa came to watch, and Archie struggled not to notice, though inside he was proud that his master took the time.

The next two days passed in much the same way, and on the third morning, Archie and Lord Pwrådisa left early to pick up his new flexible suit of armor. After Kótan's apprentices helped Archie into the new suit, Kótan looked it over, smiled, and announced, "Perfect. Perfect. One of my best jobs ever."

After the standard courtesies, Archie and Lord Pwrådisa departed. As they stood on the canal-level sidewalk waiting for the neroh-broughm, Archie spoke: "I really appreciate the dolphin and the new suit of armor, and I am honored by the opportunity to serve as your squire and participate in the jousting tournament."

Lord Pwrådisa replied, "You are quite welcome, but just so you know, it is very unusual for a new squire to have such an honor. Jousting is really a sport for knights, but because all squires are in training to become knights, from time to time we hold special tournaments in which squires deemed ready for knighthood are given the opportunity to display their skills. It is unheard of for a *new* squire to earn this honor."

Before Archie could respond, Lord Pwrådisa's neroh-brougham arrived. As his master descended the stairs and entered the carriage, Archie's attention was diverted to an approaching girl, who bowed her head. Glancing up at Archie's sandy blond hair, she asked, "Are you Archie?"

"Yes. Why?" Archie replied.

Thrusting a scroll into his hand, she replied, "This is a message from Mókea."

Archie broke the seal, removed the ribbon, and stood motionless as he read the contents of the note:

> I need to see you as soon as possible. Please meet me at dusk tonight at the skybridge intersection of the tower canal leading to my grandfather's manor house and the third dining and entertainment ring from the center of the city.

When he looked up, Lord Pwrădisa beckoned for him to descend the stairs and enter the neroh-brougham, and so Archie did.

Chapter Ten
The Tournament

At least an hour before nightfall, Archie was already at the skybridge intersection where Mókea said she would meet him. It had not been easy, but Archie managed to break away from his jousting practice early, leaving Sloth to care for Splasher. He had then run along the skywalks, the broad walkways that tracked the canals at rooftop level, until he had arrived at the designated meeting place.

During his entire run, Archie's thoughts had been focused on Mókea, but now, as he stood waiting for her, his mind relaxed enough for him to take a look at his surroundings. For several blocks all around him—perhaps stretching for miles—he could see only grassy parks pleasantly filled with large shade trees, exotic shrubs and flowers, broad walkways leading in many directions, and occasional benches. Here and there he saw T'lantim men, women, and children—young lovers strolling together through the broad walkways, oblivious to all else around them, families having picnics, and children playing games not unlike soccer and baseball in large unbroken grassy areas. The view of the city at rooftop level was certainly different from the view at canal level.

"It is good to see you again."

Archie turned toward the direction of the familiar and melodic voice and looked into the eyes of Mókea. As his heart raced, he thought how much more beautiful she was than he had recalled. Finally gathering his wits, Archie replied.

"Yes, it is." Then, he blurted out, "You are so beautiful."

Mókea blushed, and so did Archie. She turned and walked away from the skybridge and soon left the skywalk, turning onto one of the broad tree-lined walkways that made their way through the park. Archie followed, and for some time, the two walked without talking. As darkness descended, the walkways began to glow green, lending a mysterious underglow to the trees. They were alone now, for the other T'lantim who had populated the park just half an hour earlier had left.

Breaking the silence, Archie finally asked the question that was on his mind. "Your note sounded urgent. Why did you want to see me?"

Mókea turned to look at Archie and began to cry. Archie took her hand, and they walked together in silence a little while longer. After the painfully long pause, Mókea finally spoke.

"I told you that I am betrothed to Thlū'taku, and have been since the first anniversary of my birth. But I don't love him, and I don't want to marry him. He has always been kind to me, and he comes from a powerful and respected family. I know that to marry him would be an honor, but ..."

Mókea's words trailed off as she began to cry again, so Archie simply waited for her to gather herself together. He continued to hold her hand but felt quite awkward, because he was torn by conflicting emotions. On one hand, he had known her only briefly, and she was engaged to be married, making Archie want to pull his hand away. But from the moment he had first seen her, he had felt a strong attraction to her, and holding her hand merely intensified that feeling. Besides, she needed him now, and to pull his hand away would be cruel, so Archie just walked on, still holding Mókea's hand.

Mókea sat down on a bench, rubbed her eyes, and then spoke again. "Any other girl in K'truum-Shra would love to be in my place. Thlū'taku has never done anything dishonorable or cruel, but there is just something that I don't like. I ... I ... I don't trust him!" Bowing her head, Mókea added in an almost-whispered tone, "There, I've said it."

The two sat for a while, sometimes in silence, sometimes chatting about less important matters, because it was emotionally draining to talk only about Mókea's unhappy situation. And over the next few hours, they got to know each other very well, for in an effort to take Mókea's mind off her troubles, Archie began to talk about his home and parents and school, until he, too, cried. Hours were spent discussing the joys and sorrows of their brief lives, and what they told each other provided insights that only strengthened their affection for each other.

From time to time, they would get up and walk, or sit on another bench, or on the grassy lawn near one of the many lakes that could be found in the rooftop park. In a lighter moment, Mókea explained that the rainwater-fed lakes supplied fresh, running water to the city. And because the lakes were on top of the city, gravity provided the force necessary to give them running water.

Archie and Mókea walked for miles, but the distance they covered in their hearts was even greater. Soon, Archie knew that he also disliked Thlū'taku, even though he had never actually been face to face with him and even though Mókea could not name a specific reason that she did not trust him.

Eventually the sun rose, and Archie and Mókea both realized that they should have been home many hours earlier. The tournament for which Archie had prepared was today, in just a few short hours, and deep within his heart, Archie knew that he should have slept that night. As they were about to go their separate ways, Mókea slipped her handkerchief into his hand. As Archie looked at the elaborately embroidered handkerchief, still wet with her tears, Mókea asked Archie to carry it in the tournament. He agreed and then turned around and walked away, without looking back.

Now painfully aware that his time to prepare for and get to the tournament was short, Archie began running, but his mind remained on Mókea. When he finally arrived at Lord Pwrådisa's manor house, everyone was waiting for him. Lord Pwrådisa did not ask Archie where he had been, but Archie could see the disappointment in his eyes, and this added to the melancholy that now plagued Archie's heart.

The tournament was to take place at Lord Mókato's jousting pond, for tournaments among squires were not allowed in the great jousting pond behind the Palace of Elders. But even Lord Mókato's jousting pond was a grand sight, for it had a fair-sized grandstand and was colorfully decorated for the occasion. The pond itself was identical in size and shape to Lord Pwrådisa's jousting pond, so Archie was certain that he would have no problems.

There were squires from all eight houses, but only Lord Pwrådisa's house remained independent of Lord Mókato's ruling house. Although the lords of six of those houses no longer existed, the Council of Elders had appointed a steward to rule over all six of them until knights who had proven their worth could be elevated to the rank of lord. But Archie had never been told who the steward was and was shocked when he saw the tunics worn by the other squires representing those six fallen houses. Their tunics bore the shields of the six fallen houses, each a field of gold bordered with black and having both a black chief and a black inescutcheon. On the black chief there were white representations of the fruit, fish, and grain for which the house was responsible, and on the inescutcheon, a smaller black shield inside the gold field, there was a single white tower.

What Archie did not expect to see on those shields were the three green sharks that surrounded the inescutcheon. He realized from this that Thlū'taku, though not himself a lord, had been named steward of all six fallen houses! Before this shock wore off, the trumpets sounded for the first match, a match in which Archie would compete.

Already wearing his new flexible armor, he waded into the pond and mounted Splasher, who appeared eager for the competition. Archie tied Mókea's handkerchief to the tip of his lance and looked for her in the grandstand, but she was nowhere to be seen. At the signal, the squires sped toward each other on their steeds, and Archie was determined to unseat his opponent on the first run. Suddenly, however, Splasher submerged, and because Archie's armor was lighter than the water, he almost lost his seating. Splasher continued to descend, out of control, while Archie used all of his strength to remain on his steed. When Splasher finally surfaced, they were no longer in the jousting pond but, instead, in the nearby tower canal!

Dismounting, Archie quickly tied Splasher to a hitching post and walked back to the jousting pond. Almost immediately, he wished he had not. The spectators were laughing, and he knew why. But that would not be the end of his troubles, because he was soon approached by a group of men, including Thlū'taku, Lord Mókato, and Archie's master, Lord Pwrádisa. Mókea was with them. Archie expected that they might be disappointed in his performance, but what he heard next he did not expect.

"Were you alone all evening with Mókea?" Lord Mókato inquired. "And did you not know that she was betrothed to Thlū'taku?"

"Well, yes," Archie answered, giving a questioning glance to Mókea.

Her eyes returned his silent inquiry with a cold, hard stare that did not seem to belong to the Mókea he thought he knew. At the same time, she slipped her arm into Thlū'taku's arm, pulling him closer, and spoke. "The outsider tricked me into meeting him last night. He sent me a message that it was very important that I meet him. I only went because he was an honored guest of our city, and I believed him. Once with him, I could not get away, and he tried to persuade me that I should not marry my beloved, Thlū'taku. I managed to escape at dawn."

Archie stood dumbfounded, looking into Mókea's eyes, as Lord Mókato spoke next.

"You have dishonored yourself, Lord Pwrádisa, Mókea, Thlū´taku, and me. Your fate is now in the hands of the Council of Elders."

Chapter Eleven
The Second Tower

Thlū'taku's men arrested Archie, bound his hands and feet, and escorted him to a dungeon in the second of the eight towers, called the Tower of Mourning. As they crossed the threshold, Archie thought just how ironic it was that this tower, his new prison-home, had such a name, for he had much to mourn. He wished that he had never met Mókea, never become a squire, never come to K'truum-Shra, and never even used his kayak on the day of the terrible storm.

The dungeon cell was small and dark, but unlike the T'lantim bedrooms, it was completely unfurnished. Instead of a comfortable bed, the dungeon cell had only a pile of straw in one corner. With his training, he could easily make the straw comfortable enough, but for the moment, his thoughts were concentrated on what he had lost: his freedom, perhaps his life, the respect of both Lord Mókato and Lord Pwrádisa, Splasher, the new flexible suit of armor, and the prestige of being a squire. Stripped of his armor and even the tunic signifying his connection to Lord Pwrádisa's house, Archie sat on the cold floor of the dungeon, wearing only his pantaloons and a rough tunic that smelled and felt like burlap.

No one had told him how long he would be in the dungeon, or when his trial would take place, but Archie suspected that he would never again see the outside world. The dungeon had no windows and was perpetually dim, because its keepers did not see the need to furnish any lamps. The only source of light came from a small slit at the bottom of the door, and the only way Archie could tell whether it was night or day was by discerning between two degrees of darkness—dim and pitch-black. There were no visitors, at least not human, for there were some rather nasty-looking rats. In all the time Archie had been in K'truum-Shra, he had never seen any rats, squirrels, or non-marine mammals, at least until he had been thrown into this unhappy prison.

Just once a day, long before there was sufficient light to see anything at all in his cell, Archie would hear the sound of footsteps, after which a meager meal would be passed through the slit at the bottom of the door. He quickly learned to grab the food immediately. If not, the nonhuman inmates in the cell would conclude that he did not want the food and take it for themselves.

It did not take long to lose track of time, and Archie occupied himself by thinking about what led to his imprisonment. Anger and hatred soon filled his heart and occupied his thoughts. Most of all, he despised Mókea and could not believe that she had betrayed him. Over and over again, he replayed in his mind what she had done to him—how she had used her charms on him since he first arrived, how she called him out to meet her at nightfall, and how she lied about him. He could not figure out why she had betrayed him. And when he could no longer bear to think about Mókea, Archie allowed his anger and hatred to spread. He soon concluded that his parents should have known that a storm was coming and that they should have kept him out of the ocean. The T'lantim people should have helped him find his way home instead of treating him like he was the fulfillment of some stupid legend. Lord Mókato should have told him what his "quest" was. And perhaps most important of all, Lord Pwrádisa and T'lôt'aris should have told Archie the rules of their society—*all* of the rules! The more that Archie realized that his predicament was not his own fault, the angrier he got. But what made this imprisonment worse was that he was separated from all human contact. That was more than Archie could bear, and he soon found himself intermittently sobbing in despair and screaming in anger.

The days passed, and Archie soon abandoned hope that he would ever leave the dungeon. Then, one day he heard some footsteps, louder than usual and during what seemed to be the middle of his dimly lit day. Suddenly the door creaked open. Archie had to shield his eyes, for whoever had come into his cell carried a lamp that was brighter than he could stand.

In the Dungeon

"So, the light is already too much for you, Sleeper?"

Archie's heart pounded, for he immediately recognized the voice of T'lôt'aris, the old bearded knight.

"Why are you using such a bright lamp?" Archie complained.

"The light of this lamp is but that of a moonlit night."

Archie was stunned that he could no longer tolerate light but was nevertheless very happy to have company. "Am I to rot in this dungeon, or will I have a trial?"

The voice of the old bearded knight replied, "Soon, you will be summoned before the Council of Elders, but that is not why I have come."

"Then why have you come?" asked Archie.

"To ask of you a single question."

"And what is that question?"

"Why are you here?"

"Because a storm took me out to sea and carried me to your awful city," Archie replied.

"No, why are you *here*?" the old bearded knight insisted.

"Because Mókea tricked me into meeting her at nightfall, because she lied about our meeting, and because no one told me the rules of your society," Archie replied.

Archie still could see nothing, but what he heard caused him to panic: the door creaking shut, footsteps, and then silence. While all of this was happening, Archie cried out, "Please don't leave me alone. Come back! Come back—*please!*

For at least half an hour, Archie continued calling to the old bearded knight. And then, with the realization that he was alone again, Archie began sobbing. He cried for so long that he was soon exhausted and fell asleep.

On the following day, the old bearded knight returned and asked again, "Why are you here?"

Archie gave essentially the same answer, blaming everyone but himself. But this time, the voice of the old bearded knight asked another question.

"Were you not aware that what you were doing was wrong?"

"How could I," Archie blurted out. "No one told me your laws."

The old bearded knight left again, and Archie cried again. But he also began to think about what the old knight was saying.

On the next day, Archie eagerly awaited the visit from the old bearded knight and was not disappointed. And once again, the old knight asked him the same questions.

Taking time to carefully compose his reply, Archie politely asked, "Please tell me how I could have known that Mókea would deceive me and how I could have known your laws if no one ever told me?" He did not expect the answer he received, for it, too, was a question.

"Did you tell Lord Pwrádisa that you were going to meet Mókea?"

Archie did not reply, and the old bearded knight left.

The night he had met Mókea, Archie had carefully slipped away, hoping that no one would notice. Deep within his heart, Archie understood the implication of the old bearded knight's question. Even without being told that he should not meet Mókea, he had *already* known that it was wrong, and yet, he did it anyway.

But still he was innocent, Archie thought. All that he had done with Mókea was to talk and walk with her. What could be wrong with that? For the rest of the day, Archie played over and over in his mind the events that had led to his arrest and imprisonment, and he kept drawing the same conclusion: even if he knew it was wrong to meet Mókea that night, he had not done anything that hurt anyone else.

When the old bearded knight appeared the next day, Archie was ready, or so he thought, and he confidently explained that no one had been hurt, for he and Mókea had done nothing other than walk and talk in the park. And once again, Archie did not expect the question he received in return.

"Are you so certain that no one was hurt?"

Again, Archie did not know how to reply but remained silent as the old bearded knight departed. For hours, he occupied himself with the deepest thought that his sixteen-year-old mind had ever entertained. And for the first time in his life, he opened his mind to possibilities that he would have brushed aside only a few days earlier.

Perhaps his meeting with Mókea was not so innocent after all. Even though she was only fifteen, she was engaged to be married, and being out all night with Archie might have soiled her reputation, no matter how they conducted themselves during their rendezvous. But then *she* had asked to see him, and *she* was the one who was betrothed to another, and against her will, or so she had told him.

Although Archie's anger at Mókea prevented him from having any sympathy for her, the old bearded knight's question was having an effect, perhaps because all that Archie could do in the dark little cell was think. Having entertained the slightest possibility that he had any blame in the whole matter, Archie had unwittingly opened the door to the truth, for he suddenly remembered that he had held Mókea's hand as though she did not belong to another. Even while he held her hand, he had felt awkward precisely because she was engaged. He also realized that his actions were based entirely on emotion—what he desired and what felt good—rather than his conscience. He had suppressed any thought that what he was doing was wrong, though even that had been unsuccessful, as his awkward feeling about holding Mókea's hand had demonstrated.

Archie began to wonder whether this was the first time that he had acted solely on emotion. A flood of memories came pouring into Archie's mind, and he realized that on countless occasions in his life, he had "pushed the edge," thinking only that if no one was hurt or no one found out, all would be well. Had he come in when his mother had instructed him, and had he not paddled out beyond the point of safety, he would not have been lost. He would not be sitting here in this dark and lonely prison, awaiting who knows what.

Archie chuckled, because he suddenly understood just what his father meant all the times he said, "The boy thinks he invented the wheel." Archie's arguments with his father were almost invariably about actions he never fully thought through, and he would resist his father's instruction whenever it was contrary to whatever Archie desired at the moment. Then, when it became clear that Archie had closed his mind, his father would vent his frustration by making this declaration about Archie's ego.

Although he remained angry with Mókea, all the anger he had harbored against everyone else dissolved, and even his anger with Mókea slipped to the back of his mind. All that he felt was terrible loss, terrible guilt, and the desire for a second chance. *If only I had not met Mókea that night,* he thought, *or disobeyed my parents. If only I had done what I knew was right.* For the rest of the dimly lit day, Archie cried in his cell. Not the kind of childish sobbing that had marked the moments in his life when things had not gone as he wanted, but a wailing that was rooted in deep despair, a wailing that marked Archie's slowly growing recognition that throughout his whole life he had done things—or failed to do things—based only on what he wanted.

When the old bearded knight returned the following day, Archie spoke first.

"I realize now that secretly meeting Mókea at night was wrong, even if she deceived me, and that I really knew, deep down in my heart, that it was wrong when I did it. I also know that there is nothing I can do to change what I have done. To tell you the truth, I am not really sure that I could keep from doing it again. *That* is why I am here."

The old bearded knight said only one thing, and once again, it was not what Archie expected. "Will you permit Lord Pwrádisa to defend you at your trial?"

Overcome with emotion, Archie replied, "Yes, if he is willing to defend me. Will he, after all of this?"

With gentleness in his voice, the old bearded knight replied, "He has already forgiven you and wants only your commitment to do your best to obey him in the future."

Archie's answer was instantaneous. "Yes! Yes! Yes, I will obey him and serve him in *any* position, for I know that I am not fit to be a squire."

On the following day, Thlū'taku's men came for Archie, bound him, and escorted him to the Palace of Elders. Still wearing the rough, burlap-like tunic, it occurred to Archie that this second trip to the chambers where the Council of Elders met did not compare favorably to his first visit. Then, he was an honored guest; now, he was a prisoner. Then, he wore the shield of Lord Mókato, the Elder of Elders, the ruler of this people; now, he wore only a filthy rag. Then, he was escorted by Mókea; now, by armed guards. Even the Council chambers looked different, for everything had been rearranged for his trial.

Lord Mókato sat at the center of an elevated desk, much like the judge's bench in an American courtroom. Beside him on both sides, at a slightly lower level, were other T'lantim Elders. There were also two other desks, presumably for the prosecution and the defense. In the middle of all this was a cage, into which the guards led Archie, still bound. He could see that he would have to stand during the entire trial.

As Archie looked up, he saw that the room was filled to capacity, and there were even T'lantim standing in the aisles. His trial was apparently going to be great sport. Had television cameras existed in this society, the room would have been filled with them.

Lord Mókato hammered a gavel, and a hush fell over the chambers. No sooner had the room grown quiet than he asked the prosecution to read the charges.

The prosecutor arose and cleared his voice. Archie immediately recognized him: it was Thlū'taku! "The accused is charged with dishonoring a maiden, the only grandchild of the ruling house, by tricking her into secretly meeting him for an all-night rendezvous. He is further accused of dishonoring Lord Pwrádisa's house by leaving without permission and by failing to focus his attention on the single task to which he had been assigned, the jousting tournament. Thus, the accused has, through a single set of actions, placed into jeopardy the only two houses legally authorized to rule the realm."

Looking directly at Archie, Lord Mókato asked, "How does the accused plead?"

Archie looked at Lord Pwrádisa, whose facial expression told Archie that he should reply. Taking a deep breath, Archie answered. "I am guilty, but not exactly as charged, for it was Mókea who deceived me. But I did secretly meet Mókea, without Lord Pwrádisa's permission and knowing in my heart that it was wrong. In doing this, I neglected to sleep the night before the tournament, making me tired and unprepared. And at the time, I was fully aware that Mókea was engaged to be married. In short, I am guilty."

There was an immediate commotion in the Council chambers, causing Lord Mókato to use his gavel again. When the commotion died down, Lord Mókato spoke. "By your own words, you have adduced sufficient evidence of your guilt. Based on your confession, this Court finds you guilty and sentences you to be put to death by torture."

But before the sentence could sink in, Lord Pwrádisa arose and spoke. "I refer this Court to an ancient authority that is not often invoked, the Sacred Writ of the Founder."

An uproar arose in the council chambers, as various Elders rummaged through a large pile of scrolls. For a brief moment, Archie was amused, for these Elders appeared to be flustered, until finally one of them found the ancient writ, carried it to the bench, and handed it to Lord Mókato. After reviewing the scroll, he spoke. "What, precisely, do you mean by invoking this writ?" he asked.

"What I mean," said Lord Pwrádisa, "should be quite clear. This Court should acquit the accused, return him to his position, and substitute me in his place. I will serve his sentence."

Chapter Twelve
The Third Tower

The Council chambers again erupted, and for the first time, Lord Mókato and his gavel were powerless to stop the disturbance. The T'lantim spectators were actually taking sides: some were cheering and some were hissing. Hardly anyone remained seated in the thousands of theater-like seats, and armed guards ran here and there, intervening in fistfights and arguments. Lord Mókato continued to bang his gavel, but to no avail.

Before long, dozens of soldiers had entered the Council chambers and began removing all of the spectators. It took at least half an hour before the riot had been quelled. Finally, Lord Mókato spoke.

"So, you are saying, Lord Pwrǎdisa, that you are willing to forfeit your position, your title, your lands, and even your very life, all for this criminal—this outsider?"

"That is what I said, is it not?"

"And you understand that this leaves K'truum-Shra without anyone qualified to be elected Elder of Elders when I am no more?"

"I have no doubt that a leader will arise, that K'truum-Shra will not be forsaken."

For the first time since Archie had met him, Lord Mókato appeared lost. He fumbled through some writs, looked at Thlū'taku, then at the other Elders on the bench with him, and finally spoke. "Then, this Court reverses its judgment, acquits the accused, and restores him to his position. This Court further accepts your plea, finds you guilty, and sentences you to be put to death by torture in the place of the accused. And because you will no longer be the lord of the First Tower, T'lôt'aris is named steward in your place, until one is proven worthy of the title and honors of lord of that tower."

Archie was looking at Thlū'taku when Lord Mókato named the old bearded knight as steward of Lord Pwrádisa's house, and it appeared to Archie that Thlū'taku winced as the pronouncement was made. Was it possible that Thlū'taku, who was already steward of six fallen houses, had presumed that he would be named steward of Pwrádisa's house as well?

Soon the guards released Archie from the cage, and he looked over at Pwrádisa, who was being bound. Archie's eyes met Pwrádisa's, whose gentle smile stabbed at Archie's heart. As soon as he could, Archie ran to Pwrádisa, but he found no words. Pwrádisa responded to Archie's questioning eyes, saying, "Listen to T'lôt'aris, for he will guide you in my place."

The guards then removed Pwrádisa while Archie stood, unable to move or speak. After some time, he looked up at Lord Mókato, who still looked confused, and then at Thlū'taku, whose glare Archie did not quite understand. Was it anger, contempt, hatred, or was there something else? When Thlū'taku turned his attention elsewhere, Archie suddenly realized that it was *fear* he had seen in Thlū'taku's eyes!

Archie left the Council chambers and wandered for some time, eventually finding himself in the same park where he had spent that fateful evening with Mókea. He sat for several hours, thankful for his freedom and for the opportunity to be outside and in the light, but wondering what was next. As nightfall approached, he arose and reluctantly began walking toward the manor house, for he had nowhere else to go.

It was already quite dark when Archie finally came to his master's home. He did not feel like seeing anyone, and after his long captivity, he did not relish the thought of sleeping in a cramped T'lantim bedroom, so Archie walked out into the pomegranate orchard and made himself a shelter. But the sky was clear, the evening warm, and even his primitive shelter appeared too cramped, so Archie lay out under the stars, pondering the trial and Pwrádisa's sacrifice. After hours of reflection, Archie finally fell asleep.

The next morning was bright and clear. Still affected by his imprisonment, Archie wanted to stay outside, so he decided to take a run along the great wall of the city. He ran through the tunnel beneath the manor house, up the spiral stairway within the Tower of Humility, and out onto the wall. As he approached the Second Tower, the Tower of

Mourning, Archie's heart filled with fear and he picked up his pace. Before long he was approaching the Third Tower, when suddenly, T'lôt'aris stood before him. Archie stopped running.

"Where are you going in such a hurry, Sleeper?"

"Nowhere. I am just confused and needed to think about everything that has happened."

"Did you not promise to serve Lord Pwrådisa?" the old bearded knight inquired.

"Of course, but he is either dead or as good as dead."

"For one so young you seem to be so certain of everything. Are you so sure that your master is dead?"

Archie's heart leaped. "Do you mean that he was not put to death after all?"

"No, he was tortured and put to death yesterday, as ordered by Lord Mókato."

"Then what are you trying to tell me," Archie demanded. "I am confused enough already!"

"Did your promises die with your master? Did your hope? Are you not alive now because of his sacrifice, or does that mean nothing to you?"

"Of course it does, but how can I serve a dead master?"

With a penetrating gaze from which Archie could not avert his eyes, the old bearded knight asked, "What was the last thing Lord Pwrådisa said to you?"

Thinking for a moment, Archie finally replied, "He told me to listen to you and that you would guide me in his place."

"Then that is what you must do if you truly trust him."

Looking into the eyes of the old bearded knight, Archie thought how peculiar he was. Even from his first encounter with T'lôt'aris, Archie knew that he was unusual, but he seemed to grow more mysterious with each encounter. And yet, Archie felt drawn to the old knight and simply replied, "I do trust him, and I trust you, and I will listen to you."

With that, the old knight turned around and entered the Third Tower, the Tower of Surrender. Archie followed, though all of the towers now made him uncomfortable, and he secretly hoped that they would soon be outside again. But the old bearded knight led him to a room within the tower. Archie did not really want to enter but was comforted by the fact that the room was not only much larger than his dungeon cell had been but was also much brighter. In fact, the room appeared to be brighter than he would have expected from the single narrow window that appeared to be its only source of light. Still, Archie insisted on leaving the door open.

Inside the room, there were a large table and two chairs. On the table, on the floor, and scattered everywhere throughout the room were dozens of scrolls. Archie realized that it was a library of sorts. The old bearded knight gestured for Archie to take a seat and said, "You never completed your training, and that shall be our first order of business."

Unhappy even in this bright room, Archie blurted out, "But why here? All of the other training was outside. You even made us sleep outside."

"Do you not recall that one of the first things I told you was that there are three qualities of character that mark a knight? Do you recall what they are?"

Thinking back to that first day in the pomegranate orchard, Archie replied, "Physical strength, mental acuity, and moral might."

"That is correct," said the old bearded knight, "and what else did I tell you about them?"

"That they cannot be taught," Archie said, "but only developed through rigorous discipline and testing."

"Correct again. Do you still think that your classroom is restricted to the narrow confines of the pomegranate orchard and the cornfield, the arenas, and the jousting ponds? Has it not yet occurred to you that there are many places in which to learn and many situations from which wisdom might be gained?"

"I see," Archie said weakly.

"Then let us begin," said the old knight. "These are the sacred scrolls of our people, most of whom are not even aware that they exist. Indeed, some of these scrolls have been neglected even by the priests. You shall read and commit to heart everything within these scrolls."

Archie looked around the room, thinking that even here, "school" was going to involve some drudgery. If not impossible, the task was certainly daunting, and it would take him a long time. Even his homework at William McKinley High School had never been this intimidating. The old bearded knight picked up three scrolls and thrust them into Archie's hands.

"You will study these first," he said, and then departed.

For a minute, Archie sat silently considering the task before him. Then, he opened the first scroll and began to read. It was difficult to understand, and several of the initial passages Archie had to reread. But as he continued, he slowly began to understand more of what he read. Hours passed, and Archie lost track of time. Just as he finished reading the third scroll, setting it back down, the old bearded knight returned.

"Do you understand everything that you have read?" the old knight asked.

"I think so," Archie replied. Then, sensing that his answer did not please the old knight, Archie added, "Well, I do have a few questions."

For the rest of the day, Archie asked his questions, but instead of answering the questions, the old knight just asked questions in response. At first, this frustrated Archie, but before long, he began to see that by making him answer questions, the old bearded knight was leading him to think about what the scrolls said. The questions were, in fact, the best answers to Archie's own questions. By nightfall, the lessons were finished, and although Archie was certain that he did not completely understand the three scrolls, he also knew that he understood as much as he would that day.

They left the Tower of Surrender and walked along the great wall of the city. Archie felt more relaxed than he had in days and enjoyed the nighttime view of the ocean. Upon reaching the manor house, Archie was greeted by familiar faces, including Liar, Whiner, Sloth, and Glutton.

In the days and weeks that followed, Archie continued his studies in the Tower of Surrender. They began each day with a run, but they did not run the entire distance of the great wall, something that the old bearded knight declined to explain to Archie. And once inside the Tower of Surrender, the old knight would hand Archie some scrolls, sometimes one, sometimes as many as four, but each time exactly enough scrolls to occupy his attention for the remainder of the day. And the old knight also mysteriously returned each day just as Archie had finished reading the last scroll. Ultimately, the studies became easier, and before he expected it, Archie had read and studied every one of the scrolls.

On the next day, the old bearded knight opened a map and placed it on the table before Archie. Colored lines were drawn all over the map, dividing it into sections. Pointing to the section containing Lord Pwrādisa's manor house, the Tower of Humility, the Tower of Mourning, and the Tower of Surrender, the old knight shocked Archie by what he had to say.

"I have not permitted you to leave this sector for several weeks, because there is now a civil war within the city. When the Council of Elders refused to elect Thlū′taku as Lord Mókato's successor, he imprisoned Lord Mókato, his granddaughter, Mókea, and many of the other Elders. Only about one-third of the Elders and people have sided with Thlŭ'taku, but because he already controlled the army, he easily seized control of most of the strategic points in the city. All that you have learned will soon be put to test."

Chapter Thirteen
The Command

rchie thought back to his arrival at Lord Pwrådisa's manor house, when he had been told that K'truum-Shra had not been at war for more than two thousand years. He could not help but think that the civil war now engaging this strange floating city was somehow his fault. If he had never come to these people, if he had never met Mókea, if he had never saved Pwrådisa, if he had never been put on trial, would this war have come to the T'lantim? But these thoughts were soon interrupted, for the old bearded knight still required Archie's attention.

"Fewer than one thousand of the thirty-six hundred nobles stood with us, and half of those were caught outside this sector before the lines stabilized, so they have been imprisoned by Thlū'taku. Of the eight divisions, we kept two full divisions and part of another, for a total of twenty-seven thousand soldiers. Thlū'taku has the sixty-nine thousand remaining soldiers, though we do not know how many are really loyal to him and how many were simply caught in territory he controls. However, thousands of refugees migrated to this sector at the outset of the conflict, substantially swelling the population of this sector. We have recruited the most able among them, and they are undergoing refresher training even now."

Archie remembered that all T'lantim citizens were required to serve in the military for a minimum of two years. The old knight continued.

"At the present, it is all that we can do to defend this sector, but plans for an offensive are now being studied by our officers, and that brings me to you. Ordinarily, a squire serves at least seven years before he is even considered for knighthood. But because we are now at war and have a shortage of knights, you must accept the responsibilities of knighthood at an earlier age. On your knees, Sleeper."

Archie complied, and the old knight drew a sword that was long and slender, like the old knight himself. Tapping Archie on each shoulder, he pronounced, "By the power vested in me as the Steward of the First House, of the Tower of Humility, I dub you 'Sir Archie the Bold,' knight of the Loyalist Alliance, and I hereby command your fealty to the lord of the First House, Lord Pwrådisa."

At the mere mention of Pwrådisa's name, Archie cringed, for he felt terrible shame and guilt, and even loss, but then he began to think how odd it was that the old bearded knight commanded loyalty not to himself but instead to a dead master.

Without further ceremony, T'lôt'aris simply said, "Come," as he turned and began running. Archie followed. First climbing the stairs, the two exited the Tower of Surrender at the top of the great wall and turned toward the Tower of Humility and the manor house. But when they entered the Tower of Mourning, a wave of fear washed over Archie, as he recalled the time he spent alone in the dark and lonely cell, not knowing his fate. The two descended the spiral stairway and continued well past the cell in which Archie had been imprisoned. When they reached the bottom of the stairs, they entered the tunnel that ran from the Tower of Mourning to the manor house associated with that tower but stopped about half way through the tunnel. Looking up and down the tunnel, and then at Archie, the old bearded knight reached out and with his slender fingers, felt the wall. After a moment, he pushed against the wall, and on the opposite side, a concealed door opened.

Passing through the door, the two entered a large, well-lit room in which no fewer than fifty knights stood and sat around a table. Although engaged in an obviously serious debate, the men stopped what they were doing and bowed to T'lôt'aris, who said simply, "Continue."

Only one of the knights, whom Archie thought was rather large by T'lantim standards, did not bow. He spoke next, and in a manner that indicated he was a man of authority.

"We have a plan to make a push in this direction," he said, pointing to the Fourth Tower, "but must first overcome a simple problem of logistics."

"Simple problem!" another knight bellowed. "More like a fatal flaw! Without adequate supplies, this invasion proposed by N'derlex is doomed to failure. We cannot afford to take the risk!"

"We cannot win the war without taking risks from time to time," replied N'derlex, whose tunic displayed his simple coat of arms, a white anchor on a blue shield.

"Yes, but sometimes the potential risk outweighs any possible tactical advantage," another knight offered.

"Then let us minimize that risk." Taking his time to look at least five or six knights squarely in the eye, including the two knights who had voiced their opposition, N'derlex asked, "Have we fully considered every possible way to supply the invasion force?"

For a moment, there was silence as the knights examined the map on the table. As he looked on and listened to the discussion, Archie realized that the logistical problem facing the invasion force was caused by its inability to move supplies rapidly by any means other than the canals. Without invitation, the newest knight spoke up. "You can move supplies across land as quickly as you can through water. Just convert some of your vehicles by adding wheels."

Some of the men laughed, but most simply stared at Archie in disbelief, for he was yet a boy and could not possibly offer anything of value.

"Are we now going to receive our orders from the lips of a mere boy?" asked the brassy and bellicose knight who had earlier challenged N'derlex. "And not just any boy, but the boy who brought us this grief?"

"Silence!" N'derlex commanded. "What harm will it do us to hear him out?" Turning to Archie, N'derlex asked, "What is this 'wheel' that you say can make vessels cross the land?"

Archie explained, "In America, where I come from, there are very few canals. We use paved streets and highways to get around." Then, demonstrating with his fingers the circular shape of a wheel, Archie continued his explanation: "We drive cars across our land at speeds many times faster than the fastest dolphin."

Several knights once again laughed, and because he could bear their disbelief no longer, Archie turned the circular table over on its side and began rolling it around the room. N'derlex immediately understood and betrayed that fact with a smile. After a few moments of thought, other knights also began to understand, and one asked—and very respectfully, Archie thought—how the vehicles were connected to the wheels.

With every knight now listening carefully, Archie explained the use and function of axles, the configuration of wheels, and everything else associated with wheels that came into his mind. When it became obvious that no one understood what he was saying, T'lôt'aris handed Archie a pen and paper. Archie quickly drew a vehicle resembling the dolphaeton, in which he had

89

toured the city, but then added wheels and axles. This simple drawing made the concept clear to everyone in the room.

"How shall we make these wheels and axles," N´derlex asked. From a corner in the back of the room, a familiar figure arose and moved into the crowd of knights around the upturned table.

"With your permission," Kótan said, "I will turn the efforts of my workshop to this immediately, for the war will end someday, and I anticipate that there will be great demand for this wheel even after the war is long over."

"Your offer is accepted," N´derlex replied quickly, "and Sir Archie the Bold shall be appointed to oversee your efforts."

This time it was Archie on whose face the smile crept, for he had not yet heard himself referred to as "Sir." It was going to be great fun to be a knight, he thought.

The meeting ended for Archie almost immediately, as he now had a very important task, and N´derlex did not want to delay the invasion any more than was absolutely necessary. Archie and Kótan departed for Kótan's workshop, and for most of the journey, neither spoke. When they were only a short distance from the workshop, Kótan broke the silence.

"How are these wheeled vehicles pulled?" Kótan asked, smiling. "After all, dolphins cannot swim out of water."

Archie did not like what he saw in Kótan's smile, though he was not quite sure what it was. But he responded anyway.

"Where I come from, they have engines so they can move themselves. In the past, they were pulled by horses and oxen, just as dolphins pull your carriages."

"I have never heard of engines or horses or oxen," Kótan said. "What kind of animals are they?"

"Engines are not animals. They are manufactured."

Kótan flashed a wicked smile and then asked. "Tell me how to make these engines!"

Kótan's request caught Archie off guard, for it seemed that Kótan was more interested in the technology that Archie could offer than in helping the Alliance win the war. Fortunately, they had arrived at Kótan's workshop, which gave Archie an opportunity to avoid answering Kótan's request until he had thought about it. The workshop—which occupied the entire city block—was heavily guarded by soldiers, because it was already a source of war production. This is why Kótan was in the war council. But Archie now doubted that Kótan's heart was in the struggle.

In the days that followed, vehicles of every description were brought to the workshop and stored in a warehouse area. In the meantime, Archie made several drawings, which Kótan studied very carefully. After a brief period of experimentation with various mixtures of k'truum, Kótan announced that he had just the right formula, one that would give the wheels immense strength. The workshop was soon making dozens of eight-spoked wheels and axles and fitting them on the vessels that had previously been used exclusively for canal transit.

One day, N'derlex came to the workshop to see Archie and Kótan. With him were eighty soldiers. After examining the wheels, axles, assemblies, and fully converted vehicles, he turned to Archie and said, "You have done a good job, but now have new orders. You are to supervise transport of these vehicles to a staging area at skywalk level and then test them. This company has been formed for that purpose, and you are to assume command of the company."

Surprised, Archie stood mute for a moment.

"Have you nothing to say?" asked N'derlex.

"I did not expect to be put in command of anyone. I'm just sixteen years old!"

"But you are now a knight, and from what I have been told of your training, you are ready for command." Looking into Archie's eyes and seeing his concerns, N'derlex added, "Don't worry. Every leader has a first command, and everyone feels as you do this very moment. It will pass quickly if you will but focus on your mission."

Turning to his side and summoning some soldiers, N'derlex continued. "You will need the suit of armor that Lord Pwrádisa had Kótan prepare especially for you." A small group of soldiers came forward, carrying that armor. Summoning two other soldiers, N'derlex said, "As you know, all knights are awarded a distinctive design for their shields, a coat of arms." The two soldiers came forward, bearing a shield and carefully turned it for Archie to see. The field was blue, and on the field, there was a single white, eight-spoked wheel.

"T'lôt'aris thought that this would be the most appropriate design. We are happy to have you as part of the Alliance."

Arms and Armigers

(Colors Represented by Traditional Heraldic Patterns)

Sir Archie the Bold

Sir T'lôt'aris

Lord Pwrădisa

Sir N'derlex

Lord Mókato

Sir Thlü'taku

Chapter Fourteen
The Invasion

'derlex turned and departed quickly, for he was a busy man and had an invasion to plan. But most of the soldiers who had accompanied him to Kótan's workshop stayed behind, and Archie soon realized that they were awaiting his orders.

"Get some ropes and pulleys," Archie told the two soldiers who had brought his shield, "and you men come with me," he told the others.

The two men looked at each other and then one spoke. "What are pulleys?"

"Never mind," said Archie, realizing that the pulley was a form of wheel, "just come with me."

The company moved through the workshop like a wave, seizing the attention of every worker it passed and briefly disrupting the work. When the company finally arrived at the warehouse portion of the workshop, where the converted vehicles were stored, Archie told most of the men to stay there, including the men now bearing his armor and shield. Then, turning to the two he had instructed to obtain ropes and pulleys, he again asked them to follow him as he sought Kótan.

They found Kótan busily supervising some of his best apprentices, who were engaged in building more of the eight-spoked wheels. When Kótan finally looked up, Archie said, "I have something else for you to make, another sort of wheel."

Kótan smiled, and Archie could briefly see the love of profit in his eyes. But Kótan soon gave Archie his full attention as Archie explained how pulleys work. When he was done, Kótan said, "It will take less than a day to make what you need."

Archie then sent the two men accompanying him to retrieve as many ropes as possible and instructed them to return to the warehouse before nightfall. When they had left, Archie turned to Kótan and asked how many pulleys he could make and how soon. Without offering any details, the master craftsman told Archie that the workshop could—in the space of a single day—produce as many pulleys as would be required to lift all of the vehicles that had already been converted to wheeled vehicles.

Archie returned to the warehouse and, after putting on his suit of armor, took five men with him to the skywalk level. It was immediately apparent that the entire skywalk level had been militarized, for several squads of soldiers were camped adjacent to the closest skybridges crossing the canal below. Archie wondered whether all of the skybridges were guarded. The city was very large, and there were four bridges at every intersection of a tower canal and a ring canal. Calculating in his head— eight tower canals by sixty ring canals—Archie figured that there were at least four hundred eighty intersections in the entire city, and about a third as many in the sector controlled by the Alliance. That was a large number to defend!

But then Archie also realized that this was the "high ground," in fact, the highest of the high ground in the whole city. Archers at the skywalk level could easily defend against any invasion force utilizing the canals. This was why N'derlex wanted to mount his invasion where there were no canals, and this is why the wheeled vehicles would be so critical in supplying and resupplying the invasion force.

At Archie's direction, the five men with him began to look for suitable places to locate the pulleys. After they finished, they returned to the warehouse portion of Kótan's workshop. Archie divided his men into two groups, keeping one group in the warehouse with the wheeled vehicles and taking one with him to select and set up a campsite at the skywalk level.

As his men set up camp, Archie decided to inspect the area surrounding them. Although the skywalk level in the workshop district had grassy lawns, lakes, trees, and walkways, it seemed very different from the area where Archie had been alone with Mókea. Kótan's workshop was closer to the center of the city, and the blocks in the workshop district were, therefore, smaller in area. There were also fewer trees, which, because they were smaller, provided less shade. The walkways were about the same size, about the width of a street in the average American subdivision.

During his inspection of the area, Archie crossed several skybridges, which he observed were not all guarded. Apparently, Kótan's workshop was so important to the war effort that every skybridge leading to that block was guarded. In crossing the skybridges, Archie took note of their width and length and attempted to memorize these facts. As nightfall approached, Archie returned to camp, where his men had erected several tents and were now preparing a meal. One of the men, a middle-aged man, approached and introduced himself to Archie.

"I am L'teif, your company first sergeant. I did not come with the other men, because T'lôt'aris wanted to see me. I arrived this afternoon, after you had already left for your walk. T'lôt'aris sends this scroll."

Accepting the scroll, Archie broke the seal, removed the ribbon, and eagerly read its contents:

> I have arranged for the man who has given you this scroll
> to be your first sergeant. He is an experienced soldier, and
> you may trust him. Exercise a healthy distrust of all others
> under your command until you know them well.

Archie looked into the eyes of his new first sergeant and thought that the man was probably older than Archie's own father and yet, was now under Archie's command. Sadness swept over him as he thought of his own parents. Archie's father was a professor of English literature at a small college, and his world was full of dusty old books and endless papers to grade. In contrast to Archie, he was an extraordinarily disciplined man, and the friction between father and son most often arose when Archie's actions were most impulsive. Archie's mother was less disciplined and more outgoing, and yet, he also struggled with her. Suddenly, and for the first time, Archie realized that the source of his friction with his mother was *her* impulsiveness—the very trait in him that irritated his father.

Before Archie could think about this startling revelation, L'teif interrupted his thoughts. "I took the liberty of having your tent placed next to mine, and I assumed that you would want me to get the men fed. Do you have any orders?"

"Not at this time," Archie replied.

As L'teif walked away, Archie felt almost as lonely as he had in the dungeon in the Tower of Mourning. He missed his parents and his home, and he had absolutely nothing in common with the people who surrounded him. Not only were they of a different race and culture, but they were all older than Archie. And now that he was placed in command of these men, there was yet another barrier isolating Archie. The last time he had felt really close to anyone was the night he had talked with Mókea ... and that had resulted in disastrous consequences.

Archie went to his tent and sat down on the cot. After a while, he lay down and thought about everything that had happened since he had come to this strange city—meeting Mókea and Lord Mókato, the jousting tournament, saving Lord Pwrádisa, his imprisonment and trial, and the war now engaging the city. Eventually, his weariness caught up with him, and he fell asleep.

Early the next morning, Archie took L'teif with him to see Kótan. When the pair found him, Archie thrust a drawing into Kótan's hands and asked, "Can you make these simple modifications to half the vehicles?"

Kótan looked puzzled, but replied, "Absolutely, we can make just about anything in my workshop. But this new work will take three more days."

Archie left with L'teif, but before they returned to camp, Archie asked L'teif to take a message to N'derlex. While L'teif patiently waited, Archie wrote out his note:

> I have another idea that I would like to share with you, but
> I do not want to put it into writing. I have already asked
> Kótan to make some changes that will take another three
> days. I hope that this will not create a problem.

Not having a seal, wax, or ribbon, Archie simply folded his note and handed it to L'teif and instructed him to take the note directly to N'derlex without delay.

Before two hours had passed, L'teif returned, bringing N'derlex with him. Archie was embarrassed and apologized immediately.

"Sir, please accept my apology. I know that you have much to do, and what I really expected was that you would send me a reply telling me where *I* should go to meet you."

"Do not trouble your mind. As the commander of our army, I would be a fool if I never took the time to visit with my own soldiers, see how they are living, and get a feel for everything that falls under my command. You would do well to remember this in connection with your own responsibilities. Besides, I suspected that what you have in mind would be easier to understand if I allowed you to show me rather than simply tell me."

This made sense to Archie, and he invited N'derlex to go with him to Kótan's workshop. There, Kótan met them and showed them the modifications that had already been made to the first vehicle. When the two walked away, Kótan followed, but N´derlex turned around.

"Do you share all of your secrets with your customers?" he asked.

"Of course not!" Kótan thundered.

"Neither do I," said N´derlex. "Now please excuse us."

When the two were alone, Archie explained his idea to N´derlex, who enthusiastically approved it, saying, "You have done it again, Sir Archie. Good work!"

In the days that followed, weapons and supplies were delivered to the campsite, while half the wheeled vehicles were converted to the new design. Some of Archie's men lifted the vehicles to the skywalk level as they were completed, and others tested the vehicles, pushing them around a course that Archie had selected. Then, when they had lifted and tested the last vehicle, Archie was summoned to a meeting at which N´derlex explained to all subordinate commanders the final invasion plans. Though it was late at night when Archie returned to his camp, he did not sleep. Instead, he awakened L´teif, who, in turn, awakened the rest of the men.

The company broke camp and loaded all of its equipment, together with the weapons and supplies for the invasion, into the wheeled vehicles that had not been converted to the new design. Those vehicles were left empty. The company then pushed all of the vehicles for several miles, across many skybridges and through many blocks of the city. Archie thought how nice it would be to have some horses to pull the vehicles. He also realized that the absence of draft animals was the reason the wheel had never been invented in this society.

About an hour and a half before dawn, they arrived at one of the large market district blocks, where it looked like the entire army was assembling. Archie knew that part of the invasion force would gather on the great wall surrounding the city and advance as far as possible before resistance stopped those men. Their mission was then to simply hold their position. But the greater part of the invasion force was forming here, in the market district, and would make a sweep parallel to the great wall before turning down both sides of the tower canal leading toward the Fourth Tower.

Archie sent half of his men to the rear, together with the vehicles laden with weapons and supplies. Those men and vehicles would transport weapons and supplies to the army as it advanced and transport the wounded on their return trips. Archie then took the other half of his company, together with the converted vehicles, and moved to the front, where he met N´derlex. From this point forward, Archie and these men would constantly be in close proximity to the commander and to three companies of skilled archers.

As they approached the bridges crossing the border into enemy territory, enemy sentinels sounded a warning. While enemy troops gathered at each skybridge to block the Alliance advance, Archie directed his men and their converted vehicles toward skybridges on the right and left that had been targeted for the invasion. Once the vehicles were near the skybridges, but still out of range of enemy archers, Archie's men prepared them for the attack. Though wider than the skybridges, the vehicles had platforms high enough that they could easily pass over the bridge railings. At the front of the large platforms, there were V-shaped parapets, armored walls with narrow windows through which archers could fire their weapons. Once the vehicles had been properly configured for combat and the skilled archers had climbed aboard, Archie's men began pushing the vehicles across the skybridges.

The crossing was easier than expected. Although initially determined to resist the advance, the enemy soldiers soon realized the futility of their defense. The new "tanks," as Archie called them, changed everything. In prior engagements, those defending the bridges had an easy advantage, because the attacking forces were funneled directly to them in manageable numbers. Such an attack would, more often than not, result in the massacre of the attacking forces. But the new "tanks" protected the attackers. And once across the skybridge, these "tanks" did not stop but began forming a protective V-shaped line that allowed the invading army to cross the bridge in numbers that had been unthinkable in all prior battles.

The army easily poured into enemy territory, sweeping through the entire block before finally turning toward the Fourth Tower. By midmorning the enemy was retreating, not only from the districts in which the invading army was sweeping but also from all parallel districts. Word soon came that the enemy had retreated from the Fourth Tower, and thousands of citizens came out to greet the conquering army. The majority of the T'lantim did not like Thlū'taku and had been waiting anxiously for this day.

At about noon, N'derlex summoned Archie to his temporary command post, a tent that had been erected in the heart of the conquered territory. When Archie arrived, he saw that N'derlex, T'lotaris, and L'teif were all there.

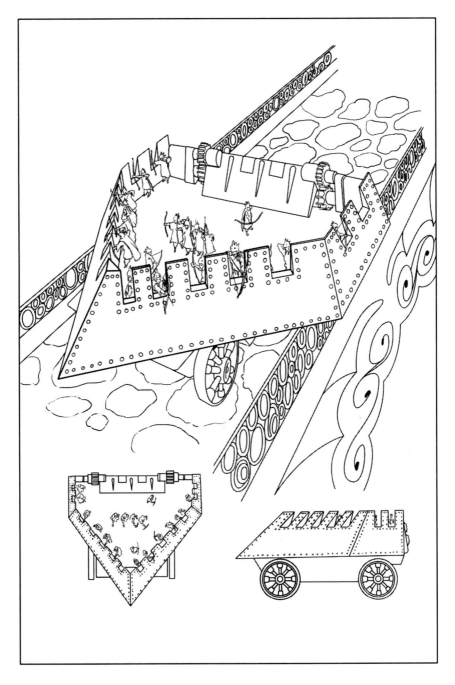

Archie's Tank

"You have done well today, very well," said N´derlex, "and have proven that it was no mistake to make you a knight. I am reassigning you to my staff, for you have demonstrated an ability to think strategically, and this should not be wasted."

Archie beamed with pride, and in a rather cocky voice asked, "Why don't we just continue the advance?"

"A prolonged advance would require more men and resources than we currently have," said N´derlex. "K´truum-Shra is very large, our army is much smaller than the enemy army, and sooner or later, Thlū´taku would have to turn around and fight. And you must think in multiple dimensions; the skywalk level is not our only concern. Thlū´taku still has the ability to wage war at the other levels, especially the canal level, and I don't want to leave our forces and citizens vulnerable to attack just to press this advance. You see, the greater the territory we control, the more we must defend. If we press the attack much more, our forces will be insufficient to defend against a canal level attack."

N´derlex paused and looked into Archie's eyes and then continued. "There is something else. Do not expect our next advance to go as well, for Kótan has gone over to the enemy. Your wheel and tanks were just too valuable, and he has no doubt received a hefty prize from Thlū´taku."

Chapter Fifteen
The Fourth Tower

Archie was enraged. In the space of mere moments, he enjoyed a number of fantasies in which he took revenge against Kótan for stealing his ideas and selling them to the enemy. Since Kótan was so interested in his inventions, Archie thought, perhaps he should "invent" something else especially for Kótan: the rack, the thumbscrew, the iron maiden, or some other medieval torture device. Or perhaps something more modern would be better, like an electric chair. Watching Kótan "fry" in his mind's eye, Archie began to smile.

"What is it that amuses you so, Sleeper?" asked the old bearded knight.

Startled by the question, Archie said nothing. As he looked into the eyes of T'lôt'aris, he felt uneasy, for if ever eyes could speak, the old master's eyes could. They reproached Archie for his malicious thoughts, and yet they simultaneously comforted him as he grappled with Kótan's betrayal. Without speaking a word, the old knight managed to turn Archie's feelings about Kótan from anger to pity, from hatred to compassion. For just a brief moment, a real insight tarried in Archie's mind: that the person most betrayed by Kótan was Kótan himself. Having seen Archie's tanks, Thlũ'taku and his forces sooner or later would have been able to create their own, with or without Kótan's assistance. But Kótan, having betrayed Archie, N'derlex, and T'lôt'aris, would never again be trusted by anyone. Even Thlũ'taku would likely keep Kótan at a distance, and perhaps even imprison him as he had Lord Mókato and Mókea. Yes, it was pity, not anger, that Kótan's foolish betrayal had earned.

N'derlex interrupted Archie's thoughts. "Although we cannot safely advance any farther at the present, I do not intend to give Thlū'taku sufficient time to regroup. We must plan quickly so that we can continue our offensive within the next twelve hours." Handing Archie a sealed scroll, N'derlex then instructed him, "Take these orders to my new command post in the Fourth Tower. T'lôt'aris and I shall join you within the hour."

Archie took L'teif and some other soldiers with him and departed. As they walked along the skywalk toward the Fourth Tower, they began to see throngs of refugees, who begged for food and water. Some only looked at Archie with hollow eyes. Archie directed his soldiers to pass out what food and water they had with them. As a result, refugees began joining Archie and his entourage, and before he realized it, there were at least a thousand T'lantim following him. Archie asked a few what had happened to them, and each told a similar tale.

Thlū'taku originally promised them whatever they desired: wealth, power, position, fame, even new lands. Once they had agreed to support him, he not only broke his promises to them, he began to take away what they already had. First, Thlū'taku's soldiers collected all of their money and valuables. Then they collected all of the food and clothing and other necessities of life. Finally, they separated families, first taking the men away from their wives and children and then taking the children away from their mothers. Once all of this had been accomplished, the people were no better than mere slaves and had to serve Thlū'taku just to be fed and clothed. Resistance had become impossible, because the social fabric had been torn apart, and no one knew—much less trusted—those around whom he or she worked, and all had been placed in circumstances that made it easy to betray a confidence in exchange for a few more crumbs to eat.

Those who complained or tried to escape were punished harshly. At first, they were merely imprisoned. Once the dungeons in the territory he controlled were full, Thlū'taku began to execute prisoners in increasingly barbaric ways. Indeed, the execution of prisoners became a "sport" for the entertainment of Thlū'taku's most loyal followers. This fact amazed Archie, because the T'lantim had been a very gentle people who had been at peace for more than two thousand years. How, then, could any of them become so bloodthirsty in a matter of just a few weeks?

When they reached the Fourth Tower, the Tower of Morality, Archie was faced with one of the most difficult decisions of his young life. For security reasons, he could not permit the thousands of refugees who had joined him to enter the tower, yet he had no more food or water to give to them. The refugees did not complain but only looked at him with a sadness unlike any he had ever seen. Archie decided right then that he would ask N'derlex and T'lôt'aris to help these people.

To gain entry to the tower, Archie showed the guard the scroll that N'derlex had given him. He was immediately ushered inside and taken to a large room, where a number of knights had gathered. Several maps were spread out on a table in the center of the room, but Archie's attention was still on the refugees outside. He paced back and forth, wondering what could be done for them.

When N'derlex and T'lôt'aris arrived, Archie wanted to talk to them about the refugees, but they went immediately to the maps and began to discuss plans for consolidating their gains against Thlū'taku. As Archie listened to the war planning, the refugee problem began to slip to the back of his mind, though it never completely left his consciousness. The refugees presented a real problem, but until he heard N'derlex and T'lôt'aris discussing the invasion, he did not realize how precarious the position now held by the Alliance was. Looking at the maps and listening to N'derlex and T'lôt'aris, it became obvious why the invasion had been halted. Although the army could have easily continued its advance on the skywalk level, it had become necessary to defend against a counterattack that Thlū'taku had mounted at canal level. While Archie's tanks had been sweeping toward the skybridges spanning the tower canal that ran between the Palace of Elders and the Fourth Tower, hundreds of knights fighting for Thlū'taku had mounted a dolphin attack down another tower canal, the canal that ran between the Palace of Elders and the Second Tower. At the same time, thousands of Thlū'taku's soldiers had advanced along the skybridges running parallel to the canal. With his superior forces, Thlū'taku was capable of mounting a counterattack on two different levels. Had N'derlex not responded quickly, this counterattack could have split the territory and forces controlled by the Alliance.

Listening to the description of the larger struggle, Archie suddenly felt his age again. It had not even occurred to him that there had been any fighting in areas other than those where Archie had been. Adding to his newfound humility was the realization that N'derlex was a master strategist, for he had not been caught off guard by Thlū'taku's maneuver and had actually prepared for a number of contingencies that would not have occurred to Archie.

But now, N'derlex was focused on gaining control of the Palace of Elders, which, being at the center of the city, had a strategic value far exceeding its size. Without the Palace of Elders, any counterattack mounted by Thlū'taku against a tower canal would have to come from the side. This would limit Thlū'taku's options and make it easier to defend against another attack by his numerically superior forces. It would also make it easier for the Alliance to drive a wedge between Thlū'taku's forces in the same way that he had attempted to divide the forces of the Alliance. But gaining control of the Palace of Elders would not be easy.

Because the inner rings of the city—those closest to the Palace of Elders—were reserved for institutions, there were height restrictions on the buildings. There were no skybridges in that district, either. Archie recalled that the bridges in the last few blocks before the Palace of Elders were narrow drawbridges, which made it impossible to seize control of the Palace of Elders with Archie's tanks. N'derlex would, therefore, use every available knight and attack the central island from the four tower canals now held by the Alliance.

By the time the meeting concluded, the knights had only a few short hours to rest, eat, prepare their mounts, and get to the assembly points. But Archie thought it well worth the effort to raise the plight of the refugees he had left just outside the tower. After most of the knights had left, he approached N'derlex and T'lôt'aris.

"There are at least a thousand refugees who followed me here. Have you seen them?"

"There are many more than that—perhaps tens of thousands," said the old bearded knight.

"I had my soldiers give them the food and water we had with us, but it was not enough. What can we do for them?"

With his usual penetrating gaze, the old knight asked, "What do you think should be done for them, Sleeper?"

"We should feed and shelter them and take care of their needs," Archie replied.

"But aren't they traitors, and don't they deserve the fate they now suffer?"

Having grown accustomed to the old knight's questions, Archie was only surprised momentarily. "But these people were deceived by Thlū'taku and have realized that following him was wrong. Shouldn't we now forgive them?" The old bearded knight did not respond, and Archie secretly swelled with pride, as he realized that for once the last word was his, that he had left the old bearded knight speechless.

N'derlex, who had silently listened, now joined the conversation, and told Archie the refugees had already been provided with food and shelter. He then added that Archie should try to get some rest before the assault on the Palace of Elders.

Archie left the Tower of Morality and walked along the great wall toward the Tower of Humility and the associated tower canal on which Lord Pwrâdisa's manor house and stables were located. It was now night, and it occurred to Archie that the starlit night provided a peaceful contrast to the civil war now being waged within the city. As he walked, he thought about how much had happened since he had first come to this strange city. It seemed like an eternity had passed since he had last taken Splasher for a ride, and yet in a few short hours, he and Splasher would ride into battle together. An uneasiness came over Archie as he pondered the coming battle. He realized that it would be very different from the tank battle that had served as his initiation into combat. For one thing, Archie had been protected not only by his armor but also by the tanks themselves. For another, he had never gotten very close to the enemy soldiers and never felt vulnerable. This time, the combat would be close and the risk of injury or even death very high.

Before long, Archie had arrived at Lord Pwrâdisa's stables. He decided to check on Splasher and made a snap decision. Even though he had not slept the previous night, Archie was too wound up to go to sleep immediately, so he decided to take Splasher for a ride. It had been some time since the two had been together, and the time might be better served riding rather than resting. Splasher was happy to see Archie, and before long, the pair was speeding through the moonlit water. Archie was careful to keep to the territory controlled by the Alliance, so he and Splasher traveled up and down the same length of canal several times, the ring canal that bordered the great wall between the Tower of Humility and the Tower of Mourning. As he turned Splasher for the sixth or seventh time near the Tower of Humility, something near the base of the tower caught Archie's eye. He rode Splasher over to the tower wall and saw an inscription just below the surface of the water. Splasher's speed had made the water choppy, and the inscription had caught Archie's eye just as the water receded from the tower. Although it took some time to read, Archie soon saw what it said: "Humility is the path to freedom."

He sat silently thinking about the words, especially "freedom." Archie remembered that when he had first arrived, he had asked Lord Mókato to call his parents and tell them to come get him. Mókato had said that the

T'lantim did not know how to find Archie's parents, but Archie would soon discover for himself how to find them. Perhaps this inscription was the key to finding his way home. Then, Archie was struck by a sudden inspiration: what if all of the towers had inscriptions!

Archie soon had Splasher speeding toward the Tower of Mourning, and before long, he was breathlessly reading another inscription: "Mourning leads to change." There were only two other towers under Alliance control, but Archie was determined to find and read their inscriptions as well. At the Tower of Surrender, he found the words, "Surrender is gain," and at the Tower of Morality, he found, "Morality is possible only when it is impossible." Because there were no other towers to which he could safely travel, Archie turned Splasher back toward Lord Pwrádisa's manor house and stables. All the way back, he pondered the four inscriptions, but none of them made sense to Archie.

Chapter Sixteen
Another Advance

$\mathcal{A}$rchie spent his remaining two hours in a largely restless half-sleep in Lord Pwrádisa's stables. After he awoke, he saddled and mounted Splasher and proceeded to his assigned staging area for the attack on the Palace of Elders. Hundreds of Alliance knights were gathering at each of four staging areas located in the Alliance-controlled tower canals. Archie's staging area was located about seven blocks from the Palace of Elders, in the tower canal running to the Tower of Humility. It was on the right flank of the Alliance and had to be prepared not only to attack the island on which the Palace of Elders sat, but also to defend possible counterattacks coming through the ring canals. There were foot soldiers, archers, and tanks on the skybridges above them, but once the knights reached the institutional rings—just two blocks away—these forces would fall behind. The tanks would not be able to advance any farther, for there were no skybridges in the institutional district. The foot soldiers would only be able to advance once the knights had secured the drawbridges located at the canal level. Thus, because Thlū'taku controlled the entire institutional district, the Alliance knights would be vulnerable on three sides in that district and would have to secure each ring canal—at least between the four tower canals through which their attack was being funneled—before they could proceed to the next.

As if this was not frightening enough, Archie did not know any of the knights in his staging area, other than T'lôt'aris. N'derlex was leading the advance on the tower canal leading from the Tower of Morality, which was on the left flank of the Alliance. Like Archie, the gathering knights all remained silent, and as Archie looked around, he could see that they all wore the same pensive countenance. They all knew that much was resting on the outcome of the attack and that many would not survive the day.

As the ranks of the knights swelled, their mounts became restless and seemed to share their masters' anxiety. T'lôt'aris summoned Archie, who maneuvered Splasher over to the old bearded knight.

"You have not been in close combat before, Sleeper. Stay near me."

"Yes, sir," Archie replied. Though he did not express it, this simple command comforted Archie, making him feel that if he simply remained with the old knight and obeyed his commands, everything would work out.

At the sun's first light, T'lôt'aris gave the command to advance, and the knights moved forward. As expected, the Alliance forces received no resistance before they reached the institutional district. Nevertheless, at each ring canal, a number of Alliance knights were detailed to sweep through and secure the ring canals that linked the tower canals serving the Towers of Humility and Morality before the advance proceeded. Even the ring canal forming the border between the institutional district and the market district was free of any substantial resistance. But at the very next ring canal—which was out of range of the now stalled skybridge archers—the battle began in earnest. The air was suddenly filled with the sound of horns and drums. At their sounding, hundreds of Thlū'taku's knights seemed to appear out of nowhere, attacking the Alliance forces from three sides. Archie froze in terror, but a single glance from the old bearded knight comforted him. Then, he was too busy to even think about his fear, for Thlū'taku's knights were everywhere.

Almost immediately, an enemy knight engaged Archie. In mere seconds, Archie thrust his blade into his attacker's torso, taking advantage of an opening that appeared in his armor as the enemy knight turned. The wounded knight fell into the water and floated helplessly. Before Archie could think about what he had just done or react to his adversary's predicament, he was attacked by two more enemy knights, one on each side. Archie felt their swords strike his armor, almost dismounting him, but he fought them off successfully.

In addition to being much larger than his attackers, Archie was the only knight wearing flexible armor, and that gave him two significant advantages. First, while the traditional armor they wore restricted the other knights' movements, Archie's flexible armor did not restrict his. Second, the stiff traditional armor worn by the attacking knights would move as the knights moved and sometimes expose parts of their bodies to attack. In contrast, Archie's flexible armor stretched as he moved, thereby completely protecting him at all times.

During the space of at least two hours, the Alliance knights were unable to advance, as they absorbed waves of enemy attacks. Archie found he had little time to think about what he was doing. The fight was so intense that he seldom saw anything around him because of his own struggle to stay alive and mounted on Splasher. But there finally came a moment when Archie was surrounded by Alliance knights and not engaged in a struggle with any enemy knights. For the first time, he could see the battle all around him. He noticed the large number of dead and wounded knights and dolphins floating all over the canal, which was red with blood. Turning his attention to the living, he had the odd feeling that what he was watching was not really a single battle, but rather hundreds of little battles. This feeling soon passed, as Archie realized that the Alliance knights, who were greatly outnumbered, were weakening and that the enemy appeared ready to break through their ranks.

Then, Archie caught the glance of the old bearded knight. Without speaking, Archie felt the old knight communicate with him, letting him know that he was no longer bound to remain nearby. Almost without thinking, Archie then did something that was not part of his training and that went against every normal instinct for a sixteen-year-old boy. Indeed, had he taken the time to think about what he was doing, Archie would have decided against it. He pushed Splasher's snout into the water, and while Archie held his breath, Splasher submerged and sped forward, underwater, toward the Palace of Elders. Just when Archie felt that he could hold his breath no longer, Splasher surfaced two blocks away, and the pair caught several enemy knights off guard. In a matter of seconds, Archie unseated two enemy knights. Splasher submerged again, and Archie began attacking the enemy from below. He focused on unseating the knights, who—if fortunate—could do no more than helplessly float in the water until assisted by other enemy knights. If not fortunate, they would find themselves upside down and drowning.

Archie continued this strange new form of underwater combat, surfacing just long enough to catch his breath. The enemy seemed helpless, and it was all they could do to rescue the knights that Archie had unseated. But it took much longer to help knights up and back onto their mounts, and Archie had soon unseated dozens of enemy knights. As enemy knights at the battlefront became aware of the struggle taking place behind their lines, they began to retreat. What began as a trickle soon turned into a rout, and Alliance forces swept forward.

Once the Alliance knights in the tower canal leading to the Tower of Humility had surged forward, Archie turned his attention to the remaining tower canals along which Alliance forces were attacking. Although it was farther away, Archie rode first to the tower canal running between the Palace of Elders and the Tower of Morality. He did this for two reasons. First, he wanted to know how N'derlex was faring. Second, he was concerned about the left flank of the Alliance. Along the way, Archie surprised enemy knights whenever he surfaced, causing rumors to fly throughout their ranks. Having been shocked by Archie's tanks just one day earlier, there was widespread speculation that the Alliance had underwater war machines freely traveling the entire city, attacking from every direction.

When he surfaced in the tower canal on the left flank of the Alliance, Archie immediately unseated five enemy knights, including Thlü´taku himself. This surprised not only Thlü´taku but Archie as well. As their eyes met, Archie saw both anger and fear in Thlü´taku's face. But unlike the other knights Archie had unseated, Thlü´taku reacted quickly. He grabbed a floating lance, which he swiftly hurled, not toward Archie, whose armor provided almost total protection, but toward Splasher. The lance struck Splasher at an angle, penetrating his side about three inches. Archie immediately spurred Splasher to submerge and headed back toward N'derlex and Alliance forces.

When the pair surfaced well behind their own lines, the lance fell out, but Archie could see that Splasher was badly injured. Tears in his eyes, he slipped out of his saddle. Floating in the water, he held Splasher and whispered, "Splasher, Splasher, what have I done to you. Please don't die!"

At that moment, N'derlex rode up on his mount and, pausing only briefly to look at Archie and Splasher, spoke. "I will issue orders for my personal veterinarian to give your dolphin the best care available. But we still need you in this battle. Don't think your dolphin is the only casualty. Hundreds of knights and soldiers have been killed and wounded on both sides today."

This remark embarrassed Archie, for Splasher was the first casualty over which he had shed any tears. Yet, he was not ashamed of his feelings for the dolphin, just his lack of concern for the human casualties. At the command of N'derlex, a young boy handed Archie the reins of another dolphin and simultaneously took Splasher's reins, which Archie reluctantly yielded. As Archie watched the boy lead Splasher away, N'derlex spoke again. "Once again you have shown initiative and done a fine job. As a result of your efforts, our advance is no longer stalled, and we are moving forward everywhere. But the battle is not yet finished, and I need you to continue what you have started."

At that, N'derlex turned his mount and his attention from Archie. Taking only a moment to look at his new steed, Archie climbed on and rode forward. As he neared the front, Archie gave his signal to submerge, but the dolphin did not understand. Archie then remembered that submerging was not something that knights or dolphins were trained to do, and that in breaking dolphins, their trainers employed many techniques to discourage them from submerging. Although it was natural for dolphins to submerge, T'lantim knights would not tolerate it from their mounts. Archie had to "unbreak" this dolphin—and soon—or he would be of no further value to the Alliance.

For about half an hour, Archie rode his new dolphin, continuously pushing his snout into the water, but the dolphin did not seem to understand. Dolphins are very smart, however, and Archie's new mount finally submerged for a short distance. When they surfaced, Archie gave the dolphin a gentle pat, and before long, the pair began to understand each other. Although Archie knew that this new dolphin did not yet understand him as well as Splasher, time was short, and he had to enter the battle again, ready or not. He signaled the dolphin to submerge and was soon speeding toward the enemy rear.

When they surfaced, Archie did no more than take a deep breath and submerge again. He did this for fear that he would lose this mount, too. For several hours, Archie rode from place to place just behind enemy lines, unseating knight after knight, spending most of his time underwater. This proved helpful in several ways. First, a fair number of enemy knights were forced to focus their attention on assisting their unseated comrades instead of fighting Alliance knights. Second, enemy knights everywhere were distracted and fearful, not knowing when they might be attacked from below, while Alliance knights grew more confident as word of Archie's exploits spread. This made it easier for the Alliance knights to defeat the enemy in combat. Finally, several of the unseated knights were permanently removed from combat, because they drowned or were killed or surrendered when Alliance knights reached them before their own comrades.

By the end of the day, the enemy knights had retreated from the Palace of Elders. Alliance knights were finally joined by soldiers and archers who had fought block by block, following the knights' advance through the canals, and the Alliance claimed the island on which the Palace of Elders was located, as well as all of the institutional district.

When N'derlex halted the advance, he, T'lôt'aris, and several other leading knights dismounted and walked onto the central island. Archie started to join them, but with the conclusion of the battle, emotions that he had restrained now took center stage. He walked a short distance away, fell to his knees, and vomited. Images of dead and dying soldiers remained in his mind, and a wave of guilt swept over him. That he had killed hit Archie hard, for he was yet a teenager, whose biggest stresses had recently been how to convince his parents to let him borrow the car and how he would do on a test. But now that the battle was over and he was not too busy to think, his weary brain had released its restraint on his emotions. On top of that, he was exhausted and cold, and his skin felt like a prune because of the time spent in and under the water.

The grass and shrubs that had once grown on the island on which the Palace of Elders was located were no longer there. Thlū'taku had positioned a large garrison of soldiers on the island, which had trampled the greenery beneath their feet. The soldiers had also left pits where they had built fires and dug defensive trenches and built defensive bulwarks all around the palace, though the enemy had retreated before using any of their earthworks. The once beautiful grounds had been destroyed, and that gave the palace a sad appearance. But none of this compared to what the Alliance found inside the palace itself.

As they walked inside, Archie and the others were immediately assaulted by the sounds of moaning and crying and by the odor of urine and feces. In the place of the bright and beautiful lighting that had once adorned the palace, they found a tomb-like darkness. The exquisite chandeliers that once graced the enormous dome were gone, and the only lighting came from torches on the walls. All of the beautiful furnishings had been taken.

But most stunning of all was the carnage that met them. Dead and dying prisoners were chained to the walls. Blood, urine, and feces covered the floor by each prisoner, the strongest of whom groaned or cried as the Alliance knights passed by. When they reached the Council chambers, they found that the enormous room had been turned into an arena in which unfortunate prisoners had been cruelly executed or forced to fight each other to the death. Freed prisoners later told Alliance forces that for "sport," husbands and wives had been pitted against each other, as had parents against their own children.

N'derlex ordered the knights to release the prisoners and tend to their wounds. Archie, like the other knights, began releasing prisoners, while soldiers dressed their wounds. As Archie began to remove the shackles from one prisoner, she looked up and with deep sorrow in her eyes, whispered, "Archie."

It was Mókea.

Chapter Seventeen
The Fifth Tower

Archie swiftly drew his sword and placed it against Mókea's neck and with nothing but contempt in his heart, whispered in her ear, "This blade has already seen much blood today, and slicing through one more lying throat would make very little difference, except that this time it would give me great pleasure."

Mókea said nothing, and in her eyes, Archie saw no fear or anger or even deceit, just sadness. Already close to death, she was past crying, and yet a single tear slowly formed in one eye and rolled down her now gaunt cheek. Conflict in his heart rendered Archie unable to carry out his threat, so he put his sword back into its scabbard. Still angry, however, he felt compelled to explain his action lest Mókea think that he still cared about her.

"I'm not going to waste my strength or soil my blade on your ugly little neck."

Turning around, Archie came face to face with T'lôt'aris, the old bearded knight. Once again, Archie could see disappointment in his tutor's eyes and then the old master spoke.

"Just a few short hours ago, a young knight said to me, 'These people were deceived by Thlū'taku and have realized that following him was wrong—shouldn't we now forgive them?' Do you recall from whose lips I heard those words, Sleeper?"

Archie was ashamed, for those were the very words he had used when speaking about the refugees. They were the words in which Archie had taken pride, for the old bearded knight had not responded to them. Now,

Archie realized that he had not, as he had believed just one day earlier, left the old bearded knight speechless. Instead, the old knight was far ahead of Archie, a lesson that Archie was determined never again to forget. But the old knight was not finished with him and asked another question.

"The value of a precious jewel is determined by its price. Of what value, then, are forgiveness and compassion if they cost nothing in return?"

Saying nothing, Archie turned and freed Mókea. Then, just as her shackles were off, she collapsed, but Archie caught her before she could hit the floor. He gently laid her down and ordered some nearby soldiers to find a physician.

"And so your love for Mókea is not dead after all, is it, Sleeper?"

Although he did not acknowledge the old knight, Archie knew that his assessment was correct. And yet, Archie could not just forget Mókea's lies.

"You see, Sleeper, there are two civil wars that are now raging. One is external, the other internal. One is for control of this city, the other for control of your soul. One is waged between the Alliance and Thlū'taku, the other between love and hate."

Archie remained speechless, not out of contempt or guilt or shame, but because he was thinking about everything he was hearing, for the old knight's words were full of wisdom and opened Archie's heart to new possibilities. While Archie gave Mókea a drink of water and a small crust of bread, the old knight continued.

"When anger, like fire, is not controlled, it is very destructive and consumes everything in its path. Love and hate are not mere *feelings*, Sleeper, they are *choices*."

The soldiers returned with the physician, who immediately began to tend Mo'kea's wounds. Archie, free to turn his attention completely to the old knight, began asking his own questions. "But how can a person choose a feeling?"

In his usual manner, the old bearded knight answered Archie with another question. "How can a feeling choose a person?"

Archie thought for a moment and then asked, "So, what you are telling me is that I should *act* with love, even if I *feel* hate?"

The old bearded knight smiled and spoke again. "Feelings follow actions. If you *practice* love, you will soon *feel* love, and if you *practice* hate, you will soon *feel* hate, with all its consequences. Just look around you. In a few short weeks, Thlū'taku has developed in his followers an appetite for hatred and cruelty."

Archie thought for a moment and then asked, "What about this war—why are we killing the enemy knights and soldiers. Shouldn't we choose to love them instead?"

"Should we spare enemy soldiers who surrender? Yes. Should we forgive them and rehabilitate them if possible? Yes. But love does not require us to surrender to evil, and even when we strike the enemy down, it should not be done in anger or with hatred in our hearts, but only to resist evil. And we should mourn not only our fallen but also the enemy fallen."

With this, T'lôt'aris left Archie, who sat silently for some time, pondering all that the old bearded knight had said. After a while, he got up and wandered through the Palace of Elders, freeing prisoners, tending their wounds, and getting them appropriate medical care. Finally, one physician looked not only at the prisoner Archie had brought him but at Archie himself.

"Sir, you look exhausted, and General N'derlex has ordered rest for all knights and soldiers who fought today. Cots have been placed in some of the conference rooms for that purpose."

Archie did not resist, for he was very tired, so he went directly to the closest conference room he could find. No sooner had he laid his head down than he was fast asleep. The sleep that found him was deep, and it seemed that only a moment had passed when he was awakened, only to find out that he had slept for ten hours. When he arose, he immediately felt sore all over, for the prior day's battle had taken its toll on Archie's body. As he sat up, the young boy who had awakened him told him that Mókea had asked to see him.

As he dressed and put on his armor, Archie thought about what the old bearded knight had said and about the anger he still felt toward Mókea. He made up his mind to disregard those feelings and instead, act with compassion and love. It would not be easy, but he would try.

Archie found Mókea in a guarded conference room with other freed prisoners. Although still gaunt, she was in much better condition than she had been the prior day, and she smiled and ran to Archie as soon as he entered the room. But when she tried to take Archie's hand, he instinctively pulled it back. Archie remembered that getting too close to Mókea was what got him into trouble in the first place. Although she seemed a little hurt, Mókea was happy that Archie was willing to see her. They sat in some chairs that had been placed near the wall of the conference room and talked, at first very cautiously and about nothing important. Deceit, anger, and hatred all build barriers between people who were previously very close, and attempts to restore a damaged relationship take time.

Just as specialized equipment is required to demolish a physical wall, specialized tools must be employed to remove the walls that people erect between themselves. Small talk, like a wrecking ball, can help tear down the wall between two people, but it cannot remove the debris that is left behind. The bulldozers of the emotional realm consist of honesty, forgiveness, and humility. Those bulldozers are not cheap to operate, for they are painful. Each person in a damaged relationship must have the humility to acknowledge the wrongs that he has committed and must be willing to overlook and even forget the wrongs committed by the other. Archie and Mókea engaged in this painful and arduous process for several hours.

Finally, Archie asked Mókea the questions that had been on his mind since the day of his jousting tournament. "Why did you lie about me? Why did you say that *I* sent you a note to meet you, when *you* were the one who sent me a note? Why did you tell me that you did not trust Thlū'taku, when your actions on the very next day proved that you do love him?"

Mókea looked down, obviously ashamed, and replied. "What I told you in the park *was* true and still *is* true: I *am* afraid of Thlū'taku, and I *don't* trust him. But my grandfather caught me as I was coming home, and he made me tell him where I was. Then he summoned Thlū'taku, and they had an argument. Thlū'taku turned to me and said that he would still marry me and not dishonor my grandfather's house if I would testify against you."

Archie was stunned, for it had not occurred to him that Mókea had been forced to do what she had done.

Mókea continued, "After your trial, Thlū'taku was very angry, and he demanded that my grandfather name him as my grandfather's successor. My grandfather agreed, and Thlū'taku then demanded that my grandfather turn over power immediately. When my grandfather refused, Thlū'taku imprisoned us."

Then, Mókea looked up and made eye contact with Archie for the first time since she began telling her painful story. She asked something that would test Archie's capacity to love and his willingness to forgive.

"My grandfather has been imprisoned in the Fifth Tower. Will you save him for me?"

Archie was stunned. He was still dealing with his anger toward Mókea, and now she wanted him to save Lord Mókato, the very person who had sentenced him to death! He remained silent, not daring to expose his feelings for fear that he would destroy the work of several hours before it was even finished. Yet, he could not forget the old bearded knight's words about love and hate being choices. After a painfully long pause, Archie finally replied, "I will do my best, but we do not yet control the Fifth Tower. It lies in our path, however, and I suspect that we will soon control it."

Mókea burst into tears, crying over and over, "Thank you. Now I know that you have truly forgiven me." This, more than anything else, softened Archie's heart, but because he was confused and still unable to forget what Mókea and her grandfather had done to him, he did not know how to react. For this reason Archie simply turned and left.

After inquiring about the current location of N'derlex and his command post, Archie left the Palace of Elders. He found N'derlex in the Tower of Morality, for the command post established there before the assault on the city's central island had not been moved. When Archie entered the room, N'derlex looked up, smiled, and summoned Archie to the map table.

"Come in, Sir Archie," he said. "There is much to do, for we shall not let Thlū'taku rest. He no longer has sufficient power to attack, because we now control the greater part of the city, its resources, and its people. And we have another advantage: those fighting for the Alliance are fighting because they want to, but very few of those fighting for Thlū'taku are really loyal to him. During the last battle, you unseated hundreds of enemy knights, but hundreds of others pretended to be unseated so that they could avoid the battle and surrender when given the opportunity. They risked drowning to do this. After one or two more advances, we should expect widespread surrender." N'derlex then paused and looked directly into Archie's eyes. After a moment he continued.

"I have a dangerous mission for you, one that only you are capable of handling. I need a knight to take a scouting party behind enemy lines to probe enemy strength along the tower canal leading to the Fifth Tower and all of the intersecting ring canals. Are you willing to do this?"

Although no longer eager for combat, and feeling that it was a little unfair to expect so much of him, Archie did not want to disappoint N'derlex or T'lôt'aris, so he just replied, "Yes."

Before Archie could ask whether Splasher had recovered, N'derlex placed his hand on Archie's shoulder and said, "I understand that Splasher is not yet well enough to ride, so you'll have to take the mount you rode after Splasher was injured."

Archie wondered whether N'derlex had read his mind. Nevertheless, within the hour, he was mounted on the replacement dolphin and on his way to the ring canal bordering the great wall near the Tower of Morality. There he met five other knights, each of whom Archie was to teach the art of submerging. Archie had them ride their dolphin steeds along the ring canal from the Tower of Morality to the Tower of Surrender and back, with the expectation that with each trip, they would spend more time beneath the surface. Unfortunately, the knights and their dolphins learned the technique at widely divergent speeds and with vastly different results. Observing the knights and their steeds, Archie had all of them change mounts, some more than once. When he finally felt that he had properly matched the knights with steeds, he continued their training. The performance of three knights improved dramatically, but the other two knights just could not master the technique, so Archie decided to dismiss them and undertake the mission with only the three knights who had achieved some proficiency in the submersion technique.

It was now dusk, and the small task force dismounted, tied their steeds to hitching posts near the Tower of Morality, and went to the military dining facility within that tower. After eating a quick meal, Archie instructed the other three knights to wait for him in the dining facility while he went and talked with N'derlex. After receiving his final orders, Archie returned to the dining facility and then departed the tower with his small task force.

Their mission was not to attack the enemy but to obtain vital intelligence about troop movements and locations. They were to ride their mounts submerged and quietly surface at specific locations, hopefully without being detected. Each knight was assigned six critical points to scout, after which he was to return to the Tower of Morality. Among the points Archie selected for himself was the Fifth Tower.

When it was completely dark, the four knights mounted their steeds, wished each other Godspeed, and went their separate ways. Archie rode his steed to each of the six points for which he was responsible, surfacing as infrequently as possible. At each location, he quietly surfaced, looked around, and took note of troop deployments, defensive works, and other matters of strategic significance. All went well until he surfaced at his fourth point, where his steed, evidently tired, made some noises that aroused the attention of two enemy sentries. Archie sat frozen in the water as the sentries came to investigate. As they came within about ten feet of him, Archie held his breath. Unbelievably, however, they did not see him in the darkness and walked right past him. As soon as he felt it was safe to do so, Archie took a deep breath, signaled his mount to submerge, and they sped toward the fifth of Archie's six points. There, Archie surfaced without incident, assessed the enemy strengths and weaknesses, and departed. Just one more point—the Fifth Tower—and Archie could return to friendly lines.

Surfacing without a sound at the base of the Fifth Tower, Archie looked around, gathered in his mind every piece of information of any conceivable value, and prepared to return to the Tower of Morality. But before departing, Archie could not resist looking for the inscription at the base of the tower. He was certain that he could find and read it without being detected. He guided his mount along the base of the tower, until he was right next to the position where the inscription should be. At last, he saw the inscription: "Compassion begets compassion."

Just as he was about to submerge and return to the Tower of Morality, Archie heard a whizzing sound and then felt a burning sensation on the right side of his neck. He fell off his mount but managed to grab its tail fluke just as it submerged and sped toward the Tower of Morality. The burning sensation in his neck grew worse, and he reached out with his right hand to feel his neck and found an arrow lodged just under his chin on the right side. But reaching for his neck caused Archie to lose his grip on the dolphin's tail fluke, and he was soon separated from the steed. He floated to the surface and with his last bit of strength, struggled to turn over. As soon as he was floating face up, he looked up on the great wall, and just before passing out, he saw soldiers pointing at him and running.

Chapter Eighteen
The Face in the Water

When Archie awoke, his surroundings confused him at first. He could see that he was in a typical T'lantim bedroom, but he did not remember how he got there. As he looked around, he felt stiffness and a dull pain in the right side of his neck, and when he instinctively placed his right hand on the affected area, he felt bandages. He then remembered being shot in the neck with an arrow. He remembered falling off his mount and clinging desperately to its tail fluke. Then, as he remembered losing his grip and seeing soldiers on the great wall overlooking him, Archie was overwhelmed with fear. He must have passed out and been captured by the enemy!

But another look around the room stilled Archie's fears, for the circumstances in which he now found himself suggested that he had not fallen into enemy hands but, instead, into the hands of the Alliance. The enemy would have surely imprisoned or executed him.

Just as Archie was savoring this hopeful thought, the trapdoor opened in the ceiling above, and a figure descended the ladder that had thrust out from the wall. Archie breathlessly observed the figure, whose back faced Archie. Unlike every other knight Archie had seen in K'truum-Shra, this man's tunic and pantaloons were black rather than white. Upon reaching the floor, the figure turned and faced Archie. It was Thlū'taku!

"You have caused me immense trouble, young man," said the dark knight, "for unlike the largely mindless citizens of this city, you think and act for yourself. Your arrival and subsequent actions forced me to move up my timetable, to take actions for which I had not yet thoroughly prepared. By all rights, I ought to torture and execute you right now."

A wave of terror swept over Archie as he imagined suffering various tortures, the effects of which he had already witnessed among the freed prisoners at the Palace of Elders.

"Nevertheless," Thlū'taku continued, "you could be very useful to me. I am prepared to overlook what you have done and offer you a position as my second in command, if you will join my cause."

Stunned, Archie remained silent, unable to process what Thlū'taku had just said to him. But before he could answer, Thlū'taku said, "Do not answer me now, for I have much to explain to you. I am confident that when you hear what I have to say, you will see that my cause is righteous. I will explain all of this at dinner. You *are* hungry, aren't you?" Looking at Archie's rumpled, tattered, and soiled clothing, Thlū'taku added, "My servants will bring you more suitable attire, garments befitting the position that you have clearly earned." At that, Thlū'taku smiled, turned, and ascended the ladder. Archie could not read the smile that had flashed across Thlū'taku's face, and he wondered just what the smile meant.

No sooner had Thlū'taku departed than Archie was greeted by an entourage of servants bearing some of the finest garments that Archie had ever seen. They were made of a fine satin material, and though they were black, they were adorned with bright green trim and shoulder braid. In addition, the black satin itself was not plain but impressed with the image of towers, each of which had three sharks on it. Even though the material was black, the light reflected from the garments always highlighted one or more of the towers. On the breast was Archie's own coat of arms, with three significant differences: the field was black instead of blue, it was bordered in gold to set it apart from the tunic itself, and three green sharks—the unmistakable symbol of Thlū'taku—encircled the white, eight-spoked wheel.

Taking no more than a moment to examine the garments, Archie put them on and asked the servants where dinner would be served. They led him out of the bedroom and up to the rooftop park. A tower loomed in the distance, but Archie could not tell which one it was. The servants who had brought him the garments he now wore motioned for him to follow and then began toward the tower.

"Which tower lies ahead?" Archie inquired.

"The Tower of Peace," one servant responded. "It is our lord's headquarters."

Archie silently chuckled at the bizarre fact just conveyed to him—that Thlū'taku should be associated with anything named "Peace." This man was responsible for a civil war and so much destruction, for the separation of families, and for the torture and death of hundreds, if not thousands. How could he be peaceful? And yet, Archie was on his way to dine with that very man. Archie chuckled again.

After about fifteen minutes, they reached the Seventh Tower, the Tower of Peace. Archie strained to see the inscription at the base of the tower, but the servants accompanying him would not let him pause long enough to see the inscription. Once inside, Archie was ushered to a large and ornate dining room with a large, circular table that could comfortably seat as many as fifty people. Thlū'taku was already seated at the table, as were ten knights. The remaining chairs were all empty, and the servants appeared to outnumber the diners. As the entourage approached Thlū'taku's seat, all of the diners, except for Thlū'taku, arose and bowed to Archie, who was directed to take the seat to the right of Thlū'taku. This was an honored position, and it signified that Archie was to be Thlū'taku's second in command, his "right-hand man."

Thlū'taku wasted no time. Archie had barely taken his seat when Thlū'taku announced, "This is Lord Archie the Bold. He is second only to me, and his orders are not to be questioned."

Archie was surprised by the title "lord," and wondered how a knight who was not himself a lord could elevate Archie to that rank.

Then, the dark knight turned to Archie and directed him to enjoy the many delicacies placed before him. Archie obliged, and as he began to devour some of the more familiar items, Thlū'taku said, "I can see in your eyes that you think that I am evil, and yet you hardly know me. It is only fair that you hear from me before you judge." After a short pause, he continued, "You have only been in our city for a short time, and yet you think that you know us well enough to judge us, that you can discern who is good and who is evil."

Archie said nothing but continued to eat as he eyed the dark knight.

"What do you really know of N'derlex, of T'lôt'aris, or of the Alliance itself? And what have they told you about me? Have you observed any of these things for yourself, or have you simply taken the words of those whom you met first?"

Pausing briefly, Thlū'taku studied Archie's face, looking for a reaction to what he had already asked. Then he continued, "You have the temerity to judge me, to blame me for this awful war, but I suggest that you look back. What was the event that sparked this war, and who was responsible for that event?"

This made Archie uncomfortable, for he knew that Thlū'taku was referring to Archie's own transgression and the subsequent trial that had divided the city.

"You think that I started this war," Thlū'taku continued, "but I lay that blame at *your* feet. Had you not come to our city, had you not broken our law, had you not disrupted our way of life, we would still be enjoying the peace that we had enjoyed for two thousand years before your arrival. And what kind of man are you that you would allow another man to die for your misdeeds? I knew Pwrâdisa, and though he and I were not close, I respected him, and his death greatly affected me."

Still holding a piece of bread in his raised hand, Archie suddenly ceased eating, because Thlū'taku's words stabbed him in his very soul.

Observing Archie's demeanor, Thlū'taku then added, "You know, when Pwrâdisa offered to take your place, I knew then that war was inevitable. You looked right into my eyes at that very moment, and you saw fear, didn't you?"

Archie slowly and reluctantly nodded.

"Well, let me tell you what I feared, for I saw the future from that moment. Mókato had no lawful heirs, and Pwrâdisa alone was qualified to assume the leadership of our people upon Mókato's death. Had he done so and married well, his line could have continued unbroken for many generations. And yet you, an outsider, let him die in your place. Don't you think that was an extraordinarily selfish act, to weigh yourself against the future of an entire people and then to decide that your own puny little life outweighed that of an entire civilization?"

Archie felt ashamed, for he had never considered Lord Pwrâdisa's death in this way. But before Archie could think about this very long, Thlū'taku changed the direction of his lecture.

"Now, let us consider what is fair to you. From the moment you arrived, you have made it clear that you want to return to your home and family, to your own people. Yet, for some reason, those you first met have evaded your questions and, quite frankly, refused to help you return. Instead, they used you for their own selfish purposes. Doesn't that make you wonder whether they should be trusted? What kind of magic have they used that the memory of your parents should fade so quickly and your safe return should so rapidly diminish in importance to you?"

Tears began to form in Archie's eyes as he thought about his parents.

"I, for one, think that you are entitled to our assistance in returning to your home, and I am prepared to do what I can to help you."

Archie's heart raced, for Thlū'taku's words made sense to him, and he began to wonder how it is that he had so quickly forgotten what he desired most.

"All I ask of you is that you consider all the facts before you judge me and that you help me to win this war. Then I will help you get home."

This was the first concrete promise that any of the T'lantim had ever made to help Archie find his way home. This single fact made Archie wonder whether he had, indeed, wrongly maligned Thlū'taku.

Thlū'taku smiled. "Enough. As I told you earlier, I do not intend to pressure you, for I have given you much to think about. You may give me your decision in the morning. Now, let us simply enjoy our meal." Once again, the smile that flashed across Thlū'taku's face was inscrutable, and Archie did not know how to respond, so he simply returned the smile.

No one spoke for quite some time, but Archie did not stop thinking about what Thlū'taku had said. He began to mull over everything that he had seen and heard since he had arrived. Foremost among Archie's thoughts was the fact that his initial impression of Thlū'taku had been formed not by personal experience but through his conversations with Mókea, and Archie *knew* that she was a liar. One question Thlū'taku asked nagged at him: what did he really know about Thlū'taku, N'derlex, or T'lotaris, and from what source had he gained that knowledge?

When the meal was over, a small detachment of soldiers was assigned to Archie. Thlū'taku explained that they were Archie's personal guard. They would show him to his new quarters in the Sixth Tower, the Tower of Purity, and would respond to his commands. Thlū'taku explained that the only restriction he was placing on Archie was to keep him away from military operations, but even this restriction would be lifted as soon as Archie made his decision to join Thlū'taku.

As the soldiers led Archie to the Sixth Tower, it dawned on him that his new quarters were located as far away from Alliance forces as possible. At the opposite end of the city was the Second Tower, the Tower of Mourning, the permanent headquarters of the Alliance. Even if they wanted to, N'derlex and T'lotaris could not rescue him, so Archie would have to make a tough decision.

When they arrived at the Sixth Tower, Archie was led to an enormous residence inside the tower. He had not seen any similar residences in any of the other towers but then, he had never fully explored them—or been permitted to explore them.

Unlike typical T'lantim structures, this residence was not open; it was safely concealed within the tower and, therefore, had exterior walls. The ceilings were very high, especially for the T'lantim, and despite the existence of the exterior walls, the floor plan itself was open, punctuated only by the occasional column and the same sheer drapes that adorned ordinary T'lantim homes and shops. The absence of interior walls gave the residence the feel of being open. Indeed, the only interior walls that Archie could find separated the sleeping quarters from the rest of the residence. And unlike typical T'lantim bedrooms, the eight bedrooms in this residence, all located against the exterior walls, had ordinary doors rather than trapdoors. Archie guessed that the military nature of the residence—located within a tower and designed to accommodate a high-ranking military leader—made the typical open residence impossible, but that the open floor plan was intended to address the T'lantim taste for openness. Then, Archie suddenly remembered this was Lord Mókato's tower, and it made him uneasy.

Having only awakened a few hours earlier, Archie knew that he could not sleep. In any event, Thlū'taku had given him plenty to think about, and for the first time, he entertained serious doubts about N'derlex and T'lotaris. So, Archie decided to take a walk and simply informed the captain of the guard, into whose face he looked for any clue that might tell Archie that the guard was a prisoner detail rather than the personal guard of a high-ranking military commander. The captain merely said, "Very well, sir," and began issuing orders and making preparations to accompany Archie.

Archie was unable to detect any emotion or other thought in the captain's eyes, for he was obviously a well-trained officer. Archie decided to conduct a test and said, "Stay here. I don't want any company." To Archie's surprise, the captain again replied, "Very well, sir," and issued new orders to his men.

Archie climbed the stairs to the top of the tower and walked along the enormous city wall, looking alternately out over the ocean and then back toward the center of the city. But all along his walk, he encountered soldiers, each of whom snapped to attention and saluted Archie as he passed. Apparently Thlū'taku was serious about making Archie second in command.

After a while, desiring solitude, Archie returned to the Sixth Tower and descended the spiral stairway to the underwater passageway leading to the manor house. After exiting one of the four doors in the arched bridge supporting the manor house, Archie proceeded down the canal-level sidewalk along the tower canal. Once again, there were many soldiers patrolling the sidewalk, and Archie soon began to enjoy the respect with which they greeted him. After a while, Archie found a bench facing the canal and he sat down, determined to think through all he had been told. The lapping waves soothed his nerves as he quietly observed the various reflections in the water.

Archie's gaze was soon drawn to his own reflection, and he began to admire the new clothing he wore, the bright green braid and trim that obviously signified his high rank, and his own coat of arms. As he looked at his own face, Archie realized that he had been through quite a bit. Despite his youth, the face he saw looking back at him had aged. It seemed more the face of a man than a boy. As he studied the reflection of his own face in the water, it occurred to Archie that he had not looked in a mirror since his arrival, and so he had been unaware of how he had changed. This saddened him, and he closed his eyes.

Archie considered his options. Thlū'taku was the only T'lantim who had offered him a way home, and so for his own good, Archie thought, he should accept the offer, help Thlū'taku win the war, and then return home. As this conclusion made its way into his consciousness, Archie opened his eyes and again met the gaze of his own reflection.

Archie gasped, for what he saw truly stunned him. The reflection of his face was no longer what it had been just moments before. It no longer looked like his own face, albeit older, but was instead the face of a very different person. Archie examined each of the features of the face in the water, comparing them to his own—or at least what he remembered of his own face. The face in the water had Archie's sandy blond hair and fair complexion, but very little else. It looked familiar, and yet Archie could not make it out. Was it his father's face? The face of a teacher? That of someone else in his life before K'truum-Shra? It could not be any of the T'lantim, for they had neither sandy blond hair nor fair complexion. Or could it be a T'lantim face but with Archie's hair and complexion?

Suddenly, Archie recognized the face in the water, and he was paralyzed with fear. The face in the water was that of Thlū'taku!

Chapter Nineteen
The Decision

After the shock wore off, Archie jumped up and began walking toward the Sixth Tower again. The salutes he received no longer held any charm for him, and his heart raced as he contemplated just what he had seen. Now, more than ever, Archie felt alone, because Thlū′taku's words had planted seeds of doubt in his heart about Lord Pwrádisa, T′lôt′aris, N′derlex, and the Alliance. Yet, Archie still did not trust Thlū′taku. If only he could find his way back home!

As he walked, it occurred to Archie that he might not be as powerless as he thought. From his first meeting with Lord Mókato, he had been told that he was on a quest and that he alone was responsible for finding his way back home. The Sixth Tower, now his new quarters, was coming squarely into view just as Archie was considering his responsibility for his own fate. Almost without thinking, Archie looked up, for he had been staring at the ground as he walked, and his eyes were drawn to the waves splashing against the base of the tower. He stopped dead in his tracks, as it dawned on him that he had not yet read the inscription at the base of the Sixth Tower. Instead of entering the door in the arched bridge, Archie jumped into the water, swam under the bridge and across the last ring canal toward the tower, and searched for the inscription.

Almost immediately, he heard a splashing sound that he knew he did not make. He turned around and saw, for the first time, three soldiers who had apparently been following him. Ignoring them, he continued toward the base of the Sixth Tower, the Tower of Purity, and began searching for the inscription. Before long, he saw the inscription, but like all the others, it made no sense to him. It read, "Purity restores the blind."

Archie swam back across the canal, climbed up onto the sidewalk, and calmly turned to lend a helping hand to each of the three soldiers who had followed him. All three of them wore a sheepish expression and were obviously embarrassed at having been caught spying on Archie.

"Did you enjoy your swim?" Archie inquired, flashing a boyish smile.

Only one of the soldiers braved a reply, saying, "Thank you, sir," and then adding, almost as an afterthought, "begging your pardon, m'lord."

Archie turned and, making no effort to lose the three thoroughly soaked and humiliated soldiers, began his way back to his new quarters inside the Tower of Purity. Once there, he instructed the three soldiers to remain with him as he summoned the captain of the guard. When the young officer arrived, Archie turned toward him and simply stared into his eyes. The captain looked at Archie, then at the three wet soldiers, and then again at Archie. When his expression finally betrayed some emotion, Archie asked, "Do you recall my telling you that I didn't want any company?"

"Yes, sir."

"And did you instruct these three soldiers to follow me?"

"Yes, sir."

"And can you tell me the punishment for deliberately disobeying an order?"

After a brief pause, the young captain answered, "Death by torture."

Startled, Archie gasped, for he was unfamiliar with the harsh rules governing Thlū'taku's military forces. This, of course, betrayed his surprise to his four subordinates. Nevertheless, Archie quickly recovered his composure and continued his interrogation of the young officer.

"Why, then, did you send these three to spy on me?"

Pausing a moment to look Archie squarely in the eye, the young officer finally spoke. His answer took Archie completely by surprise. "I had these three follow you for your own safety, not to spy on you. I instructed them to protect you, even at the risk of their own lives, for Thlū'taku has ordered your immediate assassination if you attempt to escape or if you get too close to military operations."

As Archie was taking this in, the young officer drew a deep breath and then made his most stunning revelation.

"And we have orders from N´derlex not only to protect you but to help you escape. You see, the four of us are actually Alliance agents, having infiltrated Thlū´taku's forces long before your arrival. Our original mission was simply to infiltrate enemy forces, periodically send back valuable intelligence, and await further orders. Not long after your arrival, N´derlex sent new orders through the network to find you and get you back. Because I had gained sufficient trust to be made a captain, I was able to arrange our assignment to you. As soon as the logistics are worked out, we will arrange your transport back to Alliance territory."

Archie could not help but think that this was some form of trap, perhaps a perverse loyalty test to determine whether he would try to escape. When the young officer finished, Archie turned, and partly out of shock and partly out of fear, he simply walked away and into his sleeping chamber. There, he sat on the bed and pondered the evening's events. After a while, his mind returned to the inscriptions on the towers, and so he began considering what they meant. About an hour later, having made no progress, Archie opened the door and scanned the larger room for the captain or one of the three soldiers who had followed him during his walk, but none was present. He then summoned a soldier who *was* present, and after examining his face to see whether it appeared in any way different from the four "Alliance agents," Archie realized that he could discern none. He then simply asked the soldier for paper and pen.

Motioning for Archie to follow, the soldier walked over to a large desk and opened a drawer. There he pointed to a generous supply of paper, quill pens of every size, and several bottles of ink. Archie sat down, took a sheet of paper, a pen, and ink and began to write the names of the towers and their corresponding inscriptions, if he knew them:

Tower of Humility—Humility is the path to freedom.

Tower of Mourning—Mourning leads to change.

Tower of Surrender—Surrender is gain.

Tower of Morality—Morality is possible only when it is impossible.

Tower of Compassion—Compassion begets compassion.

Tower of Purity—Purity restores the blind.

Tower of Peace—

Tower of Sacrifice—

For quite some time, Archie just stared at what he had written, hoping that its meaning would somehow be revealed to him, but to no avail. The inscriptions were short and cryptic, and Archie wondered why they had been engraved on the walls of eight different towers, all separated by great distances, and beneath the water line to boot. It is almost as if the builders had meant to hide the truth that the inscriptions seemed to offer.

One phrase seized Archie's attention more than the others, and that was the phrase, "path to freedom," contained in the first inscription. These three words seemed to promise Archie a possible way home, so he focused on the entire inscription, "Humility is the path to freedom." Could it be that something in the First Tower, the Tower of Humility, would guide him home? Was there a boat in that tower, or perhaps a hidden portal that would take him home?

Archie suddenly realized that Lord Pwrådisa was the last ruler of the house associated with the Tower of Humility. Perhaps this was a clue that he should remain loyal to that house, to T'lôt'aris, its current steward, to N'derlex, and to the Alliance. To do so, he would have to escape, despite the risk.

Even if it performed no other service, the first inscription had at least guided Archie in making the decision that had been placed before him: the decision to choose the Alliance over Thlũ'taku and his promises. Archie stood and beckoned a soldier. No sooner had the soldier come than orders issued—almost automatically—from Archie's mouth, summoning the captain of the guard.

After what seemed an almost interminable time, the young officer appeared, looking apprehensive. Archie realized that it was not only he who was required to trust the young captain, but that the captain was also required to trust Archie, because if Archie had decided to join Thlũ'taku, the captain's life would surely be forfeited.

Archie motioned for the young officer to walk with him, away from ears that might not be friendly. "I want to return to the Alliance, and I am prepared to put my fate into your hands. Just how do you plan to get me out?"

Clearly relieved, the captain offered only that preparations were already under way.

Archie became concerned. "Thlũ'taku will be here in the morning, and he expects my decision then. Wouldn't it be best to leave before then?"

The captain smiled and replied, "Escape is never so simple. It is easier to move about in enemy territory than to move back and forth between the Alliance and the enemy. Because you are new, and a high-value prisoner as well, you will be watched very closely. Everything you do will be immediately evaluated to test your loyalty, no matter what you tell Thlū′taku in the morning. For that reason, we must take every precaution to make the potential success of your escape match the risk that is involved."

Archie's heart sank, for he was afraid of his scheduled meeting with Thlū′taku, now just hours away. Before Archie could speak, the captain spoke, this time in a much more compassionate tone. "But we certainly expect that we will be able to get you out of here before Thlū′taku arrives."

The captain then turned and walked away, leaving Archie to his own thoughts.

Chapter Twenty
Escape

Fearful of what the morning might bring, Archie did not sleep. Instead, he reviewed in his mind the names of the eight towers and each of the six inscriptions that he had found and wondered what they all could mean. It occurred to Archie that the names of the towers did not appear to be related. Some had positive connotations—Peace, Purity, and Compassion—while others had negative connotations—Mourning, Surrender, and Sacrifice. Humility and Morality just did not seem to fit at all, for they were just virtues. But then, so were Compassion, Purity, and Sacrifice. The tower names seemed to defy a single categorization. And what of the order of the towers: did that make any sense at all? Why was the Tower of Humility designated as the First Tower?

Archie suddenly realized that he was not alone, for the captain of the guard had appeared without making a sound. No wonder he was a covert agent. "Sir, the preparations have been made. Follow me."

With fear in his heart, Archie complied, for once again he seemed to have no alternative. Thlū́taku would soon be coming for Archie's decision, and Archie did not even want to think about what would happen after that.

Archie and the captain of the guard made their way to the spiral stairway at the center of the tower and descended to the dungeon level. There, the captain of the guard pushed against the wall, and a secret door opened, revealing another spiral stairway. For quite some time, the two descended. It seemed to Archie that the stairs were not merely descending, but descending at an angle. When they finally reached the bottom, Archie's suspicion was confirmed, for after a short walk through a tunnel, they began ascending another spiral stairway that angled upward. Seeing the puzzled look in Archie's eyes, the captain of the guard explained, "Almost no one knows this, but each tower is connected to the tower at the opposite side of the city by an underwater passageway such as this one. It is part of the superstructure of the entire city. Thus, the Tower of Purity is connected to the Tower of Mourning, into which we will soon ascend."

Archie recalled the despair he felt when he realized that the Tower of Purity was at the opposite end of the city from the Tower of Mourning, where the Alliance had its permanent headquarters. He now chuckled, for his fear that N'derlex and T'lôt'aris were so far away and could never reach him was clearly very wrong.

As they reached the top of the secret spiral stairway, the young captain pushed against the wall and the door opened. On the other side of the door were N'derlex and T'lôt'aris, together with a detachment of soldiers guarding the secret entrance into Alliance territory. N'derlex spoke first. "You did not think that you knew all of our secrets, did you, young man?"

"No, sir," Archie replied, and then grinned. "And this is one secret I will never forget!"

Embarrassed that he still wore the tunic he received from Thlū'taku, Archie quickly pulled it off and tossed it to the ground.

"You have earned a good rest, Sir Archie, but there is still much work to do. I must, therefore, make this welcome very brief. T'lôt'aris will brief you."

N'derlex turned and walked away, and the old bearded knight turned to Archie. "We are glad that no harm came to you, Sleeper, for your quest is not yet complete. Come, run with me."

Archie followed as the old bearded knight led him up through the Tower of Mourning—past the dungeon that Archie had called home for too long—and up to the top of the great wall. As they departed the tower into the crisp morning air, they were greeted by the rising sun, an ocean breeze, and seagulls busy looking for breakfast. The two ran along the wall past the Tower of Surrender and toward the Tower of Morality. When they reached that tower, the pair entered, descended the spiral stairway, and took the underwater passageway to the manor house associated with the tower. The old bearded knight did not stop there but continued out to the fig orchard, for the lord of the Fourth Tower was responsible for raising figs. Finally, well into the orchard, the old bearded knight stopped.

"What do you know of this tower?" he asked.

"That it is called the Tower of Morality and that an inscription at the base of the tower reads 'Morality is possible only when it is impossible.'" Archie did not know whether the old bearded knight was even aware of the inscriptions, and he searched his eyes for an answer, to no avail.

"And what does that mean, Sleeper?"

"I'm not sure. I was hoping that you would tell me." Archie knew, however, that it was not the old bearded knight's practice to tell him anything but rather to lead him to figure out riddles for himself.

"And when is morality impossible, Sleeper?"

"I don't know. I suppose it is not possible for an evil person."

"Then, you are also saying that only evil people are capable of morality?"

"No. No, that is not what I am saying at all." Archie hated it when the old bearded knight put words into his mouth.

"Then, who is capable of morality, Sleeper?"

"Good people."

The old bearded knight eyed Archie without speaking for what seemed an eternity to Archie. Then finally, he spoke again.

"Who is good?"

"I don't know," said Archie.

"Are you a good person, Sleeper?"

Now it was Archie's turn to pause. He thought about the transgressions that had caused him to be thrown into the dungeon in the Tower of Mourning, about the trial and how he had caused Lord Pwrádisa's death, and about the war that he had brought to K'truum-Shra. He even thought about seeing Thlū'taku's face in his own reflection. Looking down at the ground, unable to look the old bearded knight in the eye, Archie finally responded. "No, sir, I am not."

"And are you capable of morality, then?"

"No, sir, I am not."

"Then, Sleeper, I submit that you *are* capable of morality, for you *know* that you are not good and that you are not capable of morality on your own. For so long as you bear that in mind, you are capable of morality, for that is what the inscription means."

Archie was surprised that the old bearded knight had actually told him the meaning of the inscription at the base of the Tower of Morality. Then he realized that he must also know the meanings of the other inscriptions. But before Archie could speak, the old bearded knight did. "In time, you will learn the meanings of the inscriptions associated with the other towers, but for now, you must learn the lessons this tower has to offer. Do you understand what I have told you?"

"Well, I guess," said Archie, but upon a moment's reflection, added, "No, I am not really sure what you mean. How can I be moral just by keeping in mind that I am not moral?"

"What do you need if you do not know where you are going?" asked the old bearded knight.

"Directions. A map," Archie quickly replied.

"And so, if you don't know how to be moral, how can you learn to be moral?"

Archie's eyes brightened as he suddenly understood the inscription, and he blurted out with obvious confidence, "By studying the sacred scrolls and following what they have to say." Then, after a pause, he tentatively added, "And I suppose I can always ask you?"

"I will always help you when you need me," the old bearded knight replied, "but you must not forget to continue seeking answers."

The old bearded knight then turned to a fig tree, plucked two figs, began eating one, and gave the other to Archie. Archie bit into the fig and suddenly realized that he was hungry. The two were silent as they enjoyed the sweet figs, but finally, the old bearded knight turned to Archie and asked, "What do you know of the fig tree?"

Archie quickly admitted that he knew nothing at all, and the old bearded knight continued.

"The fig tree produces fruit twice a year. The first fruit in the spring comes from old growth, from last year's shoots. Then new shoots grow, and the summer fruit comes from the new growth. As a result, the summer fruit is sweeter and more abundant. Be sure that your morality is the same."

Archie's blank expression betrayed the fact that he did not understand what the old bearded knight was saying, and so the old bearded knight continued.

"The fig tree is a *living* thing. But because it is, the fig tree is also a *dying* thing. The old growth is not capable of bearing the kind of fruit that is desirable. You, too, are a living thing and a dying thing. Like the fig tree, you have old shoots and new shoots. And like the fig tree, your old shoots are dying. How, then, do you propose to be moral?"

Archie replied indignantly, "As I said earlier, by following the sacred scrolls." Then, with pride, he added, "And you know that I have read and studied them all!"

"But when did you *last* read the sacred scrolls?" the old bearded knight inquired.

Archie blushed, because he could now see where the conversation was going. "Just before I was knighted," Archie meekly replied.

"And do you recall what you read and learned?" asked the old bearded knight. "Perhaps you can recite the sacred scrolls to me now and explain what they mean."

Archie did not respond.

"What kind of fruit, then, do you think that those old shoots will now bear?" asked the old bearded knight.

Chapter Twenty-One
The Priesthood

At that, T'lôt'aris turned and began running again. He stopped, turned around, and asked Archie whether he was going to eat figs all day or follow. Archie followed, and the two runners were soon back on the great wall of the city, moving toward the Tower of Surrender. When they reached that tower, they entered and made their way to the library where Archie had studied the sacred scrolls.

"Do you recall" asked the old knight, "that I told you most of our people are not even aware that the sacred scrolls exist and that some of these scrolls have been neglected even by the priests? Well, now is your opportunity to cultivate new shoots."

Archie stared at the old bearded knight, unhappy that he had to undergo this drudgery once again. While Archie was brooding, the old knight picked up three scrolls and thrust them into Archie's hands, just as he had done on Archie's first internment in the library. Suddenly, Archie remembered something. "But aren't you forgetting something. Didn't N'derlex say something about much work to be done and you giving me a briefing?"

"Yes, he did, didn't he? Well, this is your assignment, and it came from N'derlex. How do you suppose that we knew about the secret underwater passageways and Thlū'taku did not? It is because N'derlex *knows* the sacred scrolls and everything in them. Perhaps if you had known them as well, it would not have been necessary to send a team to rescue you. Do you want to take the same risk before your next mission?"

Resigned to his fate, Archie barely acknowledged the question and instead, just weakly picked up one of the three scrolls that the old bearded knight had given him. When he opened it, he was surprised, for it was a map of the city.

"I didn't see this scroll before," Archie exclaimed.

"You were given *all* of the scrolls, Sleeper. Yet, having eyes, you did not see, and having a mind, you did not comprehend. Did I not tell you that the summer fruit of the fig is more desirable? That it is more abundant than the fruit of the old growth?"

Without giving Archie an opportunity to respond, the old bearded knight pointed to the diagram and said, "Memorize every detail of this drawing and then start reviewing the sacred scrolls to find scriptures that relate to the diagram."

"I don't understand," Archie protested.

The old bearded knight picked up one scroll, opened it, pointed to one verse, and asked, "What does this say?"

Reading the verse aloud, Archie was caught off guard, "Humility is the path to freedom."

Smiling, the old bearded knight then asked, "And how does that verse relate to the diagram?"

Archie pointed at the Tower of Humility and said, "Those words are inscribed at the base of the tower."

At that, the old bearded knight turned and departed, leaving Archie alone in the room with the sacred scrolls.

Archie got to work immediately and spent a considerable amount of time studying the drawing of the city. It was very detailed and depicted everything he had seen and much that he had not. It was really seven drawings, showing every level of the city. All of the drawings depicted the canals. The first drawing depicted the surface level, including the Palace of Elders, the beautiful parks and reservoirs, the skywalks, the manor houses, and the fields and orchards. It also depicted the uppermost level within each of the eight towers. The next four drawings depicted the four levels in the workshop, market, and dining and entertainment districts. Those drawings also depicted the next four levels within each of the eight towers. The sixth drawing depicted the underwater passageways between the manor houses and the associated towers, as well as a series of underwater chambers and passageways associated with the Palace of Elders. And the seventh drawing depicted the secret passageways between towers on opposite ends of the city.

Archie began by studying the first drawing. Studying the fields and orchards in the outer rings of the city, he noticed the fruits and grains associated with each tower. Archie recalled his first evening at Lord Pwrådisa's manor house, when Lord Pwrådisa told him that at the founding of the city, each of the eight lords undertook to harvest a different grain, a different fruit, and a different fish.

Archie began searching for the paper on which he had written the names of the eight towers and the inscriptions he knew. He found it where he had left it, inside his armor hauberk. After finding a pen, Archie studied the map and began writing down the names of the fruits associated with each tower.

Tower of Humility—Humility is the path to freedom—Pomegranate

Tower of Mourning—Mourning leads to change—Date Palm

Tower of Surrender—Surrender is gain—Citron

Tower of Morality—Morality is possible only when it is impossible—Fig

Tower of Compassion—Compassion begets compassion—Apple

Tower of Purity—Purity restores the blind—Orange

Tower of Peace—_____—Olive

Tower of Sacrifice—_____—Grapevine

When he had completed this small task, Archie sat back and looked at what he had written. It still made no sense to him. But recalling the old bearded knight's questions about the fig tree, Archie just *knew* that there had to be some significance to the assignment of these fruits to each tower. Had it not been for those questions in the fig orchard, Archie would never have connected the fig to morality. Now, if he could just figure out the other fruits before the old knight returned, he would feel like he had accomplished something without having to be spoonfed.

Archie had an idea. He began looking through the scrolls for scriptures that referred to each of these fruits. For quite some time, Archie scanned scroll after scroll, trying to find any reference to one of these fruits. He finally made a discovery as he was drowsily reviewing a scroll that discussed in considerable boring detail the priests and their rituals. The scripture prescribed the exact nature of the priests' attire; their robes were to have pomegranates embroidered at the hem.

Archie stood up, stretched, and wondered whether anything in K'truum-Shra was straightforward, for this tiny morsel of information did nothing to satisfy his curiosity. When he sat back down, he decided to limit his search to scriptures that referred to pomegranates; he would get to the other fruits later. Archie soon discovered another equally enigmatic scripture that referred to engravings of pomegranates on the columns of the temple. He did not recall seeing any temple, so he grabbed the seven drawings and began searching for the temple. After a few minutes, he found what he was looking for, but it made no sense at all. The drawing showed a temple where he knew the Palace of Elders stood. After a moment of reflection, Archie realized that he was looking at the diagram of the first underwater level. The temple, then, was located beneath the Palace of Elders!

For the rest of the afternoon, Archie continued looking for scriptures that referred to pomegranates, but he found none. Libraries had never really been Archie's favorite places, and any prolonged visit to a library generally made Archie drowsy. Because he had not slept the previous night, Archie grew weary, so he decided that he would lay his head down on the table for just a few minutes. His thoughts drifted to his time spent training to become a squire, to those happy days in Lord Pwrâdisa's service, when he lived and ate and slept in the pomegranate orchard. One by one, the pleasant memories gradually dissolved until only the fragrance of pomegranate blossoms remained in Archie's mind. Before long, he was fast asleep.

"What have you learned, *Sleeper*," the old bearded knight said, with just a little more emphasis on "Sleeper" than he normally used.

Archie awoke, and with his weary eyes looked into the face of T'lôt'aris.

"Has your study been *fruitful*, or did you just sleep on these scrolls?"

Archie sat up, hoping to clear his still slumbering brain. "I found all of the fruits that are associated with the eight towers, and then I found a few scriptures that refer to pomegranates, but I don't really understand what they mean."

"And just what do those scriptures say, Sleeper?"

"They require that pomegranates be embroidered on the hems of the priests' robes and that pomegranates be engraved on the columns of the temple."

"And what does that tell you, Sleeper?" asked the old bearded knight.

"That pomegranates are symbolic of the priesthood," Archie weakly offered.

"Very good. And what does that have to do with the First Tower, the Tower of Humility?"

"Priests are supposed to be humble?" Archie asked.

"And the rest of us are not?" the old bearded knight inquired.

"No, I suppose that we should all be humble."

"And so the priests' humility is not much of a connection to the First Tower. Once again, Sleeper, why do you think that pomegranates are associated with the Tower of Humility?"

Fully awake now, Archie thought for a moment and then ventured a guess. "Perhaps it means that the First Tower is somehow related to the priesthood."

The old bearded knight paused, gazed into Archie's eyes, and then asked, "And what does that tell you of the lord of that tower?"

Archie thought for a moment and then guessed, "That he is part of the priesthood?"

The old bearded knight smiled and asked, "What part?"

Not really certain just how he reached this conclusion, Archie blurted out, "The High Priest?"

The old knight said nothing, but Archie's mind was racing. If the Tower of Humility is associated with the priesthood and the Lord of that Tower is the High Priest, then Lord Pwrádisa is—or was—the High Priest.

"Very good, Sleeper," said the old knight. Archie thought that this must refer to his last verbal response, but deep down, he suspected that the old knight could read his thoughts.

Chapter Twenty-Two
Into the Deep

The old bearded knight motioned toward the door and spoke again, "Dusk approaches, and you are in great need of sleep. Shall we run?"

More welcome words were never spoken, for Archie was elated on two levels. He was happy to leave the library but even happier at the prospect of sleeping in a comfortable bed.

The old knight continued as the pair began running up the spiral stairway to the great wall. "You can resume your studies another time. At dawn, we will once again taste battle."

Nothing further was said as the two ran along the great wall of the city to the First Tower, the Tower of Humility, where they descended the spiral stairway to the first underwater level and then through the passage to the manor house. There they stopped.

"You will sleep here tonight. Two hours before dawn, I will return to awaken you and take you to the staging area." The old knight then paused, looked intently into Archie's eyes, and in a much softer voice, added, "You must rest, Sleeper, for the morning will bring with it great troubles. This advance will be perhaps our most difficult."

At that, the old knight turned and departed before Archie could even gather the wits to respond. It occurred to him that the old knight's words were not the most conducive to sleep, but he had been without sleep for so long that it would not likely elude him. Archie made his way to his old bedroom, thinking about Lord Pwrádisa, whose presence still echoed throughout the manor house. Once in bed, Archie soon drifted into a deep sleep, and it seemed little more than a few moments later that he was being awakened.

"It is time to arise, Sleeper."

Archie rubbed his eyes and looked into the gentle face of T'lôt'aris.

"Put on your armor quickly, for we have much to do. Here is a new tunic to replace the one you lost."

T'lôt'aris handed Archie a new white tunic that had his coat of arms—a blue shield with a single white, eight-spoked wheel. Though he knew that this was his own coat of arms, Archie nevertheless checked to ensure that it did not also bear the three green sharks that represented Thlū'taku.

When Archie was ready, T'lôt'aris led him to the Tower of Humility. But instead of ascending the spiral stairway to the great wall of the city, they remained at the lowest level of the tower, the dungeon level. They were soon joined by other knights and soldiers, and gradually, the room filled until Archie felt it could hold no more. As he stood among the others, Archie began to sweat. He was not sure whether it was because of the heat generated by the armor-clad bodies of so many men, or because he was afraid of what the day might hold. After a while, he heard a commotion. At first, Archie could not see what had caused it, but then he saw that N'derlex had arrived. The Alliance leader stepped up onto a table and began to speak.

"Men, we are about to undertake a very dangerous attack, one that required much secrecy. That is why you have not been told anything about this attack until now. There are four secret passageways in this city, each of which runs well beneath the surface of the sea between opposite towers. We control four towers, and Thlū'taku controls four. Today, we will infiltrate enemy territory en masse by using these secret passageways. You will be advancing from this tower, the Tower of Humility, to the Tower of Compassion. Sir Archie the Bold will be your commander."

At this, Archie gasped audibly, and those around him turned and looked.

N'derlex continued, "The danger of which I spoke is real. First, because the attack is proceeding from four separate towers in four different directions to four distinct targets, it will be very difficult to coordinate. Second, the secret passageways are very narrow and were not designed for large numbers of men to traverse at the same time. For this reason, it will be paramount to move as quickly as possible so that we do not suffocate. Finally, if the enemy forces have discovered our plans, or even if they have simply discovered the secret passageways, we will be walking into a massacre, because they will certainly amass their soldiers where we will exit the passageways. And if we do not all arrive at the enemy towers at the same time, it is certain that those who arrive later will meet an unpleasant welcome from Thlū´taku. But if we can pull this off, victory will be ours."

N´derlex paused to look all around the room, engaging the eyes of as many men as possible. "Good luck and Godspeed. I must now speak with your leader before proceeding to the other towers to brief the men assembled there."

N´derlex stepped down off the table, made his way to Archie, and handed him a scroll. "Do not open this scroll until you have arrived at your primary target, the Tower of Compassion. If you are able to do that, you may open the scroll and determine your secondary targets. Under no circumstances, permit this scroll to fall into enemy hands, as it also contains the sign and countersign that we will use. If you ever feel that the scroll is in danger of being captured, read it immediately if you have not already done so and then destroy it."

N´derlex added, "You may begin your advance immediately, and you must get through the secret passageway within two hours. If you arrive before two hours have elapsed, you must wait so that our advance is coordinated, and you do not endanger the other prongs of the attack."

To Archie's surprise, N´derlex embraced him, saying, "Take care of yourself. May God be with you!" At that, N´derlex turned to T´lôt´aris, motioned for him to follow, and the two walked away.

Archie wasted no time starting the advance, for he was fearful of the consequences of a late arrival. Addressing his men, he said, "Do not speak while we are in the passageway unless it is absolutely necessary. This will preserve the air, and as we approach the enemy, it will preclude disclosing our location to the enemy. Follow me."

At this, Archie pushed against the wall and opened the door to the secret passageway. Then, he began descending the narrow, angled spiral stairway. Archie immediately smelled seawater, something he had not smelled when he was making his escape from the Tower of Purity to the Tower of Mourning.

As they proceeded down the stairs, Archie became fearful. The stairs were so narrow and there were so many soldiers behind him that he felt trapped. He had never been claustrophobic, but then, he had never before descended a narrow spiral stairway beneath the sea with hundreds of soldiers behind him. To take his mind off his fear, Archie began to think about the battle ahead and what would be required to secure the Fifth Tower. He knew that all of the towers were similar and that a spiral stairway ran through the center of each tower. He also knew that in addition to the secret passageway, there were only three other entrances into each tower—two located along the great wall of the city, facing in opposite directions, and one in the dungeon level, the underwater passageway to the associated manor house. These entrances would have to be seized and secured immediately.

Archie noticed moisture on the wall of the passageway, as he was using his hands to steady himself while descending the narrow, spiral stairway. He did not know what to make of this, for he had not encountered any moisture in the secret passageway from the Tower of Purity to the Tower of Mourning. Then, as he rounded the stairs, he stopped dead in his tracks. Before him was the sea. He could not tell how deep the water was, but based on the time the group had been descending the stairs, he believed that they were near the lowest level. He could see that the water was rising and would soon make passage impossible.

Archie turned to his men. "Take off your tunics, and tie them loosely into a bag shape. When you enter the water, lie on your backs and pull the bag down as quickly as possible to capture as much air as possible, and hold the bag down over your face. Be careful not to let the air escape from your tunics; this is your only way to breathe. Don't stop or delay. If you can't do this, or if your tunic will not hold air, move out of the way and let the next man through. Only the tunics with a fine weave will hold air. Keep one column going down the stairs and another single column going back up. Pass this along."

At that, Archie lay down on the water, face up. As he submerged, he pulled his tunic quickly into the water, trapping as much air as possible, and then placed the small opening tightly over his mouth and began the awkward swim through the water. It was not nearly as simple as he had imagined, because he was not taking a leisurely backstroke across some backyard pool but rather attempting to navigate down a narrow spiral stairway while floating on his back. To make matters more difficult, Archie was soon battling his own armor, for it was lighter than the water. As a result, Archie found himself pushed against the ceiling of the narrow, spiral stairway. Even worse, it was completely dark, because the water had washed the glowing balls of k'truum out of the lamps lining the walls, and they were all now floating on the surface of the water.

Eventually, Archie made his way to the lowest level and, groping in the murky water, found the ascending spiral stairway. By now, he was getting used to swimming on his back in the dark seawater. He found the upward journey easier, for he no longer had to struggle with his armor. As he was relishing his prowess as a swimmer, catastrophe struck. He lost his grip on his tunic, which immediately deflated, shooting a mass of air bubbles up through the water toward the surface. Now, with no air to breathe, Archie wondered whether he would make it. He turned himself over and began swimming as hard as he could. But with each stroke, Archie's lungs screamed for air. He had to fight back the urge to open his mouth and take a deep breath, for he knew that all he would suck in was seawater. When he was certain that he would drown, Archie suddenly surfaced. Surprise and joy notwithstanding, it was all he could do to climb up onto the stairs and collapse.

After a few minutes, Archie lifted his head and noticed the water was still rising. So, he lifted himself up, climbed a few stairs, and then sat back down. Archie's heart filled with fear, for no one else had made it through the water yet, and he began to think that no one else would. Because the water was rising, it was unlikely that he could return, nor did he want to try this again, and that meant he might have to go into enemy territory alone. It was unlikely that Thlū'taku would be a good host this time.

Just then, a soldier surfaced, and Archie helped him out of the water. Soon another soldier exited the water, and Archie's fears were relieved. One by one, exhausted soldiers made their way out of the water, and Archie began directing them up the stairs, because the narrow spiral stairway was becoming crowded. After about fifteen minutes, no more soldiers arrived. As he walked up the spiral stairway to resume his position in front, Archie counted the soldiers who had made it through the water obstacle. Fifty-three! That was only a fraction of the men with whom he had started.

Panic seized Archie. He now knew that he would be greatly outnumbered, and because it had taken so long to make it through the water, he would also likely be late. Well, at least the force to be massacred would be smaller. Archie was determined to do what he could and to minimize any risk to the rest of the Alliance forces. He pulled out the scroll, which was thoroughly soaked, and began reading it. He knew that his orders were to read it only after arriving at the Tower of Compassion, but to destroy it if it was likely to fall into enemy hands. But the ink was running, and to get any information, he would have to read the scroll now. Archie noted the secondary targets and then the sign and countersign—

"Anchor" and "Flame"—the symbols on the shields borne by N'derlex and T'lôt'aris.

Wheeling around, Archie barked out orders for his men to ascend the narrow spiral stairway. "Run. Run like your life depends on your speed, for today it does!"

The heaving mass of men wormed its way through the narrow spiral stairway like a centipede, and it seemed to Archie that his band of soldiers was just as sluggish as that lowly creature. Archie shouted words of encouragement, hoping to get his men to their destination before they met an opposing force coming down the narrow spiral stairway.

To Archie's relief, the small band of soldiers arrived without opposition at the top of the narrow spiral stairway. Archie divided his men into four groups. Ten men each would secure the three other entrances to the tower, while Archie and the remaining men would work their way through the tower, killing, disabling, or capturing every enemy soldier they found. This, of course, depended on what they found when they opened the door that led out of the secret passageway.

Archie pushed and the door opened. Standing there before them, weapons in hand, were at least one hundred enemy soldiers.

Chapter Twenty-Three
Capturing Compassion

When the shock wore off, Archie made a snap decision and barked out to his archers, "Hold your fire, men! Hold your fire!"

Archie stepped out of the secret passageway alone and calmly strode over to the enemy commander, who smiled and then embraced Archie. It was the young captain of the guard who had helped Archie escape. Straightening up, Archie looked at the captain and said, "Anchor!"

Almost immediately, the young captain replied, "Flame!" He then turned around and issued an order to his men, "Change!"

At that, the men removed their black tunics, all of which had some variation of the three green sharks representing Thlū'taku, and revealed new white tunics, indicating loyalty to the Alliance. Archie realized that Thlū'taku had now equipped his entire army with the same black tunic he had given to Archie. The enemy now had a distinct uniform.

The young captain of the guard next divided his men into three groups, ordering them to guard the three other entrances to the Fifth Tower. At that, he turned back to Archie and spoke.

"Thlū'taku discovered the secret passageways after your escape. He reasoned that because Alliance forces already knew about the secret passageways, it would be foolhardy for him to funnel an attack through channels that most certainly were guarded at the other end. Instead, he decided to destroy the secret passageways so that the Alliance could not use them to launch an attack against his forces. He sent men to drill holes at the bottom of each secret passageway to flood it."

"But won't that sink the entire city?" Archie asked.

"No, Sir Archie. K'truum floats, and more than 90 percent of the city is above sea level. The secret passageways will continue to flood until the water reaches sea level. Only the secret passageways will be affected."

Pointing to the soldiers who had met Archie's command, the young captain continued. "I have a company of soldiers in each of the four towers under Thlū'taku's control. Each company is posted at the entrance to the secret passageway in the tower to which the company is assigned."

Pausing, the young captain studied Archie, and continued in a more somber voice. "Thlū'taku was very angry when you escaped. He began torturing anyone who had been in close contact with you. For some reason—perhaps because I had gained his trust—he was blind to the possibility that I was the one who helped you escape. Ultimately, he tortured more than three hundred soldiers, only three of whom knew anything. The three soldiers I sent to guard you on your last evening in enemy territory died protecting my secret—and yours."

Archie swallowed hard, recalling that he had suggested that the men be punished for insubordination.

The young captain continued. "Thlū'taku trusts me, and we are fortunate that he ordered me to secure the entrances to the secret passageways. He was afraid they would flood too slowly, but I that they would flood too quickly. I posted men I hand-selected for the job. During the time that I have worked in enemy territory, I have managed to bring in many Alliance soldiers, but I have also been successful in turning even more enemy soldiers. It does not take long serving Thlū'taku to realize the mistake, and very few soldiers serving him really want to continue. The only thing keeping many from turning to the Alliance is fear of Thlū'taku. The men I turned are different: they are not afraid to die."

All of this talk of torture reminded Archie of his last encounter with Mókea and the promise he had made to her.

"I have orders to secure this tower," Archie said, "and that includes liberating any prisoners loyal to the Alliance."

"The tower is already secured," said the young captain, "as are *all* of the towers. Of course, I have issued orders to my men in the other three towers not to change their tunics until they are met by Alliance forces coming through the secret passageways. As for the prisoners, all but the highest-ranking prisoners have already been released. When I sent my men to guard the three other entrances to this tower, I also issued orders for the release of all but three prisoners. Most of these men have joined our ranks, and there are now several hundred men guarding this tower. All of them are now under your command."

They were already on the dungeon level, so Archie said, "I want to see the prisoners." After issuing orders to his soldiers, Archie began walking to the dungeon, accompanied by the young captain. As they walked, he inquired, "Is Lord Mókato among the prisoners?"

With sadness in his eyes, the young captain stated simply, "No. He died just yesterday, a result of prolonged starvation and torture."

A flood of emotions—all very confusing—washed over Archie as he recalled his first meetings with Lord Mókato, his trial and the sentencing of Lord Pwrádisa to death, and finally, his promise to Mókea. Archie had been afraid that he would be unable to forgive Lord Mókato, and he had not looked forward to the day that he would be called to do so. But now that Lord Mókato was dead, Archie regretted that he would be unable to offer that forgiveness. It seemed strange to Archie, but all of his anger had dissipated. All that he felt was emptiness in his heart.

Upon arriving at the dungeon, Archie was shocked, because he recognized one of the three prisoners still in his cell: it was Kótan! He was no longer the muscular man Archie remembered but, instead, was pale and gaunt. His hair was no longer dark, nor did it bear the healthy sheen that it once had. Now his hair was long, unkempt, and mostly white. Kótan's thin face was partially obscured by an unruly, matted white beard. He was filthy, and his clothing consisted of rags that looked as if a stiff breeze would knock them off. The scarcity of clothing revealed large bruises and open wounds all over his body. But most remarkable were Kótan's eyes, which were vacant and hollow. Gone was any trace of the greed that Archie recalled seeing in the big man's eyes when he last saw him. Kótan was a broken man.

As Archie and the young captain approached, Kótan did not even look up but, instead, continued in the work that now consumed him. Sitting against the wall, he used his left hand to rub a knee that was swollen to more than twice its normal size, while he simultaneously used his right hand to pick lice from his head. After each successful extraction, he would bring his right hand back down in front of his face just long enough to see the creature. Then, with just the slightest hint of emotion in his eyes, he would place his prey into his mouth and devour it.

Archie turned to the young captain and began issuing orders. "Determine how many men are needed to guard effectively the tower entrance that opens to the underwater passage leading to the manor house. Station *exactly* that many men at that entrance, and have them fortify it any way they can. Take the remaining men to the great wall and go to the Tower of Morality. When you encounter Alliance forces, use the sign and countersign and then order those forces to return with you to join me. Along the way, secure the facilities and quarters located within the wall itself. When you return, we will then use as many men as we can to advance on the Tower of Purity."

Motioning toward Kótan and his fellow prisoners, Archie continued. "In the meantime, get these prisoners food and medical attention. If there is nothing available in this tower, get provisions from the Tower of Morality when you get there. Return in no more than one hour."

At that, Archie returned to his men, and together they took the spiral stairway in the center of the tower up to the great wall. They exited in the direction of the Tower of Purity and immediately met the new men stationed there by the young captain of the guard. In less than an hour, the young captain returned with many additional men, some from the Tower of Morality, and reported that the great wall between the two towers had been secured.

Archie then addressed the men. "It is still morning, and yet we have accomplished our primary mission—to secure this tower—and our secondary mission—to secure the great wall between this tower and the Tower of Morality, linking us to Alliance forces. Much of our success is the result of hard work by this man." Archie pointed to the young captain and was immediately embarrassed that he had never learned his name. "No matter what happens today, we have achieved our primary objectives. Now, let us commit ourselves to our final mission today: to seize the Tower of Purity. We do not know what we will find, for that tower is the primary target of another command. We do not know whether that force was able to get through the secret passageway leading from the Tower of Mourning."

Archie paused just long enough to make eye contact with several of the men. Then, he issued his orders, "Forward! For the Alliance and the city of K'truum-Shra!"

Archie expected no resistance on the great wall, but once they were within archer's range of the Tower of Purity, he knew that things could get difficult. They faced the same disadvantage they did coming out of the secret passageway: that their forces would be funneled into a heavily fortified position, and they would be easy targets for archers shooting from the tower. Of course, the secret passageway permitted no more than one or two men at a time to emerge into the tower, while the wall was wide enough to permit ten men to walk abreast. That would make some difference, but Archie still feared the odds were against him. It would be a struggle to overcome those odds.

Inspiration came like a thunderbolt. Archie called out, "Halt!" He beckoned to the young captain of the guard, and when he had come to Archie's side, Archie said, "Send some men to get their old tunics. All of the soldiers in our front ranks will wear them so that we can deceive the enemy." The young captain smiled and turned to comply with Archie's order. "Just a moment," Archie said. "What is your name?"

"Be'lak. I am Be'lak."

The detail soon returned, and Archie divided his men into four groups. The men in the front rank of each group wore enemy tunics over their armor, and the men following remained close behind. The small army resumed its march, and as they approached the Tower of Purity, Archie strained his eyes to see the flag flying over the tower. When at last he could see the flag clearly, Archie was glad that he had taken the time to retrieve the enemy tunics. The flag he saw was Thlū'taku's.

There were about fifty men stationed near the tower, and there were more within the tower, posted at strategic locations and poised to rain death down on any enemy invasion. Archie's heart raced, but he tried to remain calm. He had instructed the men to march with confidence and not to stop unless challenged. When they were within about twenty yards of the tower, the gate began to open, and Archie was relieved. They might just pull this off.

Without warning, a torrent of arrows began to fly, but it was too late for Thlū'taku's forces. The gate was open, and only the men in the tower could see that these were Alliance forces. The men guarding the gate looked bewildered and kept looking up, apparently believing that Alliance forces were attacking from above.

"Forward into the tower!" Archie commanded.

Soldiers on the Great Wall

His men ran forward, jumping over the bodies of the few who had fallen. As they reached the tower, the confused enemy forces actually helped Archie's men into the tower. In a matter of minutes, virtually all of the Alliance soldiers were inside the tower and had taken the bewildered enemy soldiers prisoner. The archers on the floors above quickly came down, dropped their weapons, and surrendered as well.

Archie then assigned a guard to each enemy prisoner. Looking bewildered, Captain Be'lak gently suggested, "Perhaps a one-to-one ratio is not the most efficient arrangement when we still have fighting to do."

With a grin on his face, Archie replied, "This is no ordinary prisoner detail." Then, as he intermingled the prisoners and their assigned guards with Alliance forces, Archie explained, "We might not have to fight if we can deceive the enemy. We are more likely to take the enemy by surprise with these prisoners in our ranks. While they might not hesitate to attack us, they will think twice before attacking their comrades."

The little army descended the spiral stairway at the center of the tower and secured each floor, one at a time. They met little resistance and caught the enemy off guard every time. Archie was amazed at the success of his little ploy, and he was relieved when they finally reached the dungeon level. As they approached the secret passageway, they encountered a force of about one hundred men awaiting the invasion force coming from the Tower of Mourning. Captain Be'lak, who had assigned them to guard the passageway, called out to them, "Anchor."

With confusion in his voice, the commander of the small detachment replied, "Flame?"

Be'lak immediately went over to the detachment and explained everything. The prisoners were all incarcerated. Then, Archie suggested to Captain Be'lak that he interview them to determine whether they could be turned to the Alliance.

Archie realized that the Alliance forces assigned to take the Tower of Purity had never made it through the secret passageway from the Tower of Mourning, and he had no idea whether the Alliance forces in the other two secret passageways had fared any better. He needed guidance from N'derlex, and he was certain that N'derlex would welcome any intelligence that Archie could offer, but he had no idea where N'derlex was. Archie sat down and wrote a message:

> Secret passageways all flooded. Got 53 men through. Met
> Captain Be'lak and joined forces. Seized and secured Fifth and
> Sixth Towers. Prisoners taken. Lord Mókato dead. Will be in
> Compassion, Captain Be'lak in Purity. Require orders.

Archie handed the note to a soldier and directed him to follow the great wall all the way back to the permanent headquarters of the Alliance in the Tower of Mourning, to inquire about the location of N´derlex along the way, and to give the message to N´derlex when he found him. When the soldier had departed, Archie turned to Captain Be´lak and instructed him to maintain control of the Tower of Purity. Archie and a small detachment of soldiers then returned to the Tower of Compassion. Once there, Archie went directly to the dungeon, where he entered Kótan's cell. "Have you been fed?" Archie inquired.

Without any emotion, and without even looking up, Kótan replied, "Yes, thank you."

"And have you received medical attention?" Archie asked.

Again without emotion or looking up, Kótan replied, "Yes, thank you."

Archie could see that Kótan did not want to talk, but he could not let it go. Digging in, he said firmly, "Tell me what happened. Tell me your story."

For the first time, Kótan looked Archie in the eye, but he said nothing. Tears began to form, and it seemed strange to Archie that a strong man with a strong will could be reduced to such as this. Finally, Kótan spoke.

"Story? There is nothing to tell, for I am a *dead* man. It does not matter to me who wins this war, for I am *lost*. And to tell you the truth, I don't miss anything that I had. It is nothing and always was. I am nothing and always was. Why should I care who wins this war or what my fate shall be? It is all *meaningless*."

"But how did you end up here?" Archie pressed.

"How?" Kótan laughed. "How? Why, I have been here from the first day I left the Alliance. I thought that I had much to offer, that I had some value. It seems that my only value to Thlū´taku was to deny my services to the Alliance."

Kótan then began laughing again, this time with a wild look in his eyes, and he started dancing a jig and singing a nonsensical song. Suddenly, he turned to Archie and spoke again. "I wronged the good and was good to the wrong. Was I wrong, or was I good? Was I wronged or was I gooded?" These crazy observations were followed by more maniacal laughter.

Archie remembered the anger that filled his heart when he first learned of Kótan's betrayal, as well as the fantasies he had entertained in that anger. But now, he found it hard to be angry with Kótan. Having killed in close combat, and having seen the effects of torture, Archie could no longer revel in fantasies of killing or torturing another man. Still, Archie did not want to let Kótan's betrayal just pass.

But Archie also thought of his own transgressions, about his betrayal of Pwrådisa's trust, about the way he dishonored Mókea and her grandfather by spending the night with her before the jousting tournament, and about how he had been tempted to accept Thlū'taku's offer to be second in command of the enemy army. Archie shuddered. The cruelest memory of all had once again invaded his mind: seeing Thlū'taku's face in his own reflection.

Afraid to entertain any more memories, Archie turned his attention back to Kótan. What he had to say did not come easy, but he felt compelled to say it anyway. "Your life is not meaningless, and you are not dead yet."

Kótan continued dancing, singing, and laughing, apparently not hearing Archie.

"It was *my* idea that you stole, and I forgive you."

This stopped Kótan dead in his tracks, and he walked back over to Archie. "You *forgive* me?" he asked slowly, relishing each word. "You forgive *me*? *You* forgive me?"

"Yes, I forgive you." Looking into Kótan's eyes, which by this time were welling up with tears, Archie added, "And I am sure that N'derlex will forgive you, too, if you ask him."

Kótan sat on the floor and began wailing uncontrollably, all while bouncing his torso up and down. "I *can* be forgiven, I *can*. I *am* worth something, I *am*." Archie knelt down and put his arms around Kótan, whose actions so absorbed Archie that he did not notice when another figure entered the cell.

"And so, Sleeper, today you have twice made the passage from humility to compassion."

Archie turned his head and saw T'lôt'aris standing before him.

"What do you mean?" Archie replied.

"Was it not once your desire to torture Kótan? Do you not still have that desire?"

"That was just anger," Archie protested. "I had every right to be mad at him, but I have now forgiven him," he added with pride.

"And just why did you have the right to be angry with him?" asked the old bearded knight. "Is it because he did something wrong, or is it because he did something wrong that *you* would not have done?"

"I don't understand," said Archie.

"Haven't you divided wrong into two types? Would you have been as angry with Kótan if he had failed at a jousting tournament because he stayed out all night with a young woman betrothed to another? Weren't you angry with Kótan because he did something wrong that you had not done? And didn't your anger subside after you did the same thing he did?"

"I didn't sell out like he did! I didn't do the same thing at all"

The disappointment on the old bearded knight's face was evident to Archie, who now realized that he wanted some affirmation that he was not a traitor. But the old knight did not relent and instead, made Archie confront his most feared memory.

"Isn't it true, Sleeper, that the reason you are so afraid of having seen Thlū'taku's face in your own reflection is that you had decided to ally yourself with Thlū'taku?"

"But I *didn't*," Archie objected, "I returned to the Alliance without accepting Thlū'taku's offer."

"Are you making yet another distinction between wrongs, Sleeper? Is there truly a difference between *doing* wrong and *thinking* wrong?"

Now it was Archie whose eyes welled up with tears, while Kótan gently placed his arm on Archie's shoulder to comfort him.

"Why are you doing this to me?" Archie demanded, "I already forgave Kótan before you came in."

The old bearded knight's eyes softened as he answered Archie. "I am trying to help you see the source of your compassion. I am trying to make you understand so that you can enlarge that compassion."

"I don't understand," cried Archie, "isn't my forgiveness enough?"

"And so you are *proud* that you have forgiven Kótan?"

Archie thought for just a moment and then answered truthfully, "Yes, I am. Of course I am. Why shouldn't I be?"

"Tell me, Sleeper, just what was the source of your anger with Kótan?"

Archie knew that any argument that Kótan had betrayed the Alliance would be rejected, and that the old bearded knight would remind him again of his own thoughts of treason. He did not want to revisit that painful memory, so he thought about what the old knight had said.

"I guess you're right," Archie offered. "I was dividing wrong into categories. I was mad at Kótan because he did something that I would *never* do."

The old knight again showed his disappointment. "Suppose that Be'lak had never come to your aid. Suppose that no one had helped you escape. Would you have accepted death rather than treason?"

Archie began to tremble, for he knew that the old knight was right. He had always known, and that was why seeing Thlū'taku's face in his own reflection was such a painful memory.

"Tell me, Sleeper, what is it that makes you want to believe that you are not capable of the same wrongs as Kótan?"

Archie looked up, for now he understood. "Pride," he offered.

"And if pride can make you so blind, why do you want to take pride in forgiving Kótan?"

Archie did not anticipate the sting of these words, and he did not want to accept the truth. Yet, that truth was already invading his mind as surely as Alliance forces had invaded this tower. Kótan was still standing with his arm on Archie's shoulder, and now the old knight put his arm on Archie's other shoulder.

"You already knew these things deep in your heart, Sleeper, for you did forgive Kótan. That is why I said, 'You have twice made the passage from humility to compassion.' The first passage was from tower to tower, the second from heart to heart. But it was necessary to make you see the source of your compassion, for you have not always had it. If you are to grow, you must understand that just as surely as anger and hatred are fruits of pride, compassion always flows from humility."

Chapter Twenty-Four
The Worst Dungeon

N'derlex entered the dungeon and summoned Archie and T'lôt'aris. He met them just outside the cell, put his hands on Archie's shoulders, and said, "I am pleased by the progress you made today, Sir Archie, and it is good that we have captured the Fifth and Sixth Towers. As you might suspect, your forces are the only ones that made it through any of the secret passageways. No one else was able to figure out how to get through the water. But your success was enough to make Thlū'taku withdraw from much of the territory that he controlled. His forces now occupy just two towers, the Seventh and Eighth, and the triangle formed by the great wall connecting those two towers and the tower canals leading from them to the Palace of Elders. But he still commands a sizable army, and his withdrawal to a smaller territory is a strategic move, for he is maximizing his defensive capability. That makes our remaining task more difficult."

N'derlex stopped, for Kótan had walked over to the three knights, and although he remained inside his cell, he was right next to them. He was down on his knees, hands clasped as though in prayer, waiting for an opportune moment to speak.

"What is it that you would like to ask?" N'derlex said.

Looking down as though embarrassed by his request, Kótan replied, "I wouldn't be asking you this, Your Grace, but Sir Archie said that you might forgive me." At this, Kótan's words trailed off, for the very word "forgive" caused him to choke up. For a few wordless moments, he merely cried as the three knights silently watched and waited for him to regain his composure. Before long, Kótan continued, "I … I … I did wrong, and I just don't know how to fix it. I don't have any hope—I didn't have any hope—until Sir Archie told me that you might forgive me."

Having said all that he could, Kótan fell to the ground and wailed. He had never actually mouthed the request, "Please forgive me," but all three knights understood that was what he was asking. N'derlex bent over, stretched his arm through the cell bars, and placed his hand on Kótan's shoulder. In a soft voice, he said, "You are forgiven."

N'derlex motioned for Archie and T'lôt'aris to follow him out of the dungeon. As they left him behind, Kótan wept, but it seemed to Archie that it was a happy sound that issued from Kótan's mouth. What a contrast there is between the wailing of a desperate man, a man with no hope, and the joyful weeping of one who has obtained the unimaginable. Archie thought back to the moment he learned that Lord Pwrãdisa had forgiven him and wondered whether he still felt that joy, and whether the humility of which the old bearded knight spoke earlier might help him hang onto that joy.

The three knights ascended the spiral stairway to the top of the tower and walked out onto the great wall. They stopped at the parapet and looked out at the ocean. The sun was setting, and there was a stiff breeze coming off the waves. Archie took a deep breath of the salty air and closed his eyes, for it had been an emotionally demanding day. And he was tired, so the brief respite was welcome.

After a while, N'derlex turned to Archie. "You mentioned in your note that Lord Mókato is dead."

"Yes, sir. That is what Captain Be'lak tells me."

"I would like you to tell Mókea of her grandfather's death. You will find her in the Tower of Mourning."

"Yes, sir," Archie replied. "But can I do it in the morning? I am exhausted."

"No, Sir Archie. I need you to do it now. I don't want Mókea to learn about her grandfather's death from a stranger."

"Yes, sir," Archie said, as he wheeled around and departed. Though tired, he was happy to be outside. After all, he had spent most of the day inside, beginning with the cramped secret passageway between the Tower of Humility and the Tower of Compassion and ending with the dark and dismal dungeon where he found Kótan. Now that he was outside in the evening air, Archie felt the need for physical exertion, even though he was exhausted from the physically demanding morning and the emotionally draining afternoon. As he had done so many times before, Archie began running along the great wall of the city. He had grown to love the feeling that running gave him.

The Tower of Mourning was a good distance from the Tower of Compassion, so even running that distance would take some time. At first, Archie's thoughts were drawn to the sea, which was shimmering with the light of the setting sun. The air was fresh and felt good in his lungs, and the breeze, though stiff, was still quite warm. Archie thought of his parents and wondered how they were, and whether they had been forced to go home without him or were still on the island resort. He had been gone so long that it seemed unlikely they would believe he was still alive. Perhaps they had even given up hope that his body would be recovered. These thoughts were too painful to entertain for long, so Archie did his best to dismiss them from his mind.

Archie's thoughts turned to Mókea, and he wondered why she was in the Tower of Mourning. He did not associate that tower with good things, for that was where he had been imprisoned before his trial. Of all the dungeons he had seen in K'truum-Shra, the dungeon in the Tower of Mourning was the worst. But these thoughts passed as he thought of Mókea, her delicate features, her long dark hair, her olive-green complexion, and her bright green eyes. He could not help himself; despite all that he had been through, he still felt attracted to her. Surely, she no longer belonged to Thlū'taku, for he had betrayed the city. Indeed, he was responsible for her grandfather's death.

Archie suddenly realized that he did not even know what to say to Mókea, for he had never been the bearer of such terrible news. Should he tell her quickly and get it over with, or should he try to prepare her for the news? *How* could he prepare her for such news? Or was she already prepared, knowing that her grandfather had been held captive by Thlū'taku? She had been Thlū'taku's prisoner, and surely she was expecting that her grandfather might not survive.

These thoughts were still on Archie's mind when he entered the Tower of Mourning. He turned to the first soldier he saw and asked, "Where is Lady Mókea?"

"In the dungeon, sir."

The soldier's reply sent a wave of fear coursing through Archie's veins. It was no ordinary fear but instead, consisted of both dread and terror— dread because he had no idea why Mókea was in the dungeon and terror because he never wanted to see that dungeon again.

After the shock wore off, Archie continued on his assigned task and slowly made his way to the dungeon. So good was his physical condition that Archie's breathing during his entire run had never been labored, but now, as he was slowly but deliberately descending the spiral stairway, he began breathing hard and sweating profusely. He tried to convince himself that it was the result of his long run, and because he was no longer outside, there was no breeze to cool him. But deep down, Archie knew it was fear that was wreaking havoc with his body.

As he entered the dungeon, he could see that it was just as he remembered it. Unlike the dungeons in the other towers, the cells in this dungeon had no bars but were walled. Even the gates were thick doors with only the tiny food slot that brought the meager fare of the condemned. As he made his way through the dark and dismal dungeon, Archie heard no one and saw no one. All of the cell doors were locked, save one, so Archie decided to check it out. Trepidation filled him as he contemplated entering the cell, but as he opened the door, he heard a familiar voice.

"Archie!"

There, sitting on the floor of the cell on a bed of straw was Mókea. She stood up, and despite the dim lighting, Archie could see that she was as gaunt and weathered as Kótan.

"What brings you here, Archie?" she asked.

Archie had decided to break the bad news quickly, but seeing Mókea in this condition, he hastily decided that he would take his time. "I just wanted to see you," he said. "I haven't seen you for several days."

As Mókea put her arms around Archie, he realized that she had no one left to comfort her if he did not, so he did not resist. For a while, the two said nothing. Then, Mókea broke the silence. "What have you been doing? No one has told me anything of you since you spared me at the Palace of Elders."

Could it be possible that Mókea knew nothing of Archie's capture, of his encounter with Thlū'taku, or of his escape? Did she even know anything about the progress of the war? Archie recalled how he had been cut off from all outside news during his imprisonment in the Tower of Mourning and wondered whether her imprisonment was the same.

Pulling back, but with his hands still on her shoulders, Archie looked into Mókea's eyes. They no longer sparkled but had a sad look. It was not the same vacant and hollow look he had seen in Kótan's eyes, but it was, nevertheless, sad. Deliberately summoning the courage to speak, Archie asked Mókea what had been on his mind. "Why are you here?" As he spoke the words, he suddenly realized that they were the very same words that the old bearded knight had spoken to him during his imprisonment.

"Because of what I did," Mókea responded.

"How long have you been imprisoned?"

"Oh, I am not a prisoner," Mókea said, somewhat surprised. "Did you think that I was?"

"Of course," said Archie. "I found you sitting in this cell, and forgive me for saying so, but you look terrible! And then, when I asked you why you were here, you said it was because of what you did."

"I *am* here because of what I did," Mókea said, "but no one made me a prisoner. I just knew that what I did was wrong, so I decided that I must pay for it."

Remembering what the old bearded knight had told him, Archie said, "Well, I forgive you. You do not have to stay in this cell."

Mókea grabbed Archie again and squeezed him. "Thank you, but I still have to pay for what I did." Studying his reaction and not seeing the approval that she sought, Mókea added, "Don't you see, I *have* to pay for what I did so I can erase it!"

Archie did not understand, but he remembered the news he had for Mókea. He took a deep breath and said, "Mókea, I am sorry, but your grandfather is dead."

Mókea said nothing. She just stared at him with a vacant expression. The silence was unbearable, so Archie continued. "I promised you that I would save him if I could, and as soon as we captured the Tower of Compassion, I looked for him. But he was already gone."

Mókea still said nothing, and she no longer seemed to be aware that Archie was in the cell. He could think of nothing else to say or do, so Archie simply turned and left. As quickly as possible, he made his way outside the tower and onto the great wall, where he stood near the parapet, thinking about what Mókea had said. By now, the sun was no longer in the sky, but the water was still shimmering in the light of an early moon. It occurred to Archie that it was brighter in the moonlit night than it had been in Mókea's cell.

"What can you see in the darkness, Sleeper?"

Archie turned and saw the old bearded knight and wondered whether he would ever see him approaching. "I am just looking at the sea," Archie replied.

"That is not the darkness of which I speak."

"Darkness is darkness," Archie retorted, not bothering to face the old knight. "And it is not really all that dark. Can't you see the moon?"

"Oh foolish one! You believe in many when there is but one, and you believe in one when there are many."

"I am tired," Archie protested, "and I don't have the energy for one of your exhausting discussions." But Archie knew that this would not stop the old knight.

"You made several types of wrongs out of just one, Sleeper, and now you refuse to see that there is more than one type of darkness. Tell me, do you see only with your eyes? And seeing with those eyes, do you always perceive?"

"I don't understand."

"Let me put it another way, Sleeper. What is it that makes it dark?"

"The absence of light!" Archie replied.

"And is there but one kind of light?"

"All right, all right! I get your point!"

"Then tell me what troubles your heart, Sleeper."

Archie finally turned and faced his teacher and looked him in the eye. Studying his gentle face, Archie softened and then opened his heart. "Mókea has not been condemned, and yet she suffers in prison."

"And so you are concerned for her welfare, Sleeper?"

"Well, she said something that upset me. She said that she chose to stay in prison to pay for what she did, to erase it. And I was thinking that what I did was just as bad. Shouldn't I pay for what I did?"

"Tell me, Sleeper, once wine has been spilled, can it be unspilled? Can a harsh word be retrieved once it has left your lips? Can a man who has been killed live again?"

Sighing, Archie asked, "So, you are saying that it is not possible for me to pay for what I have done, to erase it?"

"If by 'erase' you mean to change the consequences of your actions, then no, you cannot. That is why you must always consider those consequences before you act. But if you mean to live with a clean slate, then yes, your slate is already clean, for Lord Pwrádisa has paid the price."

"Then why can't Mókea be pardoned as well?"

With sadness in his eyes, the old knight replied, "She does not desire pardon." Then, studying Archie's face, he continued. "Mókea has not been condemned, Sleeper. Why, then, is she here?"

Out of two different mouths—his own and now the old knight's—Archie had twice heard this evening the very words spoken to him when he was imprisoned in this tower.

"Because she chose to be here to pay for what she did," Archie answered.

"And why did she make that choice?" asked the old knight.

Recalling the conversation just hours before at the Tower of Compassion, Archie replied, "Pride. It is her pride."

At that, the old knight departed, and Archie thought, of all the dungeons he had seen in K'truum-Shra, the dungeon Mókea had made for herself was the worst.

Chapter Twenty-Five
Landmarks

Archie made his way back to his bedroom in Lord Pwrådisa's manor house. As tired as he was, he could not get the day's stresses out of his mind. He lay in bed going over all that had happened. Soon, his thoughts drifted to his parents, and he began to feel an urgency that he had been too busy to feel before. He was not one of the T'lantim, and this was not really his war. And now that Lord Mókato was dead, it did not seem that there could be any good resolution to this conflict. Even if the war was won, who would rule the city?

Because these thoughts occupied his mind as he finally fell asleep, Archie's slumber was troubled, and he tossed and turned for hours. When he finally awoke some eleven hours later, he was sore all over and in a sour mood. He arose and walked to the center of the large upper deck of the manor overlooking the tower canal, where he had stood on his first morning in Lord Pwrådisa's service, just before his training as a squire had commenced. Once again, he gazed at the far distant heart of the city and at the traffic in the canal. Archie thought that it was unfair that the war had not destroyed the daily routine of the workers he observed, for they were doing many of the things he had seen on that first day. They were loading and unloading vessels and moving goods to who knows where. Archie wondered why he bore the burden of fighting *their* war. After all, he was not one of the T'lantim and was only sixteen years old!

Archie decided that he needed a return to some kind of normalcy, and he reasoned that because he had received no orders, the day was his. Besides, he had not seen Splasher for some time, and it would be good to see a true friend again, a friend whose only demands on Archie's time was for a little fun. Archie began running to the stable. So impatient was he that he literally jumped over banisters as he descended the stairway to the canal level. Before long, he was at the stable and quickly found Splasher, who seemed happy to see Archie. There was no struggle to get the saddle on Splasher, for Splasher almost jumped into it, and in no time, the two friends were speeding through the canal at Splasher's top speed, occasionally submerging and leaping through the air.

They made their way through the outermost ring canal beside the great wall and passed the gate in that wall between the Tower of Humility and the Tower of Mourning. Suddenly, it occurred to Archie that from the day he first saw the city of K'truum-Shra, he had never ventured outside. Turning back toward the gate, Archie motioned for the guards at the gate to open it. They just stared at Archie in disbelief, because no one had left the city during the entire conflict. But Archie insisted, so the guards opened the gate and Archie and Splasher were soon outside, enjoying the wide expanse of the open sea. There, Splasher was no longer constrained by canals, and he could sense that Archie wanted to play. Splasher sped along, submerged, and leaped through the air, with Archie smiling and laughing all the way.

After a while, Archie began to get hungry, but he was having so much fun that he did not want to stop, so he didn't. They continued in their revelry until Archie noticed that the sun was getting lower, and he decided that the two should return to the city. But when he looked around, scanning the horizon, he was horrified that K'truum-Shra was nowhere in sight! He pulled back on the reins to hold Splasher steady and continued to look. For several minutes, he looked back and forth, not able to believe that something as large as K'truum-Shra could be so easily lost. He strained his eyes, but to no avail.

Panic filled his heart. Archie began thinking of everything he had ever learned about finding his way if lost, but none of it had any value to him in the wide expanse of the sea. Even if he could figure out which way was north, he did not know which way to go to find K'truum-Shra. Then another terrible thought entered his mind: he had not told *anyone* that he was leaving the city because it had been an impulsive act. Now he was lost, and no one else knew it. This had to qualify as one of the most dim-witted things he had ever done. Having been lost at sea once before, he should have known better!

Archie soon became very tired, and his limbs were all sore, for the kind of play that had amused Archie and Splasher for so long was very strenuous exercise. He wanted to dismount Splasher but was afraid that if he did, they would become separated. And Splasher now seemed tired as well and was probably as hungry as Archie. Before long, the sun began to set. Archie scanned the horizon even more diligently, for he was afraid that darkness would only make it more difficult to find his way back—if it is even possible for something to be more difficult than an already impossible task.

Soon, Archie could not resist the temptation to dismount, and so he did. He reasoned that Splasher needed the rest and that because he was wearing his armor, he would float even if he fell asleep. To keep the pair together, he tied the reins to the gauntlet on his right hand. For hours, the two friends rested silently in the moonlit night. The sea was surprisingly calm, and the gentle sound of the waves had a calming effect.

Archie was becoming very drowsy when the silence was suddenly shattered.

"You are so tired, Sleeper! Why don't you return to your quarters to get some rest?"

Archie opened his eyes and saw the old bearded knight, astride his own mount. It was so unbelievable that Archie closed his eyes, rubbed them, and then opened them again. But the old knight was still there.

"Do you not believe what you see, Sleeper?"

"But you always appear out of nowhere," Archie replied. "I never hear you coming, and how could you know where I was?"

"There are many things you do not yet know, Sleeper, for you are young, and Experience is but a mere acquaintance. But she is an old and trusted friend to me." The old knight paused and then continued. "Again, why don't you return to your quarters to get some rest?"

"I don't know the way," said Archie.

"You never had any difficulty finding your way in the city," said the old knight. "Nor did you find it difficult to leave the city. Why, then, is it so hard for you to find your way back to the city?"

Without even thinking, Archie replied. "In the city I always know where I am, and if I know where I am, I can always find my way."

"Then, how is it that you know where you are in the city, but you do not know where you are now?" asked the old bearded knight.

Archie thought for a moment and then replied, "In the city there are landmarks. Here there is nothing but endless ocean."

"Then you need landmarks to guide you where you want to go?"

"Yes," said Archie.

"And where were you going when you left the city, Sleeper?"

"I wasn't going anywhere. I just wanted to have some fun with Splasher."

"And when you travel without a destination in mind, why are you surprised to find yourself lost?"

Archie thought about what the old knight was saying, and it occurred to him that there was more to his leaving the city.

"I wasn't really thinking about it, but I just wanted to leave the city and go home. I am tired of the war and dungeons and prisoners and death. I miss my parents, and I am afraid that I will never make it back."

The old knight smiled gently and then continued. "You still have not answered my question. Even if you have a destination in mind, if you do not know how to get there but nevertheless set out on your journey, why should you be surprised when you find yourself lost?"

Archie understood the old knight's point, but said nothing.

"Come, Sleeper, let me show you something."

At that, the old knight turned his mount and began to ride. Archie quickly mounted Splasher and followed. They could not have ridden more than twenty feet and there, right in front of them, was the glowing, green wall of the city. Archie could not believe that it was so close, and yet he could not see it.

They made their way along the outer wall of the city until they came to a tower. The old knight pointed to the base of the tower. Archie steered Splasher closer, and there he saw an inscription; apparently, they were inscribed on the towers both inside and outside the city. The inscription read, "Peace is the mark of true royalty."

The old knight then took off again and motioned for Archie to follow. When they reached the next tower, he again pointed to the base, and Archie read the inscription, "Sacrifice is the path to freedom." When Archie had finished reading the second inscription, the old knight guided him back past the next tower, the Tower of Humility, and back through the city gate from which Archie had exited several hours earlier.

After they had returned their mounts to Lord Pwrâdisa's stable, the old bearded knight led Archie into the pomegranate orchard where the two had first met. Without saying a word, the old knight began to build a campfire, and Archie surmised that they would be camping that night. Soon, the two were sitting by a roaring fire, warming themselves. The old knight finally spoke again. "You now know all of the inscriptions on the towers, Sleeper. Do you see anything unusual?"

"They are all unusual to me," Archie replied without really thinking.

"Let us recite them, then," said the old knight.

One by one, the old master and his pupil recited all eight inscriptions from the eight towers:

Humility is the path to freedom.

Mourning leads to change.

Surrender is gain.

Morality is possible only when it is impossible.

Compassion begets compassion.

Purity restores the blind.

Peace is the mark of true royalty.

Sacrifice is the path to freedom.

They sat in silence for a moment and then the old knight repeated his question. "Do you see anything unusual?"

"Two of them refer to the 'path to freedom,'" said Archie.

"And what does that tell you?"

"That those two towers are related in some special way?" Archie ventured.

"Perhaps, perhaps," said the old knight. "But then all eight of the towers are obviously related, Sleeper, for together they form a single, closed wall. Think again, why would the first and last towers both mention the path to freedom?"

Archie did not respond, so the old knight continued. "Think of the eight inscriptions as a single poem, Sleeper. Now, what conclusion would you reach from the first line and the last line having the same phrase?"

Archie thought for a moment and then finally just guessed. "That the entire poem is about something mentioned in the repeated phrase?"

"Very good, Sleeper. And what does that tell you about the eight towers?"

Archie's eyes widened and his heart raced. "Maybe all eight of the towers form a map to freedom!"

"And just what, Sleeper, is 'freedom'?"

"Home," said Archie. "Mom and Dad and school and everything I have lost."

"It appears, after all, that you do have landmarks to show you the way home."

No sooner had the old knight made this declaration than he turned, made a bed of straw, and went to sleep. Archie did the same.

Chapter Twenty-Six
The Legitimate Ruler

When Archie awoke the next morning, it was still very early, but the old knight had already left the campsite. Archie got up, dressed, and cleaned the campsite, leaving no trace that he and the old knight had been there. He then proceeded to the Tower of Compassion, where he planned to talk to Kótan. When he arrived, he found that Kótan was no longer in the dungeon. He looked for someone who could tell him what had happened to Kótan but found only a single soldier, half-asleep at a desk near the dungeon entrance.

"I am looking for Kótan, a prisoner held here. Where is he?" Archie inquired.

Startled out of his partial slumber, the soldier jumped up, hitting his knees on the underside of the desk. "He has been released, sir. N′derlex ordered his release."

"Where did he go?" Archie asked impatiently.

"I suppose he went back to his old workshop," the soldier said. "But I didn't ask."

Archie turned to walk away, but the soldier, now fully awake, called after him. "Just a moment, sir. N′derlex is looking for you. He wants you to attend a meeting at his new command post at the Tower of Purity."

"When?" Archie asked.

"He is expecting you at noon," the soldier replied.

Archie thanked the soldier, departed the tower, and headed directly to Kótan's workshop. He wished that he had taken the time—before departing Lord Pwrádisa's estate—to go to the stable and get Splasher.

Instead of walking or running, he could be speeding through the canals, no doubt cutting his time in half. But it was probably better that Splasher spend the day resting.

He made his way to the skywalk level. Rather than descend to canal level as he approached the institutional district and the Palace of Elders, Archie decided to turn at the last ring canal bordered by the skywalk and go around the entire institutional district. It would be longer, but certainly faster, for he would not have to descend and enter the narrower walkways in that district. There were always bottlenecks there.

As he walked along the skywalk, he looked out over the grass and trees and marveled that the war had not left its mark in many parts of the city, including this one. Here and there, he saw T'lantim going about their business, just as they did before the war. Where were all the refugees he saw after the first battle in which he had fought? Had they all assimilated so quickly? Had they recovered so quickly from their wounds, from their malnourishment, from their trauma? Or, was he only seeing those who had not been affected by the war? *If so*, Archie wondered, *then why do some people suffer so much when others remain untouched?*

When Archie finally arrived at Kótan's workshop, he could see that Kótan had wasted no time getting his business back into order. Workmen were everywhere, shaping k'truum into literally hundreds of different things. Archie thought how much the workshop looked just as it had when he first visited with Lord Pwrådisa. But as he searched for Kótan, Archie began to notice that there *was* a difference. Although Kótan had always been an armorer, his workshop was enormous, and he had also made many other things. But now *all* of the objects on which the workmen were occupied were objects of war. It occurred to Archie that it was not really possible to know the turmoil affecting an individual just by looking at him, and it must be so with the city as well. On the surface, things looked normal. But on closer examination, it was obvious that they were not.

Archie finally found Kótan, who looked genuinely happy to see him. It had not been long since Archie had seen Kótan in his cell, but he looked so much better. He was still gaunt, and his hair was still white, but Kótan's eyes were no longer vacant and hollow, nor full of greed. Instead, they suggested a far more positive emotion. Archie struggled to discern just what it was that he was seeing in Kótan's eyes and then he finally realized what it was. They were overflowing with *contentment*!

"Welcome, my friend! How are you today?"

Archie studied Kótan's eyes a little longer, wondering how a man who had endured so much, who just two days earlier was literally acting like a madman, could now be so happy.

"Is there something I can do for you, sir?" Kótan inquired. Turning to a nearby worker, he said, "Bring some hot tea and biscuits, for I am certain that my good friend could use them!"

Archie had not realized it, but he was both hungry and thirsty. Hot tea and biscuits sounded good just now, but he had never suspected that Kótan was capable of such hospitality.

"I have another idea that might help us win this war," Archie said. "And I thought that you would be able to give some substance to the idea."

Kótan's eyes did not lose the contentment they exuded, but they did fill with tears. "After all that I have done, Sir Archie, it was enough to be forgiven. But to be *trusted* again—that is more than I could have even imagined!"

Archie said nothing, for as incredible as it now seemed to him, he had not even thought about Kótan's earlier betrayal. He was so focused on his idea and knew of only one master k'truum-smith. Now, suddenly, he had doubts about trusting Kótan. But Kótan's words made it difficult to back out, so Archie proceeded cautiously. "I am really not sure that it will work at all," Archie said as he wondered how long it would take to come up with a harebrained scheme that could serve as a substitute for his real idea without hurting Kótan's feelings.

But Archie was so eager to get the project under way that his efforts to hold back were no more successful than a dam that has sprung a leak: sooner or later, the whole thing gives way to the inevitable deluge. "Do you have pen and paper?" Archie asked.

Kótan's servant returned with a tray on which there was a teapot, two cups, and several biscuits. Kótan directed Archie toward a table and then instructed his servant to get the pen and paper. The two then sat down, and Kótan poured them some tea. Archie grabbed a biscuit, took a small bite to fill his mouth so that he could think before having to talk, and then took his teacup in hand as backup.

Before long, the servant returned, and Archie began putting form to his idea. He was careful to draw just enough to permit Kótan and his workmen to make the new invention, but not enough to disclose its purpose. Soon, the drawing was complete, and Archie had already come up with a two-part plan for a quick escape. First, tell Kótan that he had a meeting to attend, something that was true. Second, give Kótan another project in order to avoid any detailed discussion about the first, more important project.

"I have got to go soon, because I have been summoned to a meeting with N'derlex," Archie said. "And I have something else I need from you," he added, without even pausing to take a breath. "Can you create eight small medallions for me to hang on this necklace that I was given? I would like it to have these words engraved on it." On the back of his drawing, Archie wrote the eight inscriptions he had seen on the eight towers.

Kótan took the paper, and as Archie had hoped, he began reading the inscriptions without turning over the paper to examine the drawing. While he was doing that, Archie stood up, said, "Thank you," and quickly walked away.

He made his way to the Tower of Purity, where he found about three hundred knights assembled and awaiting N'derlex. Before long, T'lôt'aris arrived. "N'derlex has been detained by other business," he started, "so I will give this briefing. Thlū'taku controls less than an eighth of the city, but he still has about thirty thousand soldiers. That means that any attack will face incredible resistance, because Thlū'taku has nowhere else to retreat, and he has made it clear to his soldiers that they must either be willing to risk death for him or face certain death at his hands. His borders consist of the portion of the great wall between the Tower of Peace and the Tower of Sacrifice, the two tower canals leading from those towers to the Palace of Elders, and the last ring canal bordering the skywalk between those two tower canals. We expect Thlū'taku to post his knights in the two tower canals and the ring canal. His other soldiers will be posted in each of the towers and on the walkways bordering the two tower canals and the ring canal. His knights will be supported by archers, and they will be a formidable obstacle. But that obstacle must be overcome if the legitimate ruler is to take his place."

With this last comment, there was an immediate uproar, and Archie heard many of the assembled knights grumble. Finally, one knight spoke up. "What legitimate ruler? Lord Mókato died without heirs, and there is no one left to rule the city when this war is over!"

"Hear, hear!" several other knights cheered, each just loud enough to be heard but not loud enough to be identified. Archie wondered whether their courage on the battlefield was just as lukewarm.

The vocal knight continued. "We should choose a new ruler before the next battle! If we are going to die for the city, don't we have the right to decide its fate?" Archie suddenly recognized the knight, for he was the same brassy and bellicose knight who had challenged N'derlex in the secret war room, where Archie had first met N'derlex, the secret war room just off the underwater passageway between the Tower of Mourning and the associated manor house.

Once again, the knights previously stirred by the brassy and bellicose knight came to life, murmuring their approval.

"Are you so certain that the city is without a legitimate ruler?" T'lôt'aris asked.

This caused the room to become quiet, and Archie, who had long since ceased to doubt T'lôt'aris, wondered just who the legitimate ruler could be. Archie recalled that during his trial when Lord Pwrâdisa offered to take his place, Lord Mókato expressed concern about succession when he was dead, and Lord Pwrâdisa had replied, "I have no doubt that a leader will arise, that K'truum-Shra will not be forsaken."

When no one else asked the obvious question, Archie finally did. "Who is the legitimate ruler of K'truum-Shra?"

The old bearded knight then replied, "Long ago, the lord of the Eighth Tower, the Tower of Sacrifice, was wrongfully accused and stripped of his title. But his heir is still alive."

"Who is that heir?" Archie pressed. "Who is the Lord of the Eighth Tower? Who is the rightful ruler of the city?"

"It is N'derlex."

Chapter Twenty-Seven
Archie's Leadership

The announcement was initially met with silence and stillness, but that was finally broken by the brassy and bellicose knight, who once again voiced his disapproval.

"N'derlex? It is N'derlex?" he asked with a dismay that seemed to Archie more feigned than genuine. "N'derlex can't be our ruler. He hasn't even been a good general. While we have fought and died and bear the scars of this war, he sits on his most valuable asset, pretending to be the brilliant strategist." Then, looking at Archie and gesturing toward him, the brassy and bellicose knight continued. "This mere boy has done a better job than N'derlex in that regard, for he has shown real initiative. I know, I know, when he first joined the Alliance I had my doubts, but consider what he has done. He invented the wheel, which is responsible for the success of our first major advance. When our own forces were faltering and on the verge of a rout, he showed brilliance and courage once again by submerging his mount and single-handedly driving deep behind enemy lines, attacking the enemy rear with incredible success. He literally snatched victory out of the jaws of defeat that day. And when we advanced through the secret underwater passageways, this boy led the only detachment that made it through to the objective. He alone is responsible for our victory on that happy day."

Archie would have been flattered had he been listening to the brassy and bellicose knight speak, but his mind was no longer on the sounds that issued from those vulgar lips. Archie stood in silent shock, his jaw slightly slackened, for when the knight had gestured to Archie, they had made eye contact. And for just a moment, Archie saw in the knight's countenance the face of Thlū́taku! It barely lasted a moment, so Archie just stared at the knight's face, wondering whether his own eyes had deceived him. He thought back to the day he saw that same terrible visage in his own reflection in the water, and he wondered once again what it could mean.

Archie's thoughts were interrupted by the increasing clamor, for now all eyes seemed to be on him.

"Will you, Sir Archie?" asked one of the lukewarm knights.

"Will I what?" Archie responded.

"Will you be our ruler? Will you be our king?"

Archie searched in vain for T'lôt́aris, who had apparently slipped out unnoticed. All that remained was the assemblage of knights called by N'derlex, and most of them seemed to be taking their cues from the brassy and bellicose knight. Not wanting to be a usurper, but also unable to decline such an attractive offer, Archie did not know what to say, so he just remained silent. But when that silence became unbearable, Archie finally spoke, hoping to buy some time.

"Let me think about it. After all, this is quite a surprise."

At this, the brassy and bellicose knight immediately replied, "You are quite right. Besides, the war is not won yet, and we do not know who will survive. Perhaps we are premature." He smiled at Archie and then turned and departed. A chill ran down Archie's spine, for the smile was not easily digested. Although Archie no longer saw Thlū́taku's face in the brassy and bellicose knight's countenance, the smile he had just directed at Archie was indistinguishable from the smile that had flashed across Thlū́taku's face when he had offered Archie a position as his second in command.

Taking their lead from the brassy and bellicose knight, the others began to depart. Eventually, Archie stood alone, thinking. He wondered why N'derlex was not accepted as the lawful heir and just what his ancestors had done to lose title to the Eighth Tower. And he wondered just who the brassy and bellicose knight was, why he opposed N'derlex, and why he had nominated Archie to be the new ruler. Archie also wondered why T'lôt́aris, the old bearded knight, had abandoned him. Just then, he heard that familiar and comforting voice once again.

"And so you believe that I abandoned you, Sleeper?"

Startled, Archie turned just in time to see T'lôt́aris step out of the shadows.

"You were here all the time, weren't you?" Archie demanded.

"I have never been far, Sleeper, but sometimes we fail to see clearly all that is around us."

"What should I do?" Archie asked, though deep within his heart he already knew the answer.

"What did you promise when Lord Pwrådisa agreed to defend you at your trial, Sleeper?" asked the old bearded knight.

"I promised to obey him," Archie answered.

"Very good. But do you not recall your exact words?"

Archie shook his head, for he did not know to what the old bearded knight was referring.

With a stern yet gentle look, the old bearded knight continued. "I recall a very frightened young man, a young man who knew himself and his role in this city. I recall a young man who said that he would obey Lord Pwrådisa and serve him in *any* position. I recall a young man who said that he was not fit to be a squire." Then, after a momentary pause, the old bearded knight continued. "Is a boy not fit to be a squire fit to be a king?"

The question was a stinging rebuke, but the old bearded knight was not finished.

"When I met you on the great wall just after your trial, I asked you the last thing that Lord Pwrådisa said to you. Do you recall your response, Sleeper?"

"Yes, I told you that Lord Pwrådisa told me to listen to you, that you would guide me in his place."

With a penetrating gaze, the old bearded knight then asked, "And what have I told you about the claim to the leadership of this city? Who has the legitimate claim to rule this city?"

"N'derlex," Archie meekly answered.

"And without regard to that, who do you honestly believe is better suited to rule this city, you or N'derlex?"

"N'derlex," Archie admitted. His mind was no longer clouded, and with sincere gratitude, he added, "Thank you, sir. Thank you for helping me to see the truth once again."

T'lôt'aris smiled and gently put his hand on Archie's shoulder. Archie thought just how different that smile was from the awful one he had twice seen on Thlū'taku's face and then replayed for him on the brassy and bellicose knight's face. The old bearded knight's smile was gentle and warm and loving. It was easy to read and gratefully received, and there was nothing hidden in *his* smiling eyes. But the "Thlū'taku smile," as Archie now called it in his own mind, was harsh and cold and frightening. It was hard to read and digest, and something awful lurked in the eyes that accompanied it.

While Archie was still thinking, the old bearded knight spoke again. "Come, let us go to Kótan's workshop, for I understand that you have something you want to show N'derlex."

Before Archie could respond, the old knight had turned and started running. Archie followed. The afternoon air was warm, and there was a gentle breeze that carried the fragrance of the sea to Archie's nostrils. The sky was blue and cloudless, and Archie felt at ease, though he knew that there was much to worry about. He still had no way home, the city was still at war, and now there was clearly dissension in the ranks of the Alliance. And yet, at this moment, none of that concerned him or distracted him from the simple joy he felt from the little pleasures in life. That, Archie concluded, was due to one simple fact: he *trusted* T'lôt'aris and N'derlex. Somehow, he understood that this trust would never be broken. He trusted and relied on T'lôt'aris and N'derlex in the same way that he trusted his parents, and he knew in his heart that they could and should be trusted, just as he knew this about his parents. Archie smiled, for he knew that T'lôt'aris and N'derlex *loved* him with a familial love.

Before long, the two runners arrived at Kótan's workshop and found N'derlex already there. Kótan had been very busy, for his workmen had already constructed a prototype of Archie's new device. Archie was amazed that this had been accomplished in the span of just a few short hours. Kótan and his workmen had long been masters of production. Apparently, they were now masters of speed as well. Kótan was the first to speak.

"I hope, Sir Archie, that this is what you had in mind," he said, pointing to the prototype. "You left here without telling me what this thing does, so I don't know whether I made what you had in mind. All I had was the drawing."

As he listened, Archie looked into Kótan's eyes and realized at once that his distrust was misplaced. Even though Kótan had betrayed him and the Alliance once before, Archie somehow knew that he would never again do that. And, as if confirming Archie's own thoughts, N'derlex then spoke.

"We can trust him, Sir Archie. I *know* it."

Kótan beamed, and Archie could once again see tears in his eyes.

"What is the purpose of this device, Sir Archie?" N'derlex inquired, looking at the long, cylindrical object.

"It is a submarine, sir," Archie replied. "With it, twenty men can go underwater and surface in enemy territory. We will not have to face overwhelming enemy firepower if we go deep into their territory and attack them from the rear."

"But k'truum floats," Kótan offered. "And so does anything filled with air. How can this thing submerge?"

"Easy," said Archie. "It's just a question of buoyancy. By using weights tied to the bottom of the submarine, we can descend as far as we need to avoid being seen. Here, let's open the hatch so that I can show you."

Archie stepped toward the submarine and a man-sized "tower" that sat on top. Kótan helped get the hatch open, and all three men followed Archie into the vessel. Pointing to sixteen evenly spaced holes in the bottom of the craft, Archie continued.

"Ropes will be fed through these holes, and weights will be suspended from them. When the crew is aboard and ready to descend, a signal will be given to workmen outside the craft, who will throw the ropes and their weights into the water. They will have to do this at the same time so that the submarine will not go down nose first, or worse, turn over. When the crew reaches its destination within enemy territory, the crew will simply cut the ropes and cap the holes with fitted plugs. Of course, they will not want to cut all of the ropes, just enough to permit the towers to emerge from the water."

"But how will the crew guide this submarine to its destination?" N'derlex asked.

Archie started for the hatch and motioned for the three men to follow. When they were outside the vessel once again, Archie explained, "I have already trained a few knights in the technique of submerging with their mounts. We can expand that training and select the knights who are best at the technique. One such knight will be assigned to each submarine, but in addition, a team of dolphins can be harnessed here and here." Archie said, indicating attachments at one end of the submarine, "Each submarine will be under the command of the mounted knight assigned to it, and he will not only guide the submarine to its destination but also signal the crew to cut the ropes and, once the submarine tower has emerged from the water, open the hatch."

N'derlex studied the submarine, examining various parts, and asked, "Just where do you suggest that these submarines emerge from the water, Sir Archie?"

"We should surface in the unguarded ring canals deep within enemy territory," Archie responded. "We should surface right next to the walkways beside those canals, starting from the center of each canal. Archers should be in the first wave so that they can make it to the top level and provide covering fire."

"But how do you propose to protect *them?*" N'derlex asked.

"We will have to surface at night," Archie responded. "And to be successful, we will need the element of surprise; we will have to be as quiet as possible."

As he heard himself speak, Archie thought how much more his words sounded like they were dialogue from some old war movie rather than words from his sixteen-year-old lips. He wondered at how much he had changed since his arrival.

"I will have to study this," N'derlex said. "But I think that it may work. You are right about the element of surprise, though, and we will have to keep the nature of this plan secret. In the meantime, Kótan, make fifty of these submarines."

Archie and Kótan watched as N'derlex and T'lôt'aris departed. After a moment, Kótan turned to Archie and said, "Come with me. I have something for you."

Archie followed, and the pair went to Kótan's little office in his workshop. There, he picked up eight small, octagon-shaped medallions and held them out for Archie to see. They bore the inscriptions Archie had found at the base of each of the eight towers.

After a moment, Kótan began carefully and lovingly attaching the medallions to the seashell necklace that Archie had received from Mókea. As he did, tears rolled down his cheeks. Choking back his tears, Kótan spoke as eloquently as Archie had ever heard him speak.

"I did not assign this project to any of my workmen. These I made myself, and it was the greatest pleasure I have ever had. I owe much to you, and these are just eight small tokens of my affection. But I can assure you that with each stroke of my hammer, with each cut of my blade, with each thrust of my chisel, I was thinking of you and what you have done for me. First, you forgave me. Then, incredibly, you trusted me. And finally, you shared your heart—your innermost thoughts with me—by asking me to make these very personal medallions for you. You demonstrated a vast depth of friendship for me, a man who has never had a true friend. And so, I give you these medallions with my love. For as long as I live, they will always be my greatest works, my masterpieces, for these I made for you because I love you."

Chapter Twenty-Eight
The Seventh Tower

Kótan's words moved Archie, and soon he, too, was teary-eyed. Archie grabbed Kótan and embraced him. A flood of genuine emotion washed over the young boy, for that was all he was now. A moment before he had been a knight, a military leader, and a strategist. Despite his age, Archie was a veteran who knew the sting of the blade, the frantic numbness of deeply personal combat, and the nausea that accompanies the conclusion of battle and the knowledge of its carnage. But now, confronted with the love of one he had once considered an enemy and had never considered a friend, Archie struggled to make sense of his feelings. His tears released him from the pretense of adulthood that he had almost grown accustomed to, and Kótan's undemanding embrace helped Archie remember what it meant to be a boy once again.

When the embrace had lasted as long as it could without becoming awkward, the young knight and the old tradesman pushed back from each other, each lifting a hand to brush away tears, and said their farewells. But as Archie walked away from Kótan's workshop, he recalled something that T'lôt'aris had once said to him:

> Feelings follow actions. If you *practice* love, you will soon *feel* love, and if you *practice* hate, you will soon *feel* hate, with all its consequences.

Now, for the first time, Archie finally understood these words completely, for he had just experienced what they described. He had not felt love for Kótan but had forgiven him anyway, out of obedience. And he had not believed that he could trust Kótan but trusted him out of obedience. And yet, now he did *feel* love for Kótan, and now he *knew* that he could trust him.

But Archie wanted to revel in his youth. Never banished for long, the demands of Archie's position were already on the advance, seeking an opening through which they could invade his consciousness. Archie was weary of war. Having tasted boyhood once again, he longed for his home and parents. He was determined to resist for as long as he could. He knew that defeat in *this* war was inevitable, for these grown-up demands always found a way to slip through even the best bulwarks that Archie's mind could erect. And so, he reconciled himself to loss, focusing instead on a delaying action that would permit him a few more minutes of boyhood.

Daylight was waning, and the late afternoon air was calm. The sky was still cloudless, but the warmth of the sun was giving way to an evening chill. Archie decided that it was time for a run, and so he simply started running, with no particular destination in mind. He soon found himself on the great wall of the city, near the Tower of Purity. He started running toward the Tower of Compassion, because he wanted to put as much distance as possible between himself and Thlũ'taku.

Archie soon found himself completely alone on the great wall, and his attention was drawn out to the sea. As the sky darkened, the moon in its brilliant fullness demanded notice. Not very high in the sky, the moon cast a shimmering reflection on the water, adding to the serenity that Archie now felt.

"Where are you going, Sleeper?"

Archie returned his attention to the great wall of the city and saw T'lôt'aris, standing right in front of him, causing Archie to stop suddenly. Behind the old bearded knight, not far in the distance, Archie saw the Tower of Compassion.

"I needed some time to myself," Archie replied. "So, I thought I would run from the Tower of Purity to the Tower of Humility and then return to the manor house."

"And do you think that you will make it all the way to the Tower of Humility, Sleeper?"

"Well, there's the Tower of Compassion," Archie pointed, "and that is halfway to the Tower of Humility. You know that many times we have run around the entire city more than once, so I should be able to make it." As he spoke, Archie wondered why the old bearded knight was questioning his physical fitness.

"Look again, Sleeper. Is that truly the Tower of Compassion ahead of you?"

Archie thought for just a moment and then realized his mistake. The sea was on his left, so the tower ahead was the Tower of Peace, still under Thlū́taku's control!

As he reddened with embarrassment, Archie thought just how fortunate it was that he had encountered the old bearded knight before it was too late.

But T'lôt'aris spoke again, and what he said made Archie immediately forget his embarrassment, for it filled him with an awful fear. Gesturing toward the tower, which now seemed too close for comfort, the old bearded knight said, "As long as you have come this far, Sleeper, you might as well come with me."

This single statement made all of the trust that Archie had felt just a short while earlier quickly evaporate. In its place, he found only trepidation fueled by hasty reasoning. Archie obligingly followed the old knight but kept trying to look into his face, fearful of what he might see. After all, there was no reason for the old bearded knight to go alone directly into enemy territory. That he was making this journey in darkness only made matters worse. Had the old knight defected to the enemy? Archie continued looking at T'lôt'aris, anticipating that he might see Thlū́taku's face once again, for he had just about convinced himself that there was no other explanation for the old knight's behavior.

As they drew nearer to the tower, Archie began to plan his getaway. Should he just bolt and run for it? The old knight was a pretty fast runner, and Archie knew that he could not outrun him. But there was just no other way to escape, and time was getting short, for they had almost arrived at the Tower of Peace, Thlū́taku's headquarters. Before he could put his thoughts into action, T'lôt'aris stopped and turned. Looking into Archie's eyes, he finally spoke. "And so, Sleeper, is your trust really so shallow? If you want to depart, then do so, for you alone bind yourself to me."

Archie was stunned. "You mean I can just leave. You won't stop me?"

"Why would I stop you, Sleeper? Are we not friends and allies?"

The old knight turned around and continued toward the Tower of Peace. Archie did not really understand why, but he just followed him. He could have run away, and probably could have escaped capture, but instead he just followed. The gate was open, and the guards did not seem to notice the pair as they entered the Tower of Peace. For that, Archie was relieved. The two walked in silence, descending the spiral stairway to the lowest level, and proceeded through the underwater passageway toward the manor house. Archie was now quite certain that they were headed to see Thlū́taku himself. There could be no other explanation for this strange nocturnal journey.

But when they got to the manor house, they made their way into the associated orchard, which was filled with olive trees. The old knight plucked a few olives from one tree and walked to another part of the orchard and plucked a few more olives. He then turned to Archie and held out his hands, olives from one tree in his right hand and olives from the other tree in his left hand. "What do you see, Sleeper?"

"Olives," said Archie, "many olives."

"Do you see any difference in the olives in my two hands?"

Archie carefully examined the two handfuls of olives and then pointed to the old knight's left hand and replied, "The olives in *this* hand are smaller, and they don't look as healthy."

"Very good, Sleeper. Do you know why?"

Archie thought for just a moment and then answered, "They came from two different trees?"

"And what is the difference between the two trees?"

Archie said nothing but went back to the trees from which the old knight had plucked the olives. Although he examined them very thoroughly, he did not know what he was looking for, so he eventually gave up and returned to the old knight. "I don't know. I can't see any difference," said Archie.

"Go back to each tree and look very carefully at the branches where they meet the trunk," the old knight commanded. Archie complied and soon returned with a puzzled expression on his face.

"Well," said the old bearded knight, "did you see the difference?"

"Yes," Archie replied. "On one tree, the branches look like they were cut off and then pasted back on."

"Not exactly," the old knight offered. "You see, Sleeper, it takes olive trees many, many years to produce fruit. But those same trees can live for hundreds of years. And when a man plants an olive seed, the olives produced by the newly planted tree are not very good." Holding up one handful of olives, the old knight continued. "These puny little olives grew on trees that were planted only a few years ago. But these olives," he said, holding up his other hand, "were grown on very old trees, for they have much better root systems. And so, to produce good olives, we take advantage of the established root systems in the older trees. We graft cuttings from other plants so that there are as many branches as possible. That is why the branches look like they have been 'cut and pasted,' as you put it."

Archie vaguely understood what the old knight was saying, but he wondered why it was so important. At that moment, the old bearded knight changed subjects, or so it seemed to Archie.

Pointing to the Tower of Peace, in the shadow of which the olive orchard was located, the old knight asked, "What do you know of this tower?"

"That it is called the Tower of Peace and that the inscription on the tower says 'Peace is the mark of true royalty.'"

"And just what is peace, Sleeper?"

Without thinking long, Archie responded, "The absence of war. The absence of fighting."

"Is there never peace where there is war or fighting, and is there always peace where there is not?"

"I guess not," Archie replied. "I never really thought about it."

"And is there peace in your heart, Sleeper?"

"Well, this afternoon, when we were leaving the Tower of Purity, I felt at peace." Then, holding up his seashell necklace, Archie added, "And later, when Kótan gave me these medallions, I felt peace."

"But are you at peace *now*, Sleeper?"

Archie did not answer. He knew that he was not at peace and could not be at peace as long as he had doubts about whether T'lôt'aris was a traitor.

Seeing that Archie was not going to respond, the old bearded knight asked a more pointed question. "Why do you no longer trust me?"

Stunned, Archie responded without taking the time to think. "Because you are a traitor. Because you serve Thlū'taku now!"

"Are you so certain?" asked the old knight. "Were you not nominated to be the new king?"

Archie could not understand why the old bearded knight had posed two completely unrelated questions in the same breath, so just answered the second question. "Yes, I was nominated."

"And what did you see in the face of the knight who nominated you, Sleeper?"

Archie was stunned once again. "I saw Thlū'taku. I saw his face!"

"And what does that tell you?" asked the old knight.

"That he serves Thlū'taku," Archie responded.

"And did you accept the nomination? Are you now the king, Sleeper?"

"No! Of course not."

"Why not?" the old knight pressed.

"Because you talked me out of it," Archie replied in anger.

"Then, if I now serve Thlū'taku, how is it that I oppose the work of his faithful servant who nominated you to be king? If we are on the same team, why are we at odds?"

The question caught Archie completely off guard, but it had an immediate effect on his fear, for all of his doubts quickly evaporated. But the old knight was not finished and asked yet another question. "Why did you doubt me, Sleeper? What is it that I said or did?"

When Archie did not respond, the old knight continued. "Then let me remind you. All I said was, 'As long as you have come this far, Sleeper, you might as well come with me.' Why is that reason to doubt me?"

"Because you were going into enemy territory alone in the darkness of night!"

"So were you, Sleeper, but I did not doubt you."

"But you *knew* you were going into enemy territory. I had made a mistake."

"And have you never gone into enemy territory alone, Sleeper?"

Archie suddenly recalled that he was alone on a reconnaissance mission at night when he was captured by Thlŭ'taku's men. It dawned on him that perhaps the old knight was spying for the Alliance. He now felt embarrassed that this possibility had eluded him during his "reasoning" on the great wall of the city.

The old knight just stood there silently and sternly looked into Archie's eyes. After what seemed like a painful eternity, he finally spoke again. "Fear is a terrible thing, Sleeper. It reduces our intellect, and it is the enemy of trust. And without trust, there is no peace. Just as the olive branch must be grafted onto an older, established tree to bear good fruit, so must you be grafted onto one who is far older and wiser. You will always have conflict, but to have peace in spite of conflict, you must learn to *trust*. And to trust, you must become *obedient*. You must, therefore, surrender your will and accept your circumstances, whatever they may be. When you can do that, peace will reign in your heart."

Chapter Twenty-Nine
Gaining Peace

rchie could tell that the lecture was over, because a smile soon replaced the old bearded knight's stern expression. He stepped closer to Archie and placed his hands upon Archie's shoulders, and spoke again. "We both have much to do and must be about our work. The safest way for you to return to Alliance territory is to take the secret underwater passageway from the Tower of Peace to the Tower of Surrender. You must go now, before you are discovered. I will see you to the passageway, but after that you are on your own."

T'lôt'aris turned and began walking back to the Tower of Peace. Archie followed and secretly wondered what the old knight's mission was. As they walked, it occurred to Archie that he had never seen the old knight walk anywhere, for he was always running. But tonight, in enemy territory, he walked. Occasionally, Archie would make a noise, and the old knight would stop immediately. He never grew angry with Archie, even though he never made any sound himself. And sometimes Archie lost sight of the old knight, even though he was no more than one or two feet away. He just melted into the shadows. It occurred to Archie that if he had that much difficulty keeping his eye on the old knight when he knew what he was looking for, the enemy might not be able to detect him at all. What a fantastic asset for a spy! Archie made a mental note to ask the old knight to teach him this technique.

After a while, the pair arrived at the lowest level of the Tower of Peace, where the entrance to the secret underwater passageway was located. As they approached, Archie saw a detail of about one hundred soldiers guarding the entrance and his heart sank. The old knight, however, did not seem affected by this development at all. To Archie's amazement, he simply walked right up to the door and opened it, after which he turned and ushered Archie inside.

Seeing Archie's surprise, the old knight gestured toward the door that he had now closed behind them and said, "As I told you earlier today, sometimes we fail to see clearly all that is around us. Do not worry, for those soldiers did not see us, and they will not see me as I leave you now. You will find that the lamps you see on the wall number only twelve. After that, there are no more, and the passageway is dark. To avoid detection, you must not take any of the lamps off the wall. The soldiers you saw behind this door send a patrol down every hour, and they look for any signs of disturbance. One of the things they check is whether all of the lamps are in place."

When the old knight began to turn, Archie stopped him and asked, "But what about the flooding. How can I get past the water?"

The old knight smiled and then replied, "Two of the secret underwater passageways have been repaired and the water pumped out—this one and the one between the Tower of Morality and the Tower of Sacrifice. When we advance again, some of our men will use these two tunnels to gain access to the remaining two towers under Thlū'taku's control."

Once again placing his hands on Archie's shoulders, the old knight continued. "At the same time that your men surface in the ring canals within enemy territory, others will emerge from these tunnels into the two towers, and yet other men will attack the perimeter, where they are expected. But with your men behind Thlū'taku's defenders, we anticipate that resistance will not last."

At that, the old knight turned around and exited the tunnel. Archie watched, trying to see just how he managed to get past the enemy soldiers without them seeing him, but he could not see how it was done.

When the door closed once again, Archie took a deep breath and began to descend the spiral stairway. As he did, he began counting the lamps backward. Twelve ... eleven ... ten ... nine lamps to darkness. Eight ... seven ... six ... now five lamps to go. Four ... three ... two ... then one lamp left. In no time at all, Archie was at the last lamp, and he just stopped. He did not mind the darkness outside, for he could still see by moonlight or by lamps here and there. But the darkness in the deep was different. It was going to be complete darkness, and it was damp and cold. As he stood near the last lamp, contemplating his predicament, he realized that fear had seized him. He recalled the old knight's words about fear—that fear is the enemy of trust, that without trust, there can be no peace, and that trust depends on obedience.

Archie took a deep breath, and just as he had decided to obey T'lôt'aris and continue in the secret passageway, he received additional motivation. The sound of the door opening signaled that the hourly enemy patrol was on its way. Archie took off down the stairway, moving as fast as he could without making any noise. In no time at all, he found himself in pitch-blackness, unable to see anything at all.

He continued on in darkness and in silence for quite some time, and it seemed to him that this tunnel was much longer than the one through which he and his men had attacked the Tower of Purity. Then, he had light and the company of others, but now he was alone and for all practical purposes, blind. If anything happened to him now, no one would be there to help. He could die in this tunnel, and no one would even know what happened to him.

From the beginning of the war, Archie always knew that he could be killed, but he had always imagined that if death came, it would be in the company of others, and it would be outside in the warmth of nature. He had assumed that he would die surrounded by trees and plants and other living things, or at least the vitality of the city itself. But here, death would be dark and blind, cold and damp, lonely and forsaken.

Archie began to realize that the walls were not merely damp but increasingly slimy. Soon, the stairs too were slimy, and on more than one occasion, Archie almost lost his balance. Then, when he thought that it could not get worse, he stepped down off one stair and into water, where he froze. There was no mistaking it, for even though he could not see it, he could *feel* it and he could *hear* it. For some time, the initial splash continued to be echoed by the sound of rippling wavelets hitting the walls. Fear washed over Archie now, and his instinct was to turn around and run as fast as he could back up the stairs. But as he was contemplating that, a creaking sound fueled his fear. It sounded to Archie as though the entire structure was about to collapse, and he anticipated that at any moment, the secret passageway would break free of the city and be instantly filled with cold seawater.

As he hesitated, Archie began to think about his experience with Kótan. He remembered that his experience had confirmed the old knight's declaration that feelings follow actions and that if he *practiced* love, he would soon *feel* love. Suddenly, it dawned on him that the same must be true of obedience and trust and peace, and that what the old knight had said about them worked in the same way. No more than a moment elapsed between this insight and Archie's next step, for he decided that come what may, he was going to obey the old knight. With the very next step, Archie realized that the descending stairs had ended, and that he would have to contend with no more than a foot of water on the floor of the passageway. In no time, he was climbing the angled spiral stairway leading to the Tower of Surrender.

The journey to the top of the stairway took less time than Archie had expected, and this puzzled Archie, for it was counterintuitive. It takes more effort to climb stairs than to go down, and yet in this case, it seemed easier and even shorter. Perhaps, Archie thought, the fear and anxiety he felt going down only made it *seem* longer. As he reached the top stair, he opened the door and felt a gush of warm air hit him in the face. It was good to be back.

The Alliance soldiers standing guard at the door were surprised only momentarily, but almost immediately saluted Archie. He returned the salute and made his way back to Lord Pwrâdisa's manor house, near the Tower of Humility. As he walked, it occurred to him that the secret passageway he had traversed that night ran between the Tower of Peace and the Tower of Surrender. Was it mere coincidence that T'lôt'aris had initiated that journey with a discussion about obedience and trust being necessary for peace? In essence, the old knight had been telling him that surrender leads to peace, and in this city, the Tower of Surrender literally leads to the Tower of Peace!

This epiphany immediately made Archie think about all of the other towers. After all, secret underwater passageways led from the Tower of Humility to the Tower of Compassion, from the Tower of Mourning to the Tower of Purity, and from the Tower of Morality to the Tower of Sacrifice. Did those connections also have some significance beyond the literal? Could the inscriptions shed some light on this?

Archie recalled that the inscriptions at the bases of the Towers of Surrender and Peace were, "Surrender is gain," and, "Peace is the mark of true royalty." If surrender is gain and it leads to peace, was peace the gain to which the inscription referred? And was the surrender a surrender to true royalty? That made sense to Archie, for T'lôt'aris had told him that N'derlex was the rightful heir, and he had also told him that he must surrender to someone older and wiser, although at the time, Archie had believed the old knight was referring to himself. Right then and there,

Archie made up his mind that he would pledge his obedience and loyalty to N'derlex at the earliest possible opportunity.

But what about the other secret passageways? He already knew how the Towers of Humility and Compassion were related, for the old bearded knight had told him. But how were the inscriptions, "Mourning leads to change," and, "Purity restores the blind," related? Or, "Morality is possible only when it is impossible," and, "Sacrifice is the path to freedom"? How were these inscriptions related? Try as he might, Archie could see no connection, and as he was growing weary, he simply let these thoughts fade from his mind.

He soon arrived at Lord Pwrádisa's manor house and proceeded directly to his bedroom. He hurriedly undressed and thought how good it felt to be out of his armor. Even though it was fitted and flexible, even though it was undoubtedly the finest armor in the city, it was nevertheless armor, and Archie was glad to be free of it, if only for a few hours of sleep. He sat on the bed, covered the lamp, and leaned back. In no time, he was fast asleep.

In the morning, Archie was awakened when the trapdoor in his bedroom opened, and a rather shrill voice called out, "Sir Archie! Wake up, N'derlex wants to see you."

Archie sat up, rubbed his eyes, and ascended the ladder. The soldier who had awakened him handed him a scroll. Archie, still quite groggy, said, "Thank you," and dismissed the soldier. When the soldier left, Archie broke the seal and opened the scroll.

> Our plan has been finalized. Meet me this morning in the
> Tower of Purity for details.

Archie immediately went back into his bedroom, donned his armor, and left Lord Pwrádisa's manor house. He knew that time was critical, so he went to the stable, where he saddled and mounted Splasher. The pair was soon speeding through the canals on their way to the Tower of Purity. It was still early enough that the air was crisp and cool, and the sun had barely risen above the horizon. Shadows danced on the water, where there was very little traffic.

Soon, they arrived at the Tower of Purity. Archie tied Splasher to a hitching post and then made his way into the tower. He walked into the briefing room expecting to see dozens of other knights, but there was only one other person in the room, N'derlex, who warmly greeted Archie. "Good morning, Sir Archie, please sit down." When Archie had made his way to a chair, N'derlex continued. "You have three days to select your knights and train them in the ring canals between the Tower of Surrender and the Tower of Morality, as far away as possible from Thlū'taku and his prying eyes. For security, the only people who know about the submarines are you, me, T'lôt'aris, and Kótan, and that is why you are receiving a private briefing. Train your knights first in the submerging technique that you have developed, but do not tell them why they are being trained to submerge until they are assigned to submarines. Kótan will deliver the submarines to you in the evening before we attack. You must complete your training that night in darkness, and as part of your training, you must have your knights move the empty submarines to the staging areas."

At that point, N'derlex unrolled a map for Archie to see. Pointing to the map, he continued. "Your men will commence their attack from these three staging areas." He pointed to locations on three different sides of the small wedge now controlled by Thlū'taku. Two were on the same ring canal, but on either side of that wedge, and the final location was near the Palace of Elders. When he had finished, N'derlex paused and looked into Archie's eyes with a look that could have come from Archie's own father.

"You have grown, Sir Archie, and I am proud of you. I have not lost sight of the fact that you are yet a boy but have borne the burdens of a man in this war. And I have not forgotten that you want to return to your home and family. No matter what happens in the coming battle, I have no doubt that you will make it home."

Archie was moved and felt compelled to reply. He also remembered his decision to pledge his allegiance to N'derlex, so he got down on his knees and bowed his head. "Lord N'derlex, sir," Archie began, not knowing whether he had prematurely affixed the title "lord" to the general's name. "T'lôt'aris told me that you are the lawful heir to rule this city, and I believe him and trust him, and I believe you and trust you. Let me be the first to pledge my loyalty and obedience to you as Lord and ruler of this city."

Archie looked up to see how N'derlex received his pledge of devotion, but what Archie saw shocked him. As N'derlex smiled, Archie saw another face in his countenance, one that he did not expect to see!

Chapter Thirty
The King

"Have you seen something that surprises you, Sir Archie?" N'derlex asked, still smiling. "And if so, why does it surprise you?"

Archie did not know how to respond, for what he saw in the countenance of N'derlex was the face of Lord Pwrådisa. But Lord Pwrådisa had been tortured to death; he knew that to be true because T'lôt'aris had told him. When he had collected his wits, Archie finally spoke again. "Why am I seeing Lord Pwrådisa's face?"

"Did you not know who I am?" N'derlex responded. "Did you not know that I am heir to the throne?"

Archie struggled to understand and then began questioning N'derlex. "But wasn't Lord Pwrådisa the heir, and wasn't he tortured to death? And why am I seeing his face in yours?"

"I *am* Lord Pwrådisa, and I *am* the heir. But not just the heir to a manmade title 'Elder of Elders.' I am the *king* of K'truum-Shra." As N'derlex said these words, the image Archie saw in his countenance became fixed and stable. It seemed strange to him, but he saw the faces of both N'derlex and Lord Pwrådisa simultaneously.

"But T'lôt'aris told me that you were the heir to the lordship of the Eighth Tower, the Tower of Sacrifice. If you are Lord Pwrådisa, you are the lord of the First Tower, the Tower of Humility."

"I *am* Lord of Humility, and I *am* Lord of Sacrifice. I am the beginning and the end of K'truum-Shra, and much more."

"But I thought that the eight lords were all different houses and that they elected a council of elders," Archie said.

"The eight lords to whom I referred long ago, when you first came to my manor house, were never more than stewards. And in time and the arrogance of power, they forgot that this city has a lawful king. Indeed, they misread prophecy, sometimes by mistake and sometimes quite deliberately, so that by the time of Lord Mókato's stewardship, they were quite blind. They believed that *you* had come to save this city."

Archie could scarcely believe what he was hearing, and he was puzzled. "But if you were tortured to death, how is it that you are still alive? And what should I call you, Lord Pwrádisa or N´derlex?"

"You may refer to me by my title, 'king.' It all happened to fulfill the prophecy of which I spoke. It all happened so that I could save you, Archie. And save you I did. I saved you twice."

Archie recalled the trial and how Lord Pwrádisa had offered to take his place. But he could not remember being saved more than once by Lord Pwrádisa. Apparently prompted by Archie's puzzled look, the king continued. "I saved you by dying in your place, but before that, I saved you at the jousting tournament, where you first saw me."

"But *I* was the one who saved you," Archie protested. "I gave you CPR and then I saved you from losing your title to the lordship of the Tower of Humility."

"No, Sir Archie," the king said with a gentle smile, "I first chose you. Thlū´taku did not dismount me. I *let* him dismount me so that I could save you, for I knew you would try to save me if you thought I was in trouble. I chose you and made you my servant before Thlū´taku could lay any claim to you."

Once again, Archie was stunned. Then he asked the obvious question, "How can you be two different people at the same time?"

"Why do you assume, Sir Archie, that I am two different people? Did you ever see Pwrádisa and N´derlex together, or even at the same time?"

"But Lord Pwrádisa is the lord of the First Tower, and I have learned that Lord N´derlex is the lord of the Eighth Tower. How can one person be lord of two different towers?"

The king smiled and replied, "Are you not a descendant of both your father's ancestors and your mother's ancestors? And are you not one person?"

Archie still had many questions but could not verbalize them. After a moment of silence, the king spoke again. "We both have much to do in preparing for battle, but I promise that your questions will be answered. And always remember this: when you have questions, T'lôt'aris and I are always available. Now go do your duty."

Archie turned and walked away. He was so stunned that he almost walked right past Splasher, but the mount would not let his master just pass by. Splasher chattered and splashed at Archie until he was seen. Smiling, Archie knelt down and lovingly stroked Splasher, his best friend in K'truum-Shra. Yes, he trusted and loved the king and the old bearded knight, but they were his superiors. As much as a person can love his father or mother, his boss, or his military commander, such love is never the same as that between two friends who are equal in station. And although Splasher was a mere mount, subject to Archie's authority, somehow they were also peers.

Splasher chattered again, and so Archie mounted him and rode him back to the manor house. Splasher was a simple creature and took pleasure in simple things. But he was always joyful, and Archie understood this. And when Archie was riding him, Archie, too, felt free and full of joy. Once again, Archie recalled the words of the old bearded knight, for Splasher was the picture of obedience and surrender. He was free and joyful, even though he was in captivity and forced to serve humans. But, because he had accepted that and surrendered to his master, and even loved his master, he was always at peace. Archie resolved that he would try to be the same.

When he reached the manor house, Archie sat down at a desk and pulled out paper and pen. He began writing down the attributes of the knights he would select. First, the knights must be very good with their mounts. They would have to be able not only to ride their mounts but communicate with them. Archie wrote down "good dolphinmen."

Second, the knights would have to be in excellent physical condition and able to hold their breaths for extended periods of time. He wrote "good lungs."

Third, the knights would have to be courageous, because they did not know what they would find. He wrote "fearless."

Finally, the knights would have to be flexible, able to learn new tricks and adapt to changing circumstances. He wrote "fast learners."

Next, Archie sat back and stared at his list of attributes and started comparing the list to all of the knights he knew. Based on his experience with the reconnaissance mission, he decided that he would have to start with one hundred knights to finish with fifty. He pulled out another sheet of paper and began writing down names. At first, it was relatively easy to identify candidates, but as he continued, the task became more difficult. When he had written down the names of seventy-three, he gave up, convinced that no other knight in the city fit the description.

Archie then rolled the list of knights into a scroll and called a soldier. He instructed the soldier to notify each of the knights and instruct them to meet Archie immediately in the designated training area in the ring canal between the Towers of Surrender and Morality. After Archie had issued the orders, he departed for the stable, mounted Splasher, and rode to the training area. After a while, the knights began to arrive, and Archie wasted no time beginning their instruction. The training required some individualized attention, so Archie worked with groups of five knights. The late-coming knights simply had to wait.

Archie instructed each group to ride their dolphin steeds along the ring canal from the Tower of Morality to the Tower of Surrender and back, with the expectation that with each trip, they would spend more time beneath the surface. Archie was not surprised when he saw, once again, that the knights and their dolphins learned the technique at widely divergent speeds and with vastly different results. As he had with the reconnaissance knights, Archie first observed both knight and steed and then had them change mounts until he felt that he had properly matched each knight with a steed with which he could communicate. The knights who were first to master the technique became instructors, each taking on another five knights. Those who just could not learn the technique were dismissed.

By the end of the day, Archie had sifted through the knights and selected the fifty who would become submarine commanders, though they did not yet know it. The training continued until well after midnight, and it was obvious to Archie that all of the selected knights were weary, yet they did not mumble or groan about training for extended hours. Finally, Archie instructed the fifty knights to return not the next morning but at noon the next day. To their surprise, he also ordered them to spend the time sleeping and to get up with just enough time to return to the training area by noon.

On the next day, the training continued, but now Archie had the knights tow objects while their mounts were submerged. Although the knights did not understand why they were doing this, they did not question Archie. Once again, the training continued for many hours. This time, they did not stop just after midnight but closer to dawn. Archie released the knights and ordered them to return in the late afternoon, just about an hour before sunset. He also ordered them to once again spend the time sleeping.

When the fifty knights returned as ordered, Archie had them tie their mounts and follow him to a large room in the Tower of Surrender. There, he began his briefing. "Gentlemen, you are the select few who have been chosen for a very important mission. It is dangerous and may be very costly. You will be responsible not only for your own life but also for those of twenty soldiers. For the sake of the mission, their lives are far more important than yours or mine. Each of you will covertly lead twenty soldiers, including many archers, into position behind the enemy lines. It is our job to get them safely into position and protect them so that they can do their jobs. They will not know until early tomorrow morning just what their mission is. You are fortunate, for you know tonight."

As Archie was speaking, a soldier approached. Archie was somewhat irritated that someone not involved in the mission had interrupted the secret meeting. But when the soldier got closer, Archie saw that it was Kótan. "Why are you wearing a uniform?" Archie asked.

"I have never done anything truly important in my whole life. I have never risked anything for others—not my property, not my liberty, not my life. It is long since time to do so."

Archie was dumbfounded and just stared at the old man.

"And there is something else, sir," Kótan added. "I have volunteered for *this* mission. After all, I built these vessels," he said, gesturing beyond the room to the ring canal below, "and it only makes sense that if others trust my workmanship with their lives, so should I. I did not feel that I could truly call them safe until I was willing to be the first passenger on the maiden voyage of the first submarine."

"Okay, so be it," said Archie. "Let's take a look at your workmanship."

At that, Archie and Kótan left the room and the fifty knights followed. The ring canal and its sidewalks were free of traffic, for the area was off limits to the public and even to knights and soldiers not part of the project. Archie looked around and, with a concerned look on his face, asked, "Where are the submarines?" Kótan pointed down at the water, and Archie strained to see what he was pointing at. Suddenly, he realized that all fifty submarines were right there in the canal, just below the surface. They looked somewhat different than Archie's original design, and Kótan wasted no time pointing out the changes to Archie.

"I was afraid that as designed, these submarines would glow and be easily detected, for as you know, the k'truum from which they are made glows naturally at night. I have sealed the entire outer surface with a coating that not only prevents the submarines from glowing but also suppresses sounds that might be made if they accidentally strike something. That may be useful when these submarines surface next to the ring canal sidewalks."

By now, Archie was smiling, for he was pleased. Kótan had demonstrated an initiative that Archie had never seen in him. Archie's thoughts must have revealed themselves in his expression, for Kótan straightened up some and exuded more confidence as he continued.

"I was also concerned that the air in the submarines might not last, so I created an air vent." Kótan pointed toward a slim, cylindrical object protruding from the top of the tower of the closest submarine. Archie had not even noticed the object sticking out of the water. Kótan continued, "For most of the trip, the submarines should be towed so that the vents permit fresh air to enter them. But, if it is necessary to submerge deeper, each vent has a valve that will automatically shut, keeping out the seawater."

When it was clear that Kótan was finished, Archie drew the knights together and told them about the plan and how they were responsible for guiding the submarines full of soldiers to enemy territory. He explained that teams of dolphins would pull the submarines and that while riding their mounts, the knights would guide those dolphins.

At Archie's instruction, dolphin teams had been assembled and taken to stables in the ring canal where the knights were training. Archie, Kótan, and the fifty knights now gathered those dolphins and harnessed them to the submarines. When the first team had been harnessed, Archie assigned a knight and instructed him to practice guiding the submarine. To do this, Archie commanded the knight to guide his submarine to a specific location closer to the staging area to which he would be assigned. Soon, all of the knights were guiding their submarines, with mixed results. It suddenly dawned on Archie that the task before him was daunting, and there was no guarantee of success. And now the time seemed very short, as there were only a few more hours before the submarines were due at the three staging areas.

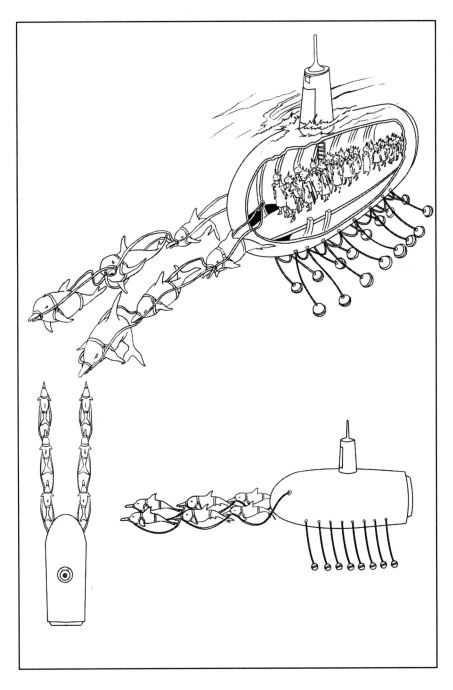

Archie's Submarine

Kótan took his leave so that he could report to his unit, and Archie spent the next several hours riding Splasher here and there to check on the progress of the fifty submarines. Some of them made it to their assigned staging areas without incident and in a short period of time. But every possible disaster seemed to confront other submarines. In one or two cases, the dolphin teams just did not respond, even though the knights and their mounts worked well together. Other submarines became entangled in the underwater structure of the city, and there seemed to be no way to free them.

But by the time the soldiers who they were to transport arrived at the staging areas, forty submarines had successfully been guided there. Archie made a snap decision to go ahead with just the forty submarines and to load twenty-five soldiers on each submarine rather than twenty. Before long, they were all under way, headed to specific locations deep within enemy territory.

Chapter Thirty-One
Victory and Loss

Archie had his hands full. While guiding the submarines to their destinations was more difficult than he had anticipated, he had no time to dwell on the fear that had momentarily gripped him when he realized how difficult his chosen task was. It was all that he could do to ride Splasher from submarine to submarine to check on their progress. And unlike their brief exercise moving the submarines from the training area to the three staging areas, the difficulties encountered by the submarines were not overwhelming. Perhaps the fact that ten submarines had been lost in moving to the staging areas was not so bad after all. Perhaps it was good that those teams were not being tested with soldiers aboard and the battle at risk.

The first teams arrived at their assigned targets about an hour early, and during the next thirty minutes, most of the other teams made it to their targets. But two submarines were struggling. One had a team of dolphins that seemed to be exhausted. The other had been snagged within the underwater structure and could no longer move. Archie rode Splasher over to the first submarine that had made it safely to its target and together with the submarine commander, unharnessed the team. He then led the team of dolphins back to the submarine with the exhausted dolphins and switched teams. That seemed to work, and the grateful submarine commander got under way immediately.

The stalled submarine was a greater problem. Not only would it not move in any lateral direction, but even when the weighted ropes were cut, the submarine would not surface. With almost no time remaining before the dawn attack, Archie was forced to leave that submarine to its commander. Before leaving, however, he ordered the commander to abort his mission and evacuate the submarine. Archie made his way back to enemy territory, and he was happy that not one of the submarines had been detected. But would they be as fortunate when they surfaced and unloaded? That would be the time when his soldiers and knights were most vulnerable not only to detection but also to attack.

Archie gave the signal to begin surfacing, and one by one, the knights under his command began carefully cutting the ropes and releasing the weights holding the submarines below the surface of the water. Kótan was right, for the coating he placed on the submarines kept them from making any noise at all as they bounced against the walkways when they surfaced. With seemingly little effort, each submarine commander opened the hatches on the submarine towers and helped his archers and soldiers exit their craft. It was still dark, and there were no enemy soldiers in sight. Archie surmised that the efforts to keep the mission a secret had been successful and that the enemy soldiers and knights were all positioned around the enemy perimeter, expecting to be attacked from without.

When fully two-thirds of the submarine crews had made it to their assigned positions without detection, Archie began to relax. The tension of the past several hours had been enormous, and he was already exhausted, even though it was not yet dawn and the battle had not yet begun. But even as he was thinking that his mission would be a complete success, he heard an enemy klaxon sound, and he knew that his men had finally been discovered. Racing to the skywalk level, where he had organized his command post, Archie realized that all was not secure yet, for he was deep within enemy territory with only forty-nine knights and fewer than a thousand soldiers. With thirty thousand men still at his disposal, Thlū'taku would have no difficulty overwhelming Archie's men. It was just a matter of time.

At first, Archie directed his archers to concentrate their fire to provide cover for the submarine crews still not in position. This was difficult, because it was still very dark, though the first light of the sun was breaking in the horizon. For quite some time, the archers held the enemy at bay. But it soon became evident that their bows could not be used exclusively to protect just a small number of archers and soldiers still trying to get to their positions. Enemy forces were beginning to surround Archie's men, and he would have to deploy his archers to protect his own perimeter.

The fierceness of the enemy attack was a surprise to Archie, and his attention was so focused on the brutal task of simple survival that time became an irrelevant concept. It seemed that in no time the sun had risen well into the sky, and everything around his puny forces was fully illuminated. What he saw struck fear in his heart. Thousands of enemy soldiers and knights were advancing on his position. Although his men enjoyed significant advantages in cover and position, the enemy numbers were simply overwhelming. It seemed that the entire enemy army was focused solely on attacking Archie's men. That was truly discouraging.

The battle intensified, and Archie's attention was demanded everywhere simultaneously. He barked commands faster than his mind could think, it seemed, and no sooner had he addressed one crisis than another arose. Then his lines began to weaken, and the enemy drove hard against one particularly vulnerable point. Enemy soldiers began to flood into his perimeter, and Archie immediately ordered his men to pull back to a single block of the skywalk level. He would no longer be in a position to support the Alliance soldiers, and this disheartened him. But he had no choice, for the sheer numbers of enemy soldiers made it impossible to retain control of the vast portion of the skywalk level that was necessary to accomplish that mission. His mission now was one of survival. That and making the defeat of his own forces as costly as possible for the enemy.

When Archie's men had successfully fallen back and secured a new perimeter, he ordered a count of his men. When it came back, he was again disheartened, for he now had just 472 men—including 32 knights, 371 archers, and 69 swordsmen. The archers would be useful only as long as they could maintain their perimeter, but if it came down to hand-to-hand combat, only the knights and swordsmen would be of any real value. Scarcely one hundred soldiers to defend against thirty thousand! Of those, at least twenty were wounded, two seriously.

They were completely surrounded now, and the enemy attacked from every direction, a luxury afforded them by their superior numbers. And though Archie observed that as many as nine or ten enemy soldiers fell for every one of his, this was little comfort, because they could afford the loss. Then, Archie was confronted with more bad news: his archers were running out of arrows. Archie immediately ordered his handful of swordsmen to gather the few enemy arrows that had landed intact within their perimeter and distribute them to the archers. At any minute, the enemy would discover this new weakness and renew their attack with greater vigor. This battle was likely to end in a massacre.

Suddenly, Archie heard the sound of enemy bugles all around them, and his heart sank. This had to be the beginning of the end. But then he noticed that enemy soldiers seemed to be retreating rather than advancing! He ran back and forth to as many positions along the perimeter as he could, and this confirmed that all around them, the enemy had turned and retreated. Archie finally realized that Alliance forces must now be attacking the enemy perimeter in force and that the enemy had drawn soldiers away from its own perimeter to attack Archie and his men.

Without pausing to think, Archie ordered his men to resume their original positions so that they could support the Alliance advance. As they began running back to those positions, right on the backs of the enemy soldiers, Archie ordered his archers to expend their last arrows to kill as many enemy soldiers as possible. When they had resumed their original positions, they had almost exhausted their supply of arrows. But Archie could see the Alliance forces and that the enemy had left only a skeletal force to protect its own perimeter. At Archie's command, his archers let fly a rain of arrows to support the Alliance advance. It did not last long, and they soon had no arrows left, but the effort paid off. Enemy soldiers everywhere were throwing down their arms and running for cover.

Within minutes, the entire enemy perimeter collapsed, and thousands of enemy soldiers and knights began to surrender. Archie sat down and took a deep breath. Disaster had been averted, but just barely.

"Congratulations, Sleeper. It seems that you have once again performed a valuable service."

Archie looked up and saw the old bearded knight standing before him.

"Victory is ours," the old knight continued. "Thlū'taku no longer has an army, and it is only a matter of time until he is arrested."

"Why did it take so long for the Alliance to attack the enemy line?" Archie asked.

"It made no sense," the old knight responded, "but Thlū'taku continued to pull men off of his line to attack your forces. It was, therefore, to our advantage to permit him to think that there would be no attack on the perimeter, and Alliance forces remained concealed until that perimeter was sufficiently weakened by Thlū'taku's own folly. Your one thousand saved several thousand."

Exhausted and emotionally drained, Archie wept. Only about one-third of his fifty knights and one thousand men had survived, and those who did not would forever be etched into his memory. He turned to T'lôt'aris and asked, "What now?"

"See to the welfare of your men, Sleeper, and then get some rest. Do not blame yourself for your losses. Your soldiers were all volunteers, and the knights you selected to lead them did not fear death. You may give your men leave to rest and visit their loved ones, for the task of processing prisoners, caring for the wounded, and preparing the dead and launching their funerary barges will be assigned to those who did not bear as great a burden in this final battle."

T'lôt'aris turned and departed. Archie sat for a few moments, contemplating all that had happened. The war was finally over, and now he could devote his energy to finding a way home. But first, he had some unfinished business. He gathered his knights and told them to dismiss their men and then made his way toward the location of the ensnared submarine. He walked, for upon arriving in enemy territory, he had deliberately chosen to leave Splasher untethered, hoping that he would return to the stable at the manor house. He had done this to prevent Splasher from falling into enemy hands.

When Archie arrived at the scene of the ensnared submarine, he found the knight assigned to command the submarine and seventeen men with him. One end of the submarine protruded from the canal, for the other end was still snagged below the surface. On the walkway were eight corpses. One of them was Kótan.

Archie immediately choked up, but decorum precluded him from crying, and he held back the tears as best he could. Turning to the knight who commanded the submarine, Archie asked, "What happened?"

"We could not move the submarine, sir. It was entangled in the superstructure just beneath the surface. The only way to get the soldiers out was to cut the weighted ropes, and that is just what I did. But you already know that. After you left, I attempted to get the submarine untangled, but I was only able to free one end. When that end went up, the tower submerged, cutting off the air supply. I then had limited time to free the submarine, but I could not enlist any help without compromising the secrecy of the mission. When I knew that the air had to be running out, I swam down and opened the hatch. Seventeen soldiers were able to get out safely before the submarine filled with water."

Then, pointing at Kótan, he continued. "Several survivors have told me that this man helped them out of the vessel. Many of the men were unconscious or close to unconscious when the hatch was opened, some from lack of oxygen and others from injuries sustained when the submarine violently tilted. One by one, this man picked them up, took them to the hatch, and sent them floating to the surface, where I pulled them out of the water. He continued this even after the submarine filled with water, and so he drowned with seven other men. But, if he had not taken the actions that he did, the number of dead would certainly be greater."

Chapter Thirty-Two
Things Remembered

Archie knelt by Kótan's body and grieved. He took Kótan's swollen, damp hand into his own and whispered, "You were a better friend than I ever realized, and I am glad that I knew you. Rest in peace, friend." He then turned to the knight in command of the ill-fated submarine and said, "Be sure that his funerary barge is launched with full honors and then prepare a report stating what you have told me. I want him honored for his actions today."

Archie left the sad scene and made his way back to his room in the manor house. He was exhausted—physically, mentally, and spiritually—and he knew that he needed rest. Word of the victory had already spread throughout the city, and everywhere he saw and heard the sights and sounds of celebration. But Archie did not feel like celebrating. He didn't really know what he felt, for his mind had not yet processed all that had happened in just a few short hours.

A solid meal and a warm bed would begin to address his physical needs, and perhaps some reflection and study in the morning would help him to mentally process all that had happened. But it seemed that there was little he could do to address the hole in his heart, for Kótan's death had affected him in ways he could not have anticipated. Kótan was nothing like a parent, but his death reminded Archie that he missed his parents and home. And perhaps that was the point. Victory belonged to the T'lantim, for this was their city and their home. They had reason to celebrate, because they had won back their home. Archie was still no closer to his.

Archie ate alone, for he did not desire company. As he ate, he watched the fireworks in the distance, over the Palace of Elders. At least, he thought, victory would free him to concentrate on finding his way back home. He recalled that the king had told him he had not forgotten that Archie wanted to return to his home and family and that he had no doubt that Archie would make it back home. He also recalled that on the day T'lôt'aris brought Archie back in from the open sea, he had suggested that the inscriptions on the eight towers could be a map back to his home.

As he made his way to his bedroom and prepared to go to sleep, Archie looked down at the seashell necklace with the medallions that Kótan had made for him. He read them over and over until he finally fell asleep.

No one disturbed him, and when Archie did awaken, he could tell that he had been asleep for a very long time. He was no longer tired, but he was sore all over. As he sat up, he decided that he would not don his armor, for the war was over. But when he grabbed for his tunic, he immediately noticed that while he slept, his combat tunic had been removed, presumably for cleaning, and that in its place was another tunic, one with sleeves. He put it on and left his bedroom and made his way to the library in the Tower of Surrender.

Archie chuckled as he entered the library, for he realized that it was the first time he had done so without being told to. He sat down and began organizing the scrolls all around him, for he was determined to unlock the mystery and find his way home. He also pulled out a piece of paper and a pen and began writing down anything that seemed relevant to one or more of the eight towers. After a very little while, he had filled several pages. But when he reviewed what he had written, he was discouraged, because it still made no sense to him.

Archie stood, stretched, and looked around the room. "I wish the old knight were here," he said.

"But I am, Sleeper, I am."

Archie wheeled around and smiled, for he knew now that his work would somehow be easier. "I am so glad to see you," he blurted out. "Can you help me find my way home?"

"The way home has been before your eyes for a very long time, Sleeper."

"Where?" Archie asked.

"What is that design on your tunic?"

Archie looked down at the shield depicted on his tunic and replied, "It is a wheel. You know that. You designed it after I invented the wheel and used it to create the battle tanks. Don't you remember?"

"I did design your shield, Sleeper. But that is not a wheel. It is K'truum-Shra!"

Archie looked at the design again and realized that it had eight spokes and that it did resemble a map of the city. But he could not see anything remarkable in the design.

Seeing Archie's confusion, the old knight spoke again. "What does your wheel do?"

"It rolls," said Archie.

"And when it rolls, Sleeper, what part of it touches the ground?"

"Well, the outside, but only one point at a time."

"And if you take away any part of the outer wheel, Sleeper, will the wheel still roll?"

"No," Archie replied.

"And if you remove the spokes, will the wheel still function?"

"No, of course not."

"Then, what does that tell you about the things that you have learned from each of the towers?"

Archie suddenly recalled his thoughts upon emerging from the Tower of Surrender. "That they are all related and that they depend on each other?"

"Very good, Sleeper. Now tell me how."

"Well," Archie said slowly as he thought about the question. Rubbing his chin, he continued, "The underwater passageway leading from the Tower of Surrender to the Tower of Peace reminds me about what you taught me about obedience—that surrender is necessary to achieve peace, at least within my own mind."

"Go on."

"And you already told me how humility and compassion are related, so it occurred to me that the other underwater passageways might be the same—that there might be a connection between mourning and purity and also between morality and sacrifice. But I could not figure those out."

"Are those the only connections you see, Sleeper?"

Archie looked at the shield on his tunic again. After a moment, his eyes lit up, and he responded, "No. The circle also connects each tower to two others."

"And what are the first two towers?"

"The Tower of Humility and the Tower of Mourning."

"Then, does humility lead to mourning, Sleeper? And if so, how?"

"I don't know."

"Were you humble when you first came to the Tower of Humility, when you entered Lord Pwrádisa's service?"

"Well, Lord Mókato said that I was. He said that I showed humility by not accepting knighthood when I learned that Lord Pwrádisa would be stripped of his title if I did."

The old knight silently examined Archie's face, shook his head, and then asked, "What is humility, Sleeper?"

"It means you don't think much of yourself."

The old knight winced and then said, "Come with me, Sleeper."

Archie followed the old knight outside the library, down the spiral stairway, through the passageway to the manor house, and finally into the barley field under the authority of the Tower of Surrender. There, the old knight instructed Archie to lie down as close as possible to the grain. Archie complied, and the old knight instructed him to look at a single grain of barley. After no less than half an hour of lying there in silence, he was finally permitted to rise, and the old knight then commanded him to once again follow.

This time, they made their way to the top of the Tower of Surrender, where the old knight instructed Archie to look out at the barley field and find his single grain. Archie laughed, and the old knight then questioned him.

"Can you not find that single grain?"

"Of course not," Archie chuckled.

"You had a full half hour to study that one grain, and yet you cannot now recognize it? Then, what do you see before you?"

"I see a whole field of barley, not just one grain."

"And so, Sleeper, the single grain, considered alone, seems more important than it really is. But its true importance lies in it being part of something much larger, being part of a community of grain. Are you then truly thinking less of yourself when you consider your relationship to others, or are you just seeing yourself as you really are?"

"I understand," said Archie.

"Do you, now?" asked the old bearded knight. "Did you see yourself more accurately after declining knighthood or after your imprisonment in the dungeon in the Tower of Mourning?"

"After my imprisonment," Archie replied meekly, not wanting to dredge up painful memories.

"Put another way, Sleeper, do you recall how you responded when I asked you why you were there in the dungeon?"

"Yes, sir."

"At first you denied that you had done anything wrong at all, and you were angry with everyone around you. But finally, you realized what you had done, wished that you had not done it, and admitted that you did not even know whether you could keep from doing it again. In short, you mourned your wrong."

"Okay. I know that."

"Then, if humility leads to mourning, as the towers do, what kind of humility are we talking about?"

"Knowing that I was wrong?" Archie ventured. "And that I would probably do it again," he quickly added.

"Very good, Sleeper. Now, how does that kind of humility lead to compassion, just as the secret underwater passageway from the Tower of Humility leads to the Tower of Compassion?"

Archie leaned against the palisade and thought for a moment. After a while, inspiration struck, and he replied, "When I see my true self, I don't look down on others, and that makes me have compassion."

"You are not far from home now, Sleeper," the old knight said. "You are very close to the truth. Let us take another step. How does mourning lead to purity?"

"Well, if humility makes me see my true self, I regret all the bad things I have done, and that restores my vision?" Archie offered.

"And what do you see with that vision, Sleeper?"

Archie suddenly realized that every time he saw a vision of Thlū́ taku's face or Lord Pwrádisa's face, it was in the Tower of Purity.

"I see myself and others as we really are!" Archie declared triumphantly.

The old bearded knight smiled and put his hands on Archie's shoulders. "You are growing wiser, Sleeper, for I see that you now think of the things that have happened at each tower."

Archie was, indeed, thinking about what he had seen and done at each of the eight towers. He looked down at the first medallion that Kótan had given him: "Humility is the path to freedom." Archie recalled that he began his training as a squire at the Tower of Humility, and early in that training, he devoured a meal naked while his clothes were drying over a fire. At the time, he had thought just how easy it was to shed the largely useless decorations of "civilized" life. Now he realized that humility was much like that cold nakedness, for many of the perceptions we have about ourselves do nothing more than hide what is just below the surface. He also recalled that his first armor was ill-fitting and musky smelling, and that the wonderful custom-made flexible armor that he had used throughout the war was a special gift from Lord Pwrádisa.

Archie then looked at the second medallion: "Mourning leads to change." Archie thought about the dark dungeon cell in the Tower of Mourning he had occupied for what seemed an eternity, and how he had come to regret not only his decision to stay out all night with Mókea but many things in his life, especially in his relationship with his own parents. And he remembered that when he acknowledged all of this, the old bearded knight had told him the wonderful news that Lord Pwrádisa would defend him at his trial. Archie also recalled that he had first met N'derlex in the secret briefing room in the underwater passageway between the Tower of Mourning and the manor house. Mourning had, in fact, led to change in Archie's own life.

Archie next looked at the third medallion Kótan had given him: "Surrender is gain." At the Tower of Surrender, Archie recalled, T'lôt'aris reminded him of his commitment to serve Lord Pwrádisa and gave him the sacred scrolls to study and commit to memory. There, he was knighted by T'lôt'aris; that was a gain of sorts. And there he emerged from his difficult journey through the darkness of the secret underwater passageway from the Tower of Peace, only to realize for the first time just what the old knight had meant by obedience and trust being necessary for peace. It was there that he first began to feel some measure of peace. Archie had surrendered to the king—not all at once, but very gradually—and the more he had surrendered, the more he had gained.

Next, Archie studied the fourth medallion: "Morality is possible only when it is impossible." At the Tower of Morality, Archie had learned about the fig tree and how its new shoots are more fruitful. He had been reminded that he could never be moral on his own and that he had to continue seeking morality by studying the sacred scrolls over and over again, and by listening to what the old bearded knight was always telling him.

Then Archie examined the fifth medallion Kótan had given him: "Compassion begets compassion." At the Tower of Compassion, Archie had obediently forgiven Kótan, in spite of his anger about Kótan's betrayal in selling Archie's wheel design to the enemy. But the effect of this forgiveness was astonishing, for Kótan changed, unexpectedly became a good friend, and even sacrificed himself to save several other soldiers from drowning. Compassion did, indeed, sire more compassion.

Archie next looked at the sixth medallion: "Purity restores the blind." At the Tower of Purity, Archie had seen in his own reflection the image of Thlŭ́taku. Later, he saw the same abhorrent face in the countenance of the brassy and bellicose knight. And most important, he had seen Lord Pwrắdisa's face in the countenance of N´derlex. It was there that he had learned—that he had "seen"—that Lord Pwrắdisa lived and was the king. Purity had restored Archie's vision, for he saw things he never dreamed possible.

Archie then looked at the seventh medallion Kótan had given him: "Peace is the mark of true royalty." At the Tower of Peace, Archie had learned about how olives grow better when grafted onto an older tree with more established roots, and he had learned that to have peace he would have to be obedient to the king, trusting him wholeheartedly. And he had known a greater measure of peace once that lesson had finally penetrated his heart.

At last, Archie looked at the eighth and final medallion that Kótan had given him: "Sacrifice is the path to freedom." But Archie had not yet been to the Tower of Sacrifice, at least no more than briefly during his daily runs, and he did not know what the inscription meant. At most, he could only guess that by seeking morality, he would ultimately have to sacrifice, and this frightened him.

When Archie looked up from his silent reflection, T´lôt́aris was gone.

Chapter Thirty-Three
Celebration and Frustration

Archie left the library and went to the stable at Lord Pwrådisa's manor house. He intended to saddle Splasher and ride, not for fun, but to seek the king himself. Surely now that the war was over, the king would be able to help him find his way home. After all, the king had said as much in the Tower of Purity just before the final battle.

Archie rode Splasher through each of the canals, methodically making his way all the way from end to end. He started with the tower canal leading from the Tower of Humility to the Tower of Compassion and then took the ring canal bordering the great wall of the city to the Tower of Purity, where he took the tower canal to the Tower of Mourning. Following this pattern, he systematically covered every tower canal in just a few hours. But he did not just ride. Along the way, he periodically stopped to question T'lantim about the whereabouts of Lord Pwrådisa. His questions were usually met by a surprised expression followed by a shrug. Occasionally, one of the T'lantim would respectfully remind Archie that Lord Pwrådisa had perished at the hands of Lord Mókato, to which Archie would cheerfully reply, "But he is alive. I have seen him." Archie was by now very well known and revered as a hero. The entire city was still celebrating the victory over Thlū'taku, so the T'lantim did not argue the point. Instead, they would politely excuse themselves after convincing Archie that they did not know where Lord Pwrådisa was.

Sir Archie the Bold

Archie continued his search over the next several hours, first completing his transit of all the tower canals and then covering every one of the ring canals. When he had finished, he started all over again. At one point, he came across Mókea, who was with a group of several other young girls. They wore flowers in their hair, bright and colorful new clothing, and they were all giggling when Archie first approached. Mókea embraced Archie, but he sensed that her actions were meant less to convey affection for him than to show off to her friends that she was close to the hero of the hour. The other girls giggled and whispered to themselves but avoided even eye contact with Archie. It seemed to Archie that these girls in Mókea's entourage had little substance.

After exchanging a few pleasantries, Archie impatiently interrogated Mókea about Lord Pwrådisa's whereabouts. This caught Mókea completely off guard and embarrassed her in front of her friends, for she had just used Archie as a prop to gain their esteem. Mókea stepped back, looked Archie in the eyes, and asked sarcastically, "Poor dear. Did you receive a head wound in the final battle? You must have, for it has affected your memory."

Archie protested, "No. No. Not at all. I saw Lord Pwrådisa just before the battle. He is alive, and he is the king!" Mókea stared in disbelief. Embarrassed even more now, she just backed away, and the group of girls turned and left without so much as a polite farewell. As he was steering Splasher back into the center of the canal, Archie glimpsed Mókea staring back at him once again. He was unable to read what he saw in her eyes, but he did not like it.

Before long, Archie encountered a group of young knights, some of whom had fought with him in the final battle. They, too, appeared happy to see Archie until he mentioned Lord Pwrådisa. They were not rude, as Mókea and the young girls had been, nor were they as superficial. One of the young knights even accepted what Archie was telling him, even though it was startling news. Rather than argue with Archie, he simply queried him about the details—where and when Archie had seen Lord Pwrådisa, how he knew it really was Lord Pwrådisa that he saw, how Lord Pwrådisa had survived when dozens of witnesses had seen him tortured to death, and how it was that he was the king when the city did not have a king.

Archie could not answer all of their questions, because the king had not answered all of his. But he told them what he knew, and after it was clear that he could tell them no more, they simply stated that they did not know where Archie could find Lord Pwrådisa. As Archie left them, some of the knights seemed puzzled, some saddened, and some barely affected by the encounter, because they had already resumed their revelry.

Suddenly, it dawned on Archie that he might find the answers he sought in the orchard associated with the Tower of Sacrifice, for that was the only tower to which he had never been, except, of course, when running around the great wall of the city. But on those occasions, Archie had only passed through the gates of the tower and through the spiral stairway and then back to the top of the wall.

Archie soon found the vineyard that stood in the shadow of the Eighth Tower and tied Splasher to a hitching post near the entrance. As he was doing this, he thought that the inscription at the base of the tower was of little value, for all it said was, "Sacrifice is the path to freedom." That meant nothing to Archie, so he thought about the secret underwater passageway leading from the Tower of Morality to the Tower of Sacrifice. How does morality lead to sacrifice? He knew that the inscription at the base of the Fourth Tower—"Morality is possible only when it is impossible—referred to the necessity of seeking morality from outside oneself and conforming his conduct to what the sacred scrolls told him. Perhaps, then, he would find the answer in one of the sacred scrolls.

But first, Archie thought, he ought to look at the vineyard and see whether it had any answers for him. Perhaps, too, the old bearded knight would show up to guide his thinking. Archie walked into the vineyard and stopped here and there to look at the grapes and the vines. He saw nothing special about them, and he realized that what he learned from the fig trees and olive trees he learned because of things the old bearded knight told him. Archie was now impatient, for this was the first time that the old knight had waited so long to show up. Where was he?

As he walked, Archie came upon a circular structure that he recognized as an old winepress in which laborers would trample grapes. He laughed at himself, for he realized that the source of his education was television. Then, he began to wonder what the old knight would ask him about the winepress. He recalled a line from the "Battle Hymn of the Republic": "He is trampling out the vintage where the grapes of wrath are stored." Archie had never really understood that line, and it did not offer any insight now. Still, for some reason, it made him very uneasy.

He had started out looking for the king. Now, he couldn't even find the old bearded knight. Where were they? As he walked back toward the hitching post where he had left Splasher, Archie noticed that although the vines had plenty of grapes on them, there were branches that appeared to be dead. He snapped off one of the barren branches and looked it over, confirming in his mind that the branch was, indeed, dead. Did this mean anything? Why wasn't T'lôt'aris coming to his aid right now?

Archie mounted Splasher and rode back to the Tower of Surrender, where he tied Splasher. He went back to the library and began reviewing the sacred scrolls diligently, looking for any references to the Tower of Sacrifice or grapes or vines, but he found nothing. Soon, he noticed that it was getting dark, and even though he was not particularly hungry, he knew that Splasher probably was. He left the library and went to find Splasher. But when he got to the hitching post, Splasher was not there. This was the proverbial last straw that made Archie lose heart, and as he began walking back toward Lord Pwrâdisa's manor house, he began to pity himself. There were fireworks over the Palace of Elders once again, and that only made Archie angry, because he did not feel that *he* had anything to celebrate.

When he had made it back to Lord Pwrâdisa's manor house, he went to the stable to find out whether Splasher had returned on his own. The stable master told Archie that he had not seen Splasher and looked at Archie with contempt. This puzzled Archie, for he could not recall doing anything to the man. This soon left his mind, however, for he wanted desperately to find either Lord Pwrâdisa or T'lôt'aris. As he searched the entire manor house, he encountered a few servants, all of whom had always been kind to Archie. But tonight, their conduct was strange. Some appeared to share the stable master's contempt, some seemed to fear Archie, and some just avoided contact altogether. None of them could or would tell Archie where Lord Pwrâdisa and T'lôt'aris were.

After a thorough search, Archie reluctantly accepted the fact that Lord Pwrâdisa and T'lôt'aris were not in the house, so he went to his bedroom. The events of the day were too disturbing to permit any thought of eating, so Archie simply sat on the bed. He continued to review the eight inscriptions on the medallions that Kótan had given to him, and soon he laid his head on the pillow. Before long, Archie was sound asleep.

He awoke to the sound of many voices and a thunderous banging on the trapdoor. As he sat up, the trapdoor opened, and the ladder pushed out from the wall. Archie rubbed his eyes, wondering what had happened. A figure descended the ladder into Archie's bedroom and turned around. As he was doing so, Archie noticed that the soldier invading his room was possibly the fattest T'lantim he had ever seen, but that was no real contest, for he had never really seen an obese T'lantim.

"Sir Archie," the portly soldier said. "You are under arrest for treason. I have orders to escort you to the Palace of Elders immediately."

Chapter Thirty-Four
Treason

𝔄rchie was stunned.

"Treason? How so?" Archie asked.

"You are charged with treason against the king. That is all I know." The portly soldier then put his right hand on Archie's left arm and said, "Let's go. We have no time to waste." The pair climbed the ladder, and upon emerging from the bedroom, they were joined by half a dozen other soldiers. Archie did not recognize any of them.

As they walked through Lord Pwrâdisa's manor house, all of the servants came out to see the spectacle. A few of them sneered at Archie, and one spat on him. Most just stood there expressionless. One or two had tears in their eyes and wore an expression of sheer terror on their faces. Archie wondered why all these servants had been so hard to find just a short time earlier, for it was still night and it was still dark.

They made their way to the tower canal leading to the Palace of Elders and there found a barge waiting for them. Archie was led onto the barge, directed to a platform within a caged area, and then bound—both hand and foot—to railings in front of him and behind him. The guards took their positions, three standing behind Archie and three standing in front of him. The portly soldier, who apparently commanded this detail, stood outside the cage and locked it.

The barge, which was drawn by a team of six dolphins, lurched forward and began its journey toward the Palace of Elders. Archie strained to see the walkways on either side of the canal, but his vision was obscured by the railing, the six guards, and the cage. Soon, however, he heard voices mixed with laughter and some indistinguishable sounds. He could not make out most of the words, but the few that he could were enough for him to understand the sentiment of the people who lined the canal.

"Traitor!"

"Barbarian!"

"Spy!"

"Turncoat!"

Suddenly, something hit Archie in the forehead and began sliding down one side of his face. It had no more substance than applesauce, as it had been filtered by the cage that surrounded Archie. The goo had a distinctly rancid smell, and although Archie knew that it must be rotten fruit, it was so foul that he could not tell what kind of fruit it was. Two of the soldiers behind him snickered, and there was no end of their amusement, for new fruit goo arrived every few minutes. Archie had difficulty comprehending why he was so despised by so many people, and he wished more than ever that he could see Lord Pwrâdisa, T´lôt´aris, or his parents.

After only ten or fifteen minutes, it began to rain. Although Archie ordinarily would have been annoyed by exposure to the downpour, on this occasion he was thankful, because the rain washed the goo from his face. It also scrubbed the air of the noxious smells and thinned the crowds intent on pelting the young knight with last month's produce. The rain was not cold but had the warmth of a late summer shower, and this, too, pleased Archie. But the occasional flash of lightning that accompanied the rain intensified Archie's growing sense of dread.

When they arrived at the Palace of Elders, Archie was taken to a tall post outside the enormous building. He did not recall seeing it before and was not sure of its function. Soon, however, that became readily apparent, for he was lashed to the post, chest forward and slightly bent over. The back of his tunic was ripped away, and a rather burly soldier began to circle him with a nasty looking whip. It had nine separate leather straps, each of which had a sharp, solid claw tied to the end. The burly soldier bent down as he passed in front of Archie so that he could look up into Archie's eyes. Just as they made eye contact, the burly soldier violently cracked the whip, causing several nearby soldiers to shudder. But the burly soldier obviously enjoyed what he was doing.

As much as Archie disliked looking into the burly soldier's sneering face, he was even more unsettled when the burly soldier finally walked back around to Archie's rear, out of sight. Suddenly, the whip whistled through the air, and Archie felt its first sting rake across his back, ripping his flesh.

He cried out in agony, and by the time he had paused just long enough to draw in another breath, the whip bit down for a second time. After the third raking, Archie lost count. The pain was now continuous, and it was difficult to distinguish just when the claws made contact. Despite the darkness, the occasional flash of lightning illuminated the mixed water and blood flowing near his feet. As he was wondering just how much blood he had lost, Archie slowly lost consciousness.

A bucket of cold water thrown in his face awakened Archie, and though the wounds in his back were still stinging and throbbing, he surmised that the whipping was over. One of the soldiers assigned to escort Archie pulled the torn back of Archie's tunic up over Archie's back, and at first Archie thought that this was a gesture of kindness. But before he could verbalize his gratitude, the soldier slapped Archie's back, grinding the tunic into the raw and bloodied flesh. This caused an eruption of guffawing among the soldiers in attendance.

Archie was then dragged inside the Palace of Elders and taken to the very same chambers where his first trial had taken place, and before that, where he had first met Lord Mókato. Just as he had been for his first trial, Archie was led to a cage. At the center of the elevated desk from which Lord Mókato had presided over Archie's first trial, a solitary figure sat, wearing a rather large, very ornate crown. There were no junior judges, as there had been at the first trial.

Archie strained to see the face of the solitary figure wearing the crown, but before he could even get close enough to recognize it, one of the soldiers escorting him kicked his knees from behind and commanded, rather loudly, "Kneel, traitor, before the king you have betrayed!" Weak from his beating, Archie's legs folded, and he collapsed onto the floor. When he finally regained his balance and managed to look up, there before him sat the brassy and bellicose knight, wearing a crown. With a sneer on his face, the new ruler addressed Archie.

"Come closer so that we may see you more clearly."

Before Archie could move, the soldiers escorting him pushed and dragged him forward.

"You disgrace yourself, treasonous fool! No T'lantim would even consider appearing before his sovereign wearing a torn and soiled garment. But then, you are a barbarian, and so we will not hold this lapse in judgment against you." The sound of laughter filled the once stately chamber. But because it was now only dimly lit, Archie could not see the faces of those laughing at him. He guessed that the circular auditorium was filled with T'lantim who had come to witness the trial.

"You served the Alliance well, Sir Archie, and so it troubles us that you have now decided to wound us so grievously." With this declaration, Archie realized that the brassy and bellicose knight was using the royal "we," as though he were now several people in one.

"In gratitude for your service, however, it pleases us to demonstrate that we can be merciful. You are charged with treason, because you have told several people that Lord Pwrádisa lives and that he is king. This, of course, is foolishness, for he was publicly executed. Treason is punishable by death, but it has been suggested that perhaps you suffered a head injury during the late war. All you must do to end this trial and be restored to your position is to confess that you were delirious, that you did not see Lord Pwrádisa, that he is not king, and that you swear allegiance to me. Will you do that?" The brassy and bellicose knight leaned forward and flashed a wicked smile.

Archie was already distraught, for he did not know why Lord Pwrádisa and T'lôt'aris had abandoned him. But now he was even more distressed. The prospect of death terrified him, and yet, he had no desire to lie about what he knew to be true, and the whole idea of swearing allegiance to the brassy and bellicose knight was out of the question. But then Archie heard the old bearded knight's voice whispering in his ear. He looked around, but he did not see his teacher. Nevertheless, the old bearded knight's voice continued to whisper in Archie's ear. And that was enough to stiffen his resolve and boost his confidence. Without hesitation, Archie repeated the words he was hearing from T'lôt'aris.

"Lord Pwrádisa lives. I know this to be true, because I have seen him. And I know him, for I have served in his house almost since the day I first arrived. He is the king. You are not. I have sworn allegiance to Lord Pwrádisa, and I will not let that oath fail."

Upon hearing this unexpectedly courageous statement, the brassy and bellicose knight exploded with rage, stood up, and shook his fist at Archie. "You worthless barbarian. *I* will show you who is king!" The sudden change from the royal "we" was obvious to everyone in the chamber, and almost immediately, the brassy and bellicose knight realized his lapse. In a markedly softer tone of voice he continued. "*We* will show you who is king!" Then, in a more sarcastic tone, he added, "Tell us, Sir Archie, just how it is that Lord Pwrádisa lives and where he may be found."

There was another burst of laughter in the chamber, and Archie slowly looked in every direction. Although the chamber was still dimly lit, Archie was no longer unable to see the spectators. As he gazed at the audience, he had the strange sensation that he was making eye contact with every person in the auditorium. But as he looked at their faces, he realized that every one of them was identical. Every one of them was the face of Thlū'taku! And what he saw was not a momentary flash. Every person in the room, including the brassy and bellicose knight, now seemed to bear the face of Thlū'taku permanently.

Once again, Archie boldly proclaimed what the old bearded knight was whispering in his ear. "You cannot see Lord Pwrádisa because you serve the evil one, Thlū'taku."

Archie had no sooner uttered these words than there arose a commotion in the chamber. It took several minutes for the imposter king to quiet the crowd.

"You are a strange one, Sir Archie, for you do not see clearly. We adored Lord Pwrádisa, and we honor his memory. We served the same cause, and our hearts have always been in accord with his. But he is *not* king. He is *not* ruler. He is *not* even alive."

With an unexpected confidence in his voice, Archie replied, "Lord Pwrádisa is alive, and he is the king. All who know him can see him. But those who serve the evil one cannot. And I can see with absolute clarity that you, a mere knight with an obviously counterfeit claim to sovereignty, serve Thlū'taku. You belong to the evil one."

Except for a few gasps, the entire chamber grew quiet. As Archie gazed around the room, he saw not merely the face of Thlū'taku in every other person but also that look of terror he saw on Thlū'taku's own face just after Archie's first trial.

"Away with him!" the counterfeit king demanded. "Show no mercy in putting him to death!"

Chapter Thirty-Five
The Eighth Tower

rchie was then led out of the Palace of Elders. The T'lantim no longer jeered at him but, instead, just stared at him in disbelief. Even the soldiers escorting Archie no longer seemed to find amusement in mocking him. Before long, the prisoner detail was back aboard the barge, which once again lurched forward. Archie did not know their destination, and he did not have the strength to ask. He simply assumed that he was being taken to a place where he would be executed.

The rain had slowed, and there was only a very slight drizzle coming down. A mist was rising off the surface of the canal, and the sky had cleared enough that the moonlight cast an eerie glow on the mist. No one spoke, and the walkways along the canal were no longer populated with T'lantim eager to scoff at Archie. The only sounds Archie heard were the occasional muffled splashes made by the team of dolphins and the ripples hitting the walls of the canal.

After a while, the barge docked. As Archie was being led out of the cage and onto the walkway, he looked up and saw one of the eight towers. The smell of grapes told him that a vineyard was nearby and that the tower now before him was the Tower of Sacrifice. Soon, the small detail entered the tower and began climbing the spiral stairway. Still no one spoke, but the portly soldier began to huff and puff. Finally, they reached the top level, and Archie was led into a dungeon. It seemed strange to him that the dungeon was on the top level, but he had seen so many strange things in this city that he was only mildly surprised. The portly soldier then shackled all of Archie's limbs to the wall, and the guard detail left.

As Archie looked around the circular room, he saw a dozen or more other prisoners, all shackled to the wall. Each of them seemed to be stretched out, and their feet barely touched the floor. Archie, who was larger than any of the T'lantim, could not stretch out but was, instead, forced to fold his body to fit the shackles. This was extraordinarily uncomfortable, but it was nothing compared to the pain he felt in his back. The blood had dried, and his tunic, which one of the soldiers had slapped onto his back, was stuck to the open wounds.

As he looked around the room, Archie saw many familiar faces. He saw some of the knights who had served with him, particularly those who had fought at his side during the final battle. He also saw several workmen from Kótan's workshop. Many were now unconscious, and apparently no one had the strength to speak. Neither did Archie.

The throbbing pain from his back and the discomfort of the awkward shackles made it difficult for Archie to rest. He found that he was bound to his pain, unable to escape consciousness. He decided to pass the time by reflecting on the eight inscriptions he found at the bases of the eight towers:

Humility is the path to freedom.

Mourning leads to change.

Surrender is gain.

Morality is possible only when it is impossible.

Compassion begets compassion.

Purity restores the blind.

Peace is the mark of true royalty.

Sacrifice is the path to freedom.

Archie now believed that he had at least some idea of what the first seven inscriptions meant, but he did not understand the last. How could sacrifice be the path to freedom? And what kind of sacrifice, and for what purpose? And how was sacrifice related to morality? After all, the two towers were opposite in this city. Perhaps sacrifice was possible only when it was impossible. Archie smiled, for he had no strength to laugh. He sure wished the pain he felt was impossible, but it was all too real.

Archie's thoughts were interrupted when one of the other prisoners, a knight with whom he had fought, finally spoke in a voice that was no more than a whisper. "Sir Archie! I had hoped that you might have escaped this injustice. How is it that they have arrested you, a true hero?"

"I was arrested for treason. They wanted me to lie, to say that Lord Pwrádisa is dead."

"So, it is true after all! We had heard that you were saying that Lord Pwrádisa lives, but we did not know what to make of it. How do you know this?"

"I saw him. I spoke to him, and he told me that he is the king. I swore my allegiance to him just before the final battle, and so I couldn't swear allegiance to that counterfeit king."

The other knight did not respond immediately, and Archie could not tell whether it was because he had nothing else to say or because he had no strength. After a while, he continued, but in a much weaker voice. Gesturing to the other knights as best as he could under the constraint of his shackles, he said, "We were rounded up and thrown into this dungeon without so much as a trial. The only thing we share in common is that we served you. And these workmen all served Kótan, who also served you."

It troubled Archie to learn that all of the other prisoners had been arrested because of their connections to him, and the emotion was just too much. He began to weep, which served only to further weaken him. After a while, the other knight spoke again. "Tell us about Lord Pwrádisa. None of us ever knew him."

Archie lifted his head and regained his composure. He began speaking with a strength that he did not believe was left in him, and he told the other prisoners everything that he knew about Lord Pwrádisa, N'derlex, and T'lôt'aris. Then he told them everything he knew about Thlū'taku, the brassy and bellicose knight, Lord Mókato, and Mókea. Finally, he started telling them about the eight towers and the inscriptions at their bases. Everyone listened intently, and finally, the knight who had broken the silence spoke again. "I believe that you are telling the truth and that Lord Pwrádisa is king. I will soon be dead, but I will swear my allegiance to him with what remains of my life."

Several of the other knights and workmen did the same, and the dungeon was soon filled with an energy that seemed impossible for the beaten and exhausted prisoners. The excitement was interrupted when the door opened, and an entire company of soldiers entered. They unshackled all of the prisoners and escorted them down the spiral stairway to the lowest level of the tower. There, they entered a large chamber. Around the walls were stadium-type seats filled with T'lantim. In the center of the room was a large pool of water, and from the sides, there were objects that resembled cranes with cages attached at the ends. As the prisoners were led into the chamber, the crowd jeered and taunted them.

"Traitors! You deserve a horrible death!"

"Ask 'King Pwrådisa' to save you now!"

"If Pwrådisa is king, he has the power! Where is he now?"

At this last taunt, the crowd cheered. Slowly, they all joined together in chanting, "Where is he? Where is he? Where is he?"

Archie looked up into the crowd and saw many familiar faces. He still could not understand how people who had loved him just a little while earlier could now be filled with such hatred. Among the faces he saw was that of Mókea, who was sitting with her entourage of teenage girls. She, too, was chanting with the crowd.

Soon, the crowd began a new chant, yelling, "We serve the true king! We serve the true king! We serve the true king!" As they taunted the prisoners, soldiers took the knight who had spoken to Archie in the dungeon and placed him in one of the cages attached to a crane-like object. While they did this, three soldiers slashed and cut him with their swords so that fresh blood dripped from him. They hoisted the crane, and as he rose above the crowd, the young knight yelled out with such force that it stopped the chanting. "Yes! Yes! I serve King Pwrådisa, the only true king. Long live King Pwrådisa!"

At that, the cage opened, and the young knight plunged into the water. Seemingly from nowhere, dozens of sharks swam to the bloody young knight and tore into his flesh. In a matter of minutes, they had devoured him. The crowd cheered wildly, and as Archie watched, he saw only the face of Thlū'taku.

One by one, the prisoners were fed to the sharks in the same manner. Each time, they took their cue from the first knight: each of them publicly proclaimed his allegiance to King Pwrådisa just before plunging to death.

Finally, only Archie remained, and the captain in command of the executioners addressed the crowd. "Before you stands the worst traitor of them all, and he has been saved for the finalé. The sharks are too quick to devour their prey, and he deserves a lingering death. Why? Because he is a barbarian!" The crowd cheered.

"Because he caused the late war!" The crowd cheered again.

"Because he caused Lord Pwrådisa's death!" Still more cheers.

"Because he mocks us by claiming that Lord Pwrådisa still lives!" By now, the crowd had been whipped into a frenzy and cheered as loudly and wildly as possible. When the cheering had finally subsided a little, the captain continued, at first in a near whisper, so the crowd grew very quiet, straining to hear him. "This prisoner does not deserve a quick death."

Then, gradually increasing his volume, the captain added, "Therefore, what awaits him is the most painful, most prolonged, most exceptional death possible. What awaits him will be the greatest spectacle you have ever seen!"

As the captain paused, the crowd cheered, and Archie was led to one of the crane-like devices that had not yet been used. All of his clothes were ripped off so that he stood naked before the crowd, which broke out in laughter. Next, the soldiers slashed and cut him with swords, just as they had the other prisoners. Then they put him in the cage and closed it. As they lifted him over the crowd, Archie heard the voice of the old knight once again whisper into his ear, and he repeated what he heard, calling out to the crowd below. "King Pwrádisa is the only true king. I am innocent, but I forgive you. King Pwrádisa will forgive you too if you will turn to him!"

With that, the entire cage, with Archie inside, plummeted into the water. Sharks attacked the cage, trying their best to get to the bloody body whose scent they smelled, but to no avail. Archie was jerked from one side of the cage to another as the sharks attacked, and it was all he could do to hold his breath. Just when he thought that he could hold it no longer, the cage was lifted out of the water. Archie sucked in as much air as he could while the cage was slowly being lifted above the crowd. The taunts began anew.

"Where is your King Pwrádisa? Where is he now? Where is he? Where is he? Where is he?"

Archie was still breathing hard when the cage plummeted again into the water. The sharks, by now very agitated, attacked even more ferociously, and Archie was certain that the cage would not protect him for long. He wanted desperately to breathe but was determined to hold his breath as long as he could. Remembering something he saw on television, Archie sucked the air in his lungs back and forth between his mouth and lungs, all while keeping his mouth tightly sealed. This was made more difficult by the violent movement of the cage as the sharks jerked it around. The cage was finally lifted out of the water just as Archie was inhaling. Some water nevertheless got into his windpipe, and he began coughing violently as the cage was lifted yet again above the crowd.

The taunting continued in a dull rhythm, "Where is he? Where is he? Where is he?" And before Archie had sucked in enough air, or even stopped coughing, the cage was once again released, plunging into the water below.

As he struggled to hold his breath, Archie thought of his parents, and his heart was torn. He knew that he would never again see them. He would never feel their warm embrace. He would never finish high school. He would never go to college, or get married, or even attend his senior prom. And worse than all of that, his parents would never know what happened to him.

The cage was starting to come apart, and the sharks were continuing to attack vigorously. Archie opened his eyes, though he was still underwater, and was amazed by what he saw. There was a bright light glowing in the water, and at first, he did not know what it was. Soon, however, he realized it must be dawn and that sunlight was now streaming into the chamber in which this deadly spectacle was taking place. The light was beautiful, and Archie smiled. He relaxed his muscles, and water came pouring into his lungs, but it did not hurt. As he lost consciousness, he could see his father and his mother, and he was content.

Chapter Thirty-Six
Freedom

Archie opened his eyes. There in front of him were his father and mother. He was lying in a bed, and his mother was caressing his face. Sunlight was streaming through a window just over the bed. Archie blinked, for he was confused by what he saw. The room did not look like a T'lantim bedroom at all. As he looked around, his mother said, "Archie, dear. We were so worried about you."

"Yes, son," his father added. "We thought we lost you."

Still confused, Archie asked, "Where am I?"

"This is your room in the vacation house," his father replied. "I guess you don't remember it. You went out with your kayak before we were even unpacked."

"What happened?" Archie asked.

"There was a terrible storm, and it drove you out to sea," his mother replied. "You lost your kayak, and you nearly drowned, but a fisherman saved you. He brought you back to us."

Archie did not remember this at all. He was still grappling with the fact that he was with his parents and no longer in K'truum-Shra, among the T'lantim. He sat up and looked around the room and then at himself. He was wearing his own pajamas, and the room was certainly what he would expect from an ordinary house, though it now seemed strange to him, because he had grown accustomed to the T'lantim ways.

"How did the fisherman find me?" Archie asked.

"You were floating in the water just off the shore of another island, an uninhabited island not far from here. Mr. Cotton was fishing nearby when he saw you. He pulled you from the water and discovered that even though you were unconscious, you were alive. We were very fortunate that he came along when he did, for you had almost drowned. But he got there just in time to administer CPR. He saved your life."

Just then, the doorbell rang, and Archie's mother got up to go answer the door. While she was away, Archie looked into his father's eyes and spoke. "I guess you're pretty mad, aren't you, Dad?"

"Son, I am just happy to have you back. Your mother and I love you very much, and we were very worried about you."

"So you are not going to lecture me about thinking I invented the wheel?" Archie asked. "Because if you are, I want you to know that I have learned that lesson. I *know* that I didn't invent the wheel, and I will never again ignore you when you share your experience with me."

Archie's father looked surprised but did not speak, because Archie's mother returned and announced, "Archie, you have a visitor. Archibald Zwick, meet Mr. Cotton, the man who saved your life."

Archie looked toward the door and what he saw surprised him. There, standing before him, was an old man who resembled Kótan. He did not have the same slender T'lantim build, nor was his complexion green. But there was no doubt that his face was the same. He smiled, removed his hat, and walked over to Archie's bed.

"I am so glad that you are well, now, my friend. I was afraid that I pulled you out of the water too late. When I heard that the doctors said you would make a full recovery, my heart jumped for joy, and I came over here hoping to see you."

Archie sat up, still bewildered. As he sat up, he heard a jingling noise near his neck, and he instinctively reached out a hand and touched it. There, he found the sacred necklace of K'truum-Shra, together with the medallions made by Kótan. As he fumbled with them, the fisherman said, "I hope you like your gift," gesturing toward the necklace. "It is not very expensive, but it carries an important message."

Archie pulled off the necklace and examined it thoroughly. It was identical to the necklace he recalled, but the inscriptions were different. Instead of the inscriptions he found on the towers of K'truum-Shra, Archie read:

Blessed are the poor in spirit, for theirs is the kingdom of heaven.

Blessed are those who mourn, for they will be comforted.

Blessed are the meek, for they will inherit the earth.

Blessed are those who hunger and thirst for righteousness, for they will be filled.

Blessed are the merciful, for they will be shown mercy.

Blessed are the pure in heart, for they will see God.

Blessed are the peacemakers, for they will be called sons of God.

Blessed are those who are persecuted because of righteousness, for theirs is the kingdom of heaven.

Watching as Archie read the inscriptions, the old fisherman continued. "My church makes these, because we believe that the Beatitudes are a summary of everything our Lord taught. If you would like, when you get better, I will explain them to you."

Looking up, Archie said, "Thank you. I believe I understand. I finally understand."

About the Book

Imagine you are kayaking in the Atlantic Ocean, just having fun, when a strong storm erupts. And when it is over, nothing is familiar. Instead of the island where your family has been vacationing, you find yourself on a strange, floating city.

That is what happens to sixteen-year-old Archibald Zwick. Though the inhabitants of this strange city have welcomed him, Archie just wants to return to his family. But, as he quickly learns, it will not be an easy task, as the city is on the verge of a civil war. Almost before he realizes it is happening, he finds himself embroiled in the politics of the strange city, receiving guidance along the way from an old, bearded knight.

Whether Archie can return to his family depends on the outcome of the civil war and on the lessons he can learn from the eight towers in the wall that surrounds the city.

About the Author

Robert Leslie Palmer, a Birmingham, Alabama attorney, received a BA from Tulane University and a JD from Georgetown University. He thoroughly enjoys writing and for many years has published law review articles, poetry, and newspaper commentaries. After twenty-seven years in practice, he is now on sabbatical to pursue a life-long dream of writing full-time.

Breinigsville, PA USA
06 February 2011
254943BV00001B/1/P